CW00419072

ALL Tнь
COLOURS YOU
CANNOT NAME

ALL THE COLOURS YOU CANNOT NAME

Joad R. Wren

SEREN

Seren is the book imprint of
Poetry Wales Press Ltd
Suite 6, 4 Derwen Road, Bridgend,
Wales, CF31 1LH

www.serenbooks.com
Follow us on social media @SerenBooks

ISBNs
Paperback – 978-1-78172-720-1
Ebook – 978-1-78172-724-9

A CIP record for this title is available from the British Library.

The publisher acknowledges the financial assistance of the
Books Council of Wales.

Cover painting: Georgina Wren.

Printed by Akcent Media Ltd.

to Georgina Wren, in lieu of a time machine

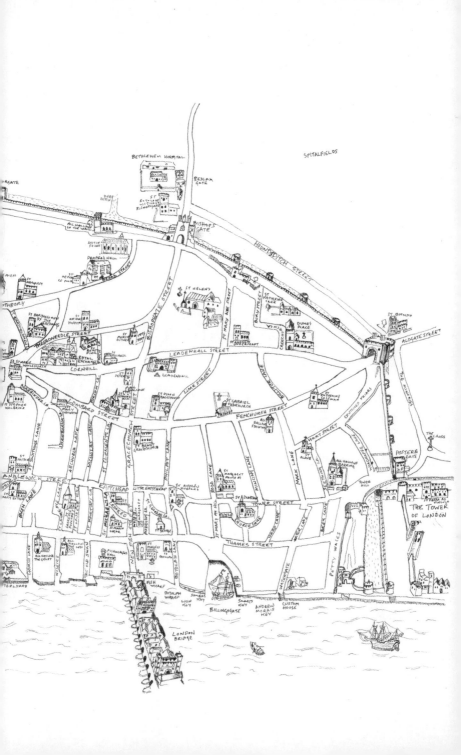

CHAPTER ONE

When he stands outside his shop he can see through the small gate in the wall, along the gravel path, into the city itself. Not Aldersgate, the main gate, but the small one, the short-cut to Paul's Churchyard. He can see the top of the tower, or thinks he can: his eyesight has weakened. He stands there every day, and looks. Not for any purpose, but because it makes him feel grounded, here, in the ward of Farringdon Without the Wall, with his back to his parish church, St Bartholomew the Less. He has lived here for six good years.

Today he does have a purpose, however. He is waiting for Solomon Eagle, who has arranged to bring him a manuscript to print. James White needs the work, and Eagle has agreed to pay promptly. James stands at his door as he does every morning, but this time he waits for Eagle's tall, gaunt figure to approach. He does not know if it is because of this, but today he does not feel as though he stands on solid, reassuring foundations. He attends to his breath, trying to slow it down and reach further into his lungs, but his heart still races, his skin prickles, birds flutter in his blood, and it feels as though there is not enough air for him. He wonders if this is what it feels like in an air-pump. He has read about birds starved of breath as the atmosphere is sucked from their glass jars, the little madness of their beating wings before they fall to the ground. Is this what it feels like? To stifle?

Around him the plague still roars, still rages, still strikes people down with its indifferent cruelty. It is not as furious nor as mortal as it was a year ago, and many Londoners have decided that they can go about their lives with impunity. They work, they go to market, they speak with neighbours. Most have stopped following so attentively the weekly numbers of plague deaths, and those who still study the Bills say that there's little to fear, that the pestilence will soon be gone entirely from London. In the countryside the story is different: there its raging is more fatal than it was last year, villages are decimated, and no one flees London to the country for safety. Here a semblance of normality has returned, though some still live in the shadow of nearly two years' isolation, worry at contact with strangers, stumble in everyday conversation, walk haunted, look over their shoulders, fear that the world they live in is no longer safe.

He does not fear the plague. He has resigned himself to the hands of providence, or to what will happen by chance. He feared the plague for many months, but by now he has decided that he may catch it, or may not catch it, and thinking about it will change nothing. Though he is inclined to think that he will not catch it. It is not fear of the plague that troubles him now. It is something else he cannot name. He looks through the small gate into the city and the roaring in his ears speaks wordlessly of catastrophe. He has had this feeling before, though, and disaster has not always come to pass. It is a feeling, a fretful disquiet, no more than that. Yet he wishes it would go away and leave him to wait in peace. He has never felt it here before, grounded on this patch of earth in front of his shop. In fact he has not felt it for years. It has invaded this new life of his, this tremor of fear and despair that seeks to invalidate his past and cancel his future. It is an old feeling, and he breathes methodically to drive it from him. It does not belong here; it does not belong to him.

'White,' a voice says behind him, and he jumps. It is a low, thin, nasal voice that pierces the roaring in his ears. He turns.

'Eagle.' He offers his hand to the grey-haired, grey-skinned man. 'I thought you would come from the city.'

'I live in Spitalfields,' Eagle says. 'I always have. I preach in the city. And elsewhere.'

He is holding a package, wrapped in brown paper and tied with thread.

'Is this your pamphlet?' James asks. 'Shall we go inside and see how long it is, and how we could lay it out on the page?'

Eagle nods. 'And how long it will take,' he says. 'Are you busy at the moment? Do you have other works to complete first?'

'I've just finished one,' James says, though this is not exactly true. 'I can start tomorrow. Though I will need payment towards the paper first.'

'I have it with me,' Eagle reassures.

They turn and enter White's printing shop.

★ ★ ★

Ellie is waiting in the shop. She makes busy with tidying the jars of ink and the inkpads. The truth is, though, that they've had no work for eight days. The plague has ruined much of the trade in the city. Now is not the time for doing small jobs like she and James do. If they were printing bibles or volumes of scholarship or collections of sermons then they would be better positioned to weather these quiet times. But when the gaps between the small jobs grow longer and longer, she knows that one day the next job will not come. And then they will have to consider what to do, because although the plague has already receded, although it's fed on so many living bodies with such malevolence that there are fewer now to devour, and life has already begun to return to normality, all the same they're still waiting for work, and still hoping that their livelihood hasn't been destroyed, and that not everything, not quite everything, has changed.

The truth is, she admits to herself, that she is trying not to say the word 'if' to herself. There are many 'ifs' here, and she has never seen anything like this before. The plague has always raged and abated, but in human memory was a plague ever this bad? What if this is a different kind of plague? What if it never completely goes away? What if God has had enough? She would not blame Him. If it goes on like this for another year, another five years, what will be left?

James enters and sees her lost in thought. He catches her eye and everything stops. This response has not changed in six years.

When he first spoke to her, outside the church, he knew that she could be everything to him. What has changed is that now when he looks at her, she represents to him everything he desires, everything he finds admirable and beautiful. He doesn't notice anyone else when she's there. The sense of her presence distracts him too much. The other change is that he now knows how to put this into words. At first he just felt dumbfounded and a little stupid. They married, set up this shop together, and slowly he became able to describe, to himself and then to her, that sense of now understanding what beauty was, how it shone through her skin from within her spirit, that knowledge that he was incomplete without her. Every day when he wakes up next to her he feels the same.

'Hello,' says a voice beside him. Eagle has reappeared.

'Ellie, this is Solomon Eagle, the preacher, the man with the pamphlet for us.'

She curtsies.

'I'm never sure about the word "pamphlet",' says Eagle. 'It makes it sound, I don't know, light or whimsical. There is a lot of judgement and philosophy in this. It's short, I admit, and I hope it won't take too much paper. But it's not without substance and weight.'

'I mean no offence. I just meant that it's a short work, and we'll print it as a cheap quarto, without ostentation or wasting any paper. Many pamphlets contain more serious matter than some big books.' James now feels guilty about using the word, though for him it has only ever been a description of a physical object, not the content. 'Shall we look at it, your book?'

Eagle places his package down on the table, unknots the string, and unfolds the wrapping. James reads the title at the top of the first page: 'The judgement and warning of the Lord against the people of England for their sins of presumption and denying the light, in which Solomon Eagle', here the letters are larger, 'goes naked before the Lord and His people in language only, and wears the fire and brimstone on his head as a presage of what will come.' Without thinking about the content, James looks through the pages, measuring with his eye the handwriting and the length of line, estimates the number of words, and translates these to the printed page.

'If we indent these notes into the margin of the page, and use a font this size' – he points to an example on the wall – 'then with a title page we will just fit it into sixteen pages; two sheets.'

Eagle nods assent.

They discuss the cost of the work. James looks up at Ellie throughout. He needs her to check his calculations at all times. She is good with numbers. She moves over to look at the manuscript, and he sees her lips move as she counts the lines. She nods.

'Two sheets, sixteen pages. No woodcuts, but perhaps some decoration on the title page?'

'No decoration,' says Eagle. 'Just the words.'

Eagle pays James ten shillings, which he will take with him to the Stationers' Hall the next morning, and collect two reams of paper. These he will then use to print the small edition. He sees Eagle to the door.

'How long?' the gaunt man asks.

James is unaccustomed to looking up at people, but he has to tilt his chin a little to catch Eagle's eye.

'Monday, a week today.' He is careful not to suggest working on the Sabbath, as he suspects that would rile Eagle, though to complete it in a week he will certainly have to work on Sunday. This does not trouble him. Churchgoing has lost its savour in recent months, and prayer seems unrewarding. It is probably best that Eagle does not know this, however. He might judge James, and choose to find another printer. He leaves, and James turns to see Ellie reading the manuscript. She is struggling with this, her fingers moving very slowly along the lines, and her lips silently mouthing the words. He had started to teach her to read from the start, even before they were married. He sits beside her and watches her read. His heart is full of colours he doesn't know the names of.

* * *

'The judgement and warning of the Lord' is part examination of the state of the kingdoms – when Eagle writes 'England' he means, as Ellie notes, England and Wales and Scotland – and part prophecy. It touches on fear, of plague, of disaster, fears about health. The plague has prevailed in London for a year and a half. Ellie and James heard rumours at first. Then they started following the numbers in the weekly Bills of Mortality. They watched the numbers creep into Farringdon Without. Then Hugh Allworth, the tapster, took ill and died. The disease became real. Then they read the orders for shutting up houses, and then they saw the searchers travelling street by street, inspecting the bodies of the dead and determining the cause of death. Then they stopped reading the Bills of Mortality.

They know that nearly 69,000 Londoners died of the plague the previous year, more than ten times as many as died of agues and fevers, accounting for about seven in every ten deaths. This year the number has fallen, having been surpassed by consumption, but death still stalks the city. The streets are quieter, not only because the citizens are more subdued, and playhouses and other forms of entertainment closed, but also because so many have fled. Last summer James watched them process through Aldersgate, the grand, tall gate nearby. They took horses and carts with their belongings, as much as they could carry, heading into the country for an uncertain duration. Some went on foot, with packs on their back, ready to sleep by the road and risk highwaymen and common robbers. Aldersgate opened the way to the north, to St Albans and beyond, and many passed under its arch. Who knows how many thousands fled, to all points of the compass? Perhaps the Lord Mayor knew the actual numbers; to James it was a multitude, all fearful of the judgement of God on the city.

James reads the sheets as Ellie finishes them. He catches up quickly, having long been a reader, then reads over her elbow. He catches her smell, closes his eyes, and falls behind. He wants to take her upstairs to bed, but they should work.

Eagle's book says that three years ago he had published a warning to the nation that there were portents of a divine judgement to come. He had walked naked as a sign, like earlier true prophets, with fire and brimstone on his head; he had been mocked and imprisoned, but he had borne true witness. The players and their filthy shows were one indication, drunkenness another, and the playing of music was a third. And now the playhouses were closed, many had fled the city of London, and all men and women were subdued. The plague was the judgement he had prophesied. And he prayed to the Lord that many would be spared, but he hoped rather than expected that they would. And, further, he had another warning, that anyone who spoke or wrote against the light, with voice, pen or press, was doomed. What was the light? The light was the spirit of God within, the spirit that moved those who walked upright, with which they bore testimony, with which they were tested. And if the men of darkness did not stop speaking and writing against the children of light then there would be a great darkness followed by a burning light pursued by darkness again. This prophecy would prove true, just as the last one had.

His writing is peppered with scriptural allusion and quotation. James will need to use a lot of italic type to mark the quotations.

Ellie finishes. 'Eagle uses too many words,' she says. 'It could be said more simply.'

James savours her accent. He adores the sing-song lilt, the lift at the end of the sentence, as though she is asking a question, which she is not. Her voice is low, except sometimes when she speaks to customers, when she raises it several notes.

And it had been higher when she spoke to Jeremiah. As he remembers this, he catches himself. How can he always find sadness in the middle of a happy thought? He does, though. It had been higher when she spoke to the baby, before he died. And then for a long time she hardly spoke at all.

★ ★ ★

John Smith enters.

'Master, mistress,' he says, but he will not meet their eyes.

Ellie sees immediately that there is something amiss. He should have been in the shop this morning, though there was nothing for him to do, but he left at dawn, without asking.

'John?' she asks, with an exaggerated rising inflection.

He walks into the store room at the back of the shop, where he sleeps, and speaks from there.

'The Fowlses,' he says in his West Country accent, 'all of them. Nathan dead, Margaret dying, their boys, and the two apprentices, all shut up indoors and going to die. It's a crime.'

James and Ellie look at each other. There is unfettered panic in John's voice.

'It's the orders and regulations,' says James. 'And they may not die. They're confined so that others don't.'

'They will die because of the orders and regulations,' says John. 'Begging your pardon, master.'

He is standing in the doorway again, with his knapsack. All three catch their breath and look to one another.

'I don't want to die.'

James shakes his head. 'It's not right.'

'I don't want to die. I'm not going to die.'

'You should trust in God to protect you,' says James, though as the words leave his mouth he realises he is no longer sure that he means them. They are hollow words, little empty sounds, scratching in the corners of the room.

'And if He doesn't intend to protect you, then running from London won't help,' adds Ellie.

'Nor will inviting Him to let me catch it,' counters John. And he bows his head. He is trembling, James sees. But he is twenty, no longer a child. He should understand. He has been rebaptised, having listened to Ellie's wisdom, so he has freely accepted the spirit, and with it responsibility for his actions. He is also an apprentice, and not even six of his agreed seven years have been completed. He is not free to break his indenture. If he leaves before his time, if he runs, then James can have him whipped.

'Your indenture,' James ventures. The reasoning feels weak.

He should say something about defying God. 'You know it's not yet complete. You know this.'

'I have to trust your pity,' says John, still staring at the floor. James is taller by two or three inches, and broad across the shoulders, deceptively strong from years of pulling the press. John won't look at him. 'Besides,' he continues, 'I would prefer a weal from a whip to buboes.' He falls silent, refusing to catch their eyes. He pauses, hesitates, caught.

Then he walks out of the shop, closing the door behind him.

James sighs.

'Well?' asks Ellie.

'I cannot make him stay. I mean, I can, but it would be wrong to do so. Imagine he catches it and dies. How would we feel then?'

'But to have stayed so long, and now to leave when it's so much safer than it was. It makes no sense. He is startled by the news of the Fowls family, frightened out of good sense. And what will he do if he doesn't complete his apprenticeship? All those years.'

James stands by the window, peering into the street along which John has disappeared. 'This will make the work for Eagle more difficult,' he groans, 'it will slow things down. You'll need to help me pull the impression.'

In the midday air, through the bends of the glass, he cannot see the signs he found in the morning. There is no disquiet in the sky, no roaring in the air, nor in his ears. Once again the ground is solid beneath his shoes. He breathes.

CHAPTER TWO

James stands at a table with a surface that slopes up away from him, covered, as it almost always is, with cases of type. There are four cases: his plain type, above that the capitals and incidentals, to the right the italic type and above this the italic capitals. He holds in his left hand a metal slide the width of a printed line, and with his right hand he takes pieces of type and places them on the slide. This way he compiles a line of type, building it from right to left, because the letters are backwards. Once the line is complete he places it on a bed on another table, and so builds up the page of the book line by line. Then he puts together the pages so they print a single side of a sheet of paper. Because paper has two sides, and because page two appears on the back of page one, he has to print one side of a sheet of paper at a time, and so if there are eight pages on a single sheet, he will first print pages one, four, five and eight, and then print pages three, two, seven and six on the back. The printing press has a strange logic. But he doesn't even think about this as he works, because the logic and the knowledge and the practice are all deep within his body, and he composes the page without needing to consider all of the things he knows.

Line by line he makes the page, letter by backwards letter he makes the lines. Eagle's manuscript lies on the case of italic capitals. He finds this position most comfortable, so he doesn't have to turn his neck, and it stops his inclination to hunch over the trays of type. Many printers are stooped; he is still upright. He mainly looks at Eagle's writing and not the cases of type, because he knows where the letters are distributed in their separate compartments. He glances occasionally at the line of type in his left hand, just to check that he has used the correct letters. Sometimes a piece of type with 'f' has been put in the compartment for the tall 's', because they look so alike, and the same is true of the pieces of type with 'si' and 'fi'. The words 'sickle' and 'fickle' are hard to distinguish. He can read backwards letters as a matter of habit. The letters are always the right way up, because a notch on the bottom side of each piece of type lets his hands check this. Again, he does not think about it: the knowledge is tacit in the touch. He has to remember to focus on the words as they appear, and not drift off into thoughts about what they mean and what they say to him and whether or not he thinks they're right and whether he would write it a different way. It's quicker if he sees only words and letters, not logic and rhetoric.

It is an art, though few see this. There is art in everything, in the knowledge his body has of the laying out of type, in the gift of his eye for assessing a line, making sure the spaces are evenly distributed, in justifying the end of each line without stretching the words too far, in making a page with the right size of type, the right length of line, the right block of printing and the correctly sized margins. There is art in the decisions he makes about how to present a book, so its material appearance is sympathetic to the meaning of the words, in how the organisation of the page supports the reader who looks for pleasure or knowledge or instruction in the words. There is art in balancing ink against white space. There is art in being able to see the contours of dark against light. There is art in knowing when to break the page, in dividing a manuscript into pages, which must take place before the typesetting begins. At every stage in the process, from weighing the manuscript, designing the page, laying out the type, through choosing or making the ink, picking out the paper, operating the press, folding and stitching the book, selecting a binding if the work is to be bound, to placing it on the table or stall for a prospective reader to admire; at every stage in this broad loop of activity there is art. Readers and writers may think that his work is merely mechanical, but printing is an art, in which meaning and beauty are inseparable.

When he completed his apprenticeship under Simmons he

had dreams of reinvigorating the art of printing in London, of shaking off the slough of drudgery and returning it to its glory. He would impregnate it with the same spirit that it had in Germany or in Italy. Eight years' work as a journeyman printer did not dull this ambition. Working for Simmons and others, composing type, inking, operating a press, he learned everything he could, not only the practical work required of an apprentice but much beyond this, through observing how master printers made decisions about pages and books, and how they organised their printing shops to make their work flow more freely. He knew that once he had seen how they did things, and compared and emulated and improved this, then he would be a great printer. He would not be ground down by numbers and profit.

He became a freeman of the Company of Stationers and established his own printing shop, a little north of where he now is, on the far side of the bent street called Little Britain, just east of Smithfield, in the summer of 1641. It was a wonderful time to be setting out as a printer, it was a dreadful time. The world was breathless. With war imminent between king and parliament, no one wanted beautiful books. They wanted pamphlets, printed as quickly as possible; they wanted them to fly from the presses like paper bullets. They wanted newspapers, weekly pamphlets of news scrambled together in the utmost haste. He was the first to admit that there was a kind of beauty in this rush of cheaply-printed news and communication, that the light of truth shone through the clouds of misrepresentation and deception, that these inky wars had their own splendour. But it meant that his ambitions to make superb volumes were shelved in favour of earning a living printing little books that were quickly born and quickly forgotten. He prospered for almost twenty years, marrying and burying a wife, living through wars and contentious peace, watching the killing of a king, seeing the creation and overthrow of new governments, the rise and oppression of seekers after new religion, wars against the Dutch, the Scots, the Irish, the settlement of Jamaica in the West Indies, plotting and conspiracy and riot, and then the return of another king, more benevolent and less trustworthy than the first. All the while he was printing the news of these matters. He prospered, but he forgot why, and all the while it seemed he was treading water in a cold river. And then he met Ellie.

★ ★ ★

It was August, and he stood in the yard of St Bartholomew the Less, looking at the flowers. Having been born in Smithfield to a butcher, then apprenticed to a printer in Aldersgate, and working all his life in the same ward, he did not know the names of flowers. He had decorative woodblocks with flowers in his shop, but did not know if they depicted particular flowers, or just the idea of flowers. No, that wasn't true: among his woodblocks there were lilies, and he knew they symbolised purity. And roses too, which signified Tudor monarchs, as well as love, and true Christian faith. And there was a poppy, which indicated the brevity of life. And the raggedy flower in a piece of decorative metal type was a carnation, he thought, and that was also a good Christian life. Once he started to think, he knew more names than he realised. But they were pictures, not real flowers in a churchyard.

He heard her before he saw her, speaking in her strange accent, which at the time he did not recognise. 'Then it would not be me who was speaking!' she said.

'Elinor!' exclaimed the woman she was with, better dressed – her employer, he saw at once. 'You have a singular mode of expressing yourself!'

It was a chastisement, though spoken kindly. She should know her place. But also, the mistress depended on the servant, and could not be too harsh. Elinor curtseyed to this younger woman, who nodded and walked away. She came and stood not far from him. He looked sideways at her, then looked away.

'Thomas Bishop,' she said. 'He is always speaking of the last things: death, judgement, heaven and hell. He is not so interested in this life.'

'He should speak about sins?' He turned to face her, and

found that she was looking directly at him. Her eyes were wide and chestnut brown, and discerned him immediately. He regretted having said it. She knew he was speaking lightly, that he thought little of Bishop the preacher, that he had his own thoughts about the resurrection of the body on the day of judgement.

'He might think about promises that were made and then broken. About toleration. Particularly of those who don't fall in with the church as it now stands.'

She had fathomed him, and she was inviting him to speak seditiously of the church, the Restoration of the monarchy, and of the crowning of the new king. He took his life in his hands in more than one sense when he said, 'Yes, he should.' He was now hers.

They walked around the churchyard, then by the small gate through the ditch and wall along the gravel path to St Paul's, then to the Thames, and then back again when it was time for Ellie to return to the Smithfield house where she was a servant. They talked about the sermon they had heard, about their earlier lives, about the days behind and ahead of them. He stood outside her doorway after she had gone in and thought that not only was he hers but that perhaps she was his.

★ ★ ★

It was Bishop who married them six months later, on St David's Day, with the churchyard bursting with daffodils. It was a small wedding, the second for both of them. Her family, still living in Brecknock, did not come. Her master and mistress and their daughter attended, though they had been unhappy that she was going to leave their household. His sister Jane came. He had long since lost contact with the youngest, Margaret, who had married above them all. He felt sad that Mary, the oldest in their family, had died four years earlier, especially because he knew she would have liked Ellie. His brothers, John and Thomas, had died long ago. He carried his years now. Mary Simmons came, the widow of his former master, who kept a prosperous printing shop near

St Botolph's Aldersgate. He can walk there in five minutes, but seldom does, not since he stopped working for her. There was John Smith, the corn merchant at Leadenhall market, with his son, also John, who would shortly be indentured as James' apprentice. There were a handful of friends. There were no bridesmaids, no bride-men. There were no children from their former marriages. There was a congeries of parishioners, who wished to attend a Friday morning service out of curiosity and a concern for the state of their own souls.

This mattered little to James and Ellie, who scarcely noticed the church or worshippers. What they did see, beyond each other, was the light moving across the flagstones. Spring light after a bitter winter. It caught the flowers on the table near the nave, shimmered on the altar cloth, and illuminated the dust rising with the air, auspicious and cheering.

Ellie was looking at the flowers when she felt him take her hand: she had not been attending to Bishop. There was his face, with its crooked lines. The creases made it familiar, made it his, now hers. She repeated her vows and he placed the ring on her finger. It was resolved. She knew this would not change.

They went to the Hand and Shears, where the landlady laid out a modest feast of mutton pie and wine, and then a cake iced with egg and sugar. For only the briefest moment, Ellie had a spasm of memory, when the sugar made her think of her first husband who died on Cromwell's Hispaniola expedition. She did not want to think of him today, or ever. And then he was gone. Her former master and mistress stayed only for a short while, took a piece of cake, and then her mistress pressed a drawstring purse into her hand, nodded and departed. She felt coins, more than she was owed. James kissed her and they, too, left the tavern. As they passed St Bartholomew the Less she squeezed his arm, and they stopped, leaned against the wall, and kissed again. People would think them unmarried and iniquitous, which was the opposite of what they were.

They turned left, towards the wall, and found the shop, all shut up. They opened the doors and shutters and let the light in.

Ellie began to sweep the floors. James had moved the contents of his old shop there, the presses and printing stuff and his furniture, but the place had not been dusted or cleaned. She put the flowers Jane White had given her in a pot on the kitchen table. Then she moved the table, so the light fell onto it and onto the flowers. Everything must be moved out of the darkness.

As she rearranged the flowers, James approached and, from behind, wrapped his hands around her breasts, pulling her back into his chest. He was warm. He did not make her feel ungainly. She turned, he took her arm and led her upstairs. They had a bedroom; he had already made the bed, with a real mattress and sheets. There was nothing else in the room, except the dust. She opened the shutters a crack to let the light in. He undressed her.

* * *

Five and a half years later, James stands at his composing table, finishing a line of type. He deliberates whether to start the next word and break it with a hyphen, but then chooses instead to add a little more spacing between words. He takes the line to the table where he has laid out the growing page, and finds that he has reached the end of the apportioned space. He thought he might have squeezed a little more in, but that won't work, so he chalks a new break into the manuscript. He places the line carefully with the others, and makes a catchword. This is the first word of the next page, placed at the bottom of the preceding page, so the printer and bookbinder and reader all know that the pages are in the right order. The catchword is 'effect', and once it is in place he surrounds it with a wooden frame, and then inserts quoins and wooden wedges within this to fix the metal type and stop it from moving. This page is done. He moves on to another out-of-sequence page.

On this page the words are different, and Eagle speaks with another kind of voice. Here there is a little humility. The fire has stopped burning at the end of the lane, and instead he reflects back on walking in the spirit of God, ashamed of his sins, hoping the fire and brimstone will purge some of the shame and grief he feels welling up inside him. James tries to ignore the sentences and just see the words. Something clouds his sense though. There is another out-of-sequence-ness in his thoughts, as he goes from Eagle, to the plague, to fire and brimstone, to Ellie, to his apprentice's fleeing, to the closing of the city gates, to thoughts of the burial pits outside the walls, to the falling numbers of fatalities, to the notion that deaths can be just numbers, back to Ellie, and to the hopes they had held when he took over this shop, and she swept out all the dust, scrubbed the floors and whitewashed all the walls.

The plans they harboured in whispers: to work together, to break bread together, to read to each other once Ellie had learned her letters, to make fine books and prosper, to make children to populate the kitchen and gather around its broad hearth. Neither was young, but they would be fruitful. They decided it separately, and found it funny when they told each other. It was something about the smell when they lay together, and the way they fitted together when they fell asleep. He feels the cold damp move in, and he nudges his thoughts so they lurch back to Eagle, the plague, to judgement. He is adept at this disciplining of unwelcome thoughts.

Eagle writes of burial, and, as his right hand collects the letters in the correct order, James's mind drifts to the grounds of St Bartholomew's hospital, near Mount Mill, where a pit was dug to bury bodies promiscuously, a shallow pit. They said that the burial pit near Aldgate in the east was deep, as deep as could be dug, three or four men in height, so body could be piled upon body, tipped straight from the cart, mingled together, into the abyss. But this one, which he saw with his own eyes, was barely deep enough to hold one man standing up, and bodies had been carted from Aldersgate and Farringdon Without, from Clerken-well and from within the city walls, thousands of corpses mangled in a small pit. He wondered if, in a rainy season, they would begin to show above the topsoil, decaying limbs swimming their way to the surface.

26

He had ventured to the St Bartholomew burial pit out of curiosity. These common graves had been excavated around London quickly to deal with the excess of dead. There was no time to bury them in churchyards, nor enough space. His curiosity took him to the edge of the pit in broad daylight, not when the carts could be heard approaching, heavy wheels cracking against the edges of cobbles. He stared down. As each layer of bodies was shot from the cart, a dusting first of lime and then of soil was thrown over, more for decency than truly to bury them. Then the next evening another layer arrived. The bodies were wrapped in shrouds, or some half naked. People feared the contagion of clothes, but not enough to prevent some from stealing and purifying them with smoke. He looked down at the shapes under the earth, the limbs contorted, not at peace. Fighting judgement, fighting God, uselessly. It would soon be full, and a final, thicker layer of earth applied, to let the elements have their say. Behind him he heard a cry, a cry of pain and fear, and his reverie was broken. This was a danger, standing so near a pit of plague victims. Even the soil might be contagious. He was risking not only his own life, which he might spare, but Ellie's, which he could not. He backed away, wanting to keep the edge in sight, wanting to be a few steps from it, before turning. He washed his face and hands before returning to his printing shop.

He finishes another page, exactly where his chalk mark on Eagle's manuscript predicted he would. His judgement is still sound. Tomorrow he will do the presswork. He will ask Smith to prepare the paper.

He has forgotten to collect the paper. And he has forgotten that Smith has deserted him. He sighs in frustration. It is too late to do this today. He will go in the morning. This will slow his progress.

'Ellie?' he calls out. She doesn't reply. 'Ellie?'

She is not in the kitchen. He looks out of the back door; she is not there either. She must be upstairs. He goes to find her.

CHAPTER THREE

James wakes at the precise moment of dawn. The hour of the nightingale has been replaced by that of the lark; the wolf has turned into the dog. Through closed shutters he sees grey light turn pink, hears birdsong. He judders awake, his mind already in full flight. He is sad, he is angry, he is fearful. He is not alone; Ellie lies beside him, in an ocean of sleep. She seldom wakes quickly, but this morning he does not know what she will do.

He rises, trying not to disturb her, uses the chamber pot in the corner of the room. He goes downstairs, smells the air in the kitchen. They will not need a fire today. They will need one soon. He pours a cup of small beer from the barrel in the larder off the kitchen. He takes a blanket which is thrown over a press, wraps it around his shoulders, and then stands outside his front door. The air and beer begin to fix him to the ground. He begins to speak his orisons in his mind. He has had six good years, and he is grateful for them, and he is alive and well. But then he looks to the east and, above Aldersgate, the sun is rising, and his thoughts run wild again. What is wrong with him? The sun is rising, and it will rise every day until judgement day, and perhaps even after then. It pays no attention to him or to anyone. It is busy and uncaring. When the good years are over it will rise and mock him, or not even care to mock him, though perhaps he will feel it does. Everything in nature is moved by God, and everything is decided by God, but it also happens by itself, through its own motions, set in motion once and for all. All of creation moves, and keeps moving, through inherent momentum, like a clock, until it is stopped.

And it is the same with the plague. If you catch it, it is God's decision. But it would be vanity to think that if you catch it, then it is because God has pointed his finger at you and said, 'You're next'. That isn't how providence works, or how probability works. If you catch the plague then you've been in contact with someone with the plague, or you've touched something they have touched, or you've breathed in their breath, shared their fluids. Staring into a plague pit risks contracting plague, going into a plague house that has been shut up risks contracting plague. Those women who are employed as nurses for people with the plague risk their lives, and thousands lie in the same plague pits as their patients. People ran from London at the height of the plague, before the gates were closed to those trying to flee, because they knew that they would reduce the danger to themselves by fleeing. Though at the same time they increased the danger to those who lived in areas of the country unaffected by plague. Now the plague is worse in the country than in London. Does this mean that the total danger was the same, but now spread among more and different people? He thinks not. Rather, a few people who fled from London were less at risk, but many more in the country were at greater risk, and villages that might have been entirely unaffected could now face desolation. So those who fled did what was right for them, but for those whose lives were consequently endangered, it was an injustice, and their lives were placed in another's hands. Was this a Christian way? But was it also not entirely understandable? Could those who fled not say that they had saved their own lives, that whatever they did was shaped by providence, and that if others died, then it was God's will?

His thoughts run wild, and what is wrong with him? More air, more beer, more sense of the weight of his feet against the cold stone. He breathes. And thinks of Ellie.

★ ★ ★

She was asleep when he went upstairs to find her in the afternoon of the day before, asleep in their wide bed. He had bought the bed when, in the flush of pamphlets about the restoration of the king, there was good money to be made. He had felt guilty about printing some of the works he had helped put into the world, fawning tracts, rhetorical tracts, some spouting lies, that cared nothing for the good of the people. But the money had let him set up the shop and buy a good, wide bed.

She lay there asleep, a familiar shape under the blankets, her face visible. Her hair spread wide on the bolster, floating over the sea of sleep, a mermaid's hair, singing to him, some wide curls, some tight, shining in the gloom. Her eyes, under thick eyelids, were heavy, sitting close to the front of her face, which meant to him that they were open, honest. Her forehead, so broad and high that he swam in it whenever she was irritated with him.

She was not quite asleep. He sat down beside her.

'Ellie?' She stirred. 'It's early.' She moaned. He laid his hand on her forehead. It was hot. 'Ellie? What's the matter?'

'Nothing,' she said, and he felt a wave of relief. 'It's just that I'm tired.'

'When did it come on?'

'I don't know. Earlier. When I brought back the bread from the baker's oven. It's in the kitchen.'

'I saw it. I smelled it.'

'I thought I would just lie down a little. It came over me suddenly. I'm sorry.'

'What are you sorry for? I was worried, that's all.' He hesitated. 'Do you think you might …?'

'No. I don't think so.'

'When did you last …?'

'It's been a month. But still.'

The topic burned in him, and he needed to change it.

'I was composing Eagle's pamphlet. I set four pages, one forme. It looks competent. I don't think it will need much proofing.'

'That's good. I can help tomorrow.'

'I forgot to fetch the paper. From Stationers' Hall. I'll have to go there first thing. I forgot about John. We needed him this week.'

'Makes me think of Mary.'

'Over a year now.'

'Yes. I wonder how she is. If she's still alive.'

Mary Richard had been their maid. She left in the summer of 1665, fleeing the city for her family on the coast in Kent. They could not have afforded to keep her in any case, but it felt like an abandonment after all they had been through. Ellie and Mary were friends. But they had not seen or heard of her since she travelled east.

'Perhaps he'll come back,' she said.

'I think he will. He was stupefied.'

'You'll forgive him.'

'If he comes back, yes. In good time, I hope. There'll be more and more work as it goes away. I think. Judging by Eagle's ability to make meaning out of others' misfortune.'

'You think it's that bad?'

'Not really. But, as you said, he uses a lot of words.'

She sank back into the bolster.

'What's wrong?'

'Nothing. I'm just tired. It came over me suddenly.'

'You're not unwell?'

'No, just tired. And I ache.'

'You should rest.'

'I'll be able to help you tomorrow. I'll ink, you can pull the press, and I'll hang the sheets. We'll make good progress.'

'I don't think we'll be finished by Monday, as I promised Eagle. The day of judgement may have to wait.'

She didn't laugh. She usually laughed; she was quick witted, liked to laugh. Perhaps he hadn't been very funny.

★ ★ ★

The sun is now clear of the rooftops, and the magic of its unpredictable colours has abated. Instead he sees pale blue descend into pink. This is his place, he thinks; he will not be shaken. He will stand here, firmly planted in Farringdon soil, and they will be together, do good work and prosper. He will not be shaken and alarmed. He will not take John Smith's flight as a sign, he will forget about Mary Richard, he will not think of the Fowls family. He will live his life as it should be lived. He finishes his beer. He will take Ellie one.

His mind, though, rebels against him, and the pink flush of the sunrise reminds him of Ellie's flushed neck. He has not completed his orisons.

He had gone down to the kitchen, eaten some broth and a chunk of the fresh-baked loaf. He chewed it slowly, making his hunger recede for longer. The small beer he had in plenty, as he brewed it himself. He wondered if the pestilence was spread by unbrewed water. Beer also suppressed his appetite. It was beginning to grow dark, so he lit a tallow candle and carried it into the shop. He stood in front of the case of shelves that he had made himself, built to fit the wall beside the fireplace. Standing here quelled the persistent gnawing sensation in his guts, which was not appetite but something else, an uneasy feeling, an apprehension. The shelves were half-full of books bound in the same blue paper, and bundles of stitched pamphlets. He and Ellie printed all of them themselves, together. So the shelves and the books are all their work.

The titles of the books are written on the blue spines, most in his hand, some in hers. The bundles of pamphlets are organised by years. There is less order in the books. They are not sorted by size, year, subject, author or by title. Perhaps the arrangement reflects how he thinks about them. He looked through them, not to find something in particular, but anticipating that something would seize his attention. Then something did. It was a book of poems, one of the first things they had printed together. An English poet, who writes about religion and faith, but also about love. Secular love, profane love, love of a woman, love of this world. He eased it from the shelf and carried it into the kitchen. He placed a chair near the hearth, the candle above the fire, stirred the embers, and started to read.

The words are still in his mind the following morning, as he watches the remaining pink steal into blue, until all is blue, even the west. The lines of verse will fade though, will slip his memory until they are half lines or phrases, and then just a few connected words, and then just a half-recalled feeling. Until he refreshes his memory by re-reading, and they come back, as hard and bright as ever.

He had read for two thumbs' width of candle, and then returned upstairs, carrying the candle and some bread and cheese and a pot of beer for Ellie. It was strange to have the house so quiet. No Mary, no John; it was as though he was alone there, creeping in the silence and near dark.

She was asleep and he didn't want to rouse her. Instead he left the food and drink on the table by her side of the bed, took off his clothes, and crept in. She stirred a little, moaned, but stayed asleep. Her neck was pink, flushed. He thought he should leave her be, and lie at a distance. But they never slept that way, without some comfort. It would be a sign that something was awry. He moved behind her until she folded into him, back against chest, buttocks into groin, kneepit to knee, and slipped his arm over hers to hold her breast. She was hot to touch, her thin smock wet with perspiration, her forehead hot and damp. She did not respond to his touch. A fear began to creep over him, as cold as she was burning. His hand over her breast was what made him feel connected to her when she was asleep, because of the pleasure it gave them both when awake, and because he sensed her slumbering body responding. But now he slipped his hand, slowly and softly, over her ribs, her waist, her hips, and down to her thighs, to the crease. He felt there, slowly and softly, into the fold of skin, looking for something amiss. There was nothing. Then back up again, over hip and waist and ribs and shoulders and to her armpits. There was nothing new there either. He wrapped his arm around her again and pulled her close.

He was jumpy, fearful. Because of John Smith and the Fowls family. And reading Eagle's broiling prose. And because of everything. That was all.

He slept uneasily, and woke at the precise moment of dawn.

★ ★ ★

He has found himself again, quashed the rebellion of fear and uncertainty in his mind, and feels his feet heavy on the ground. He won't lose himself in the sky; he is covered, protected by it. He breathes and returns inside the house.

Ellie is in the kitchen. She is wrapped in a blanket, but otherwise normality seems to have returned. She is making a fire.

'You're better now?'

'A little, I think. Still not right. Hot and cold by turns. And …' She hesitates, troubled, looking for the words. 'I can't remember going to bed. I was here, and then …'

'You were feverish.'

'I brought the bread back?'

'And then went to bed. I came up and found you there, half asleep. We talked. I came back downstairs and read. You were deep asleep when I went to bed. I don't think you broke the night at all. I woke and you didn't stir.'

'You prayed?'

'I did, a little. I was weary, and worried.'

'Don't worry.' She wraps her arms around him.

After six years, he is still brought to a standstill. He feels her height, the strength in her arms. He cannot move, cannot breathe, until she releases him. Which she does, once she feels that he is back with her.

'Will you be printing today?' she asks.

'I forgot to collect the paper yesterday. I'll have to go to Stationers' Hall this morning. I forgot that John had run away.'

'Oh!' she exclaims. He sees that she had forgotten this too.

'It's going to slow the making of Eagle's pamphlet, not having John.'

'Perhaps I can help?' she offers. He thinks that they've already agreed this, but says nothing. 'I could ink the type, if you operate the press. And I can help hanging the wet sheets. I still don't feel quite well. It'll pass. Perhaps I'll feel better by the time you return with the paper. Now I need to sit, though.' She pulls up a chair. He places a pot on the revived embers in the fireplace.

'You're kind to me, James.'

'I love you Ellie.'

'And you're very good to me.'

'I need you to be well. We do this together.'

'We do.'

He smiles. 'I was reading one of our books last night. The poems, remember them?'

She nods and smiles, but there is a hint of sadness in the smile.

He leans over her, and whispers a line of verse in her ear, one that was restored to his mind last night, and she listens intently to the words and to his voice, sonorous even in a whisper, and she feels the spirit of time stretch its wings over both of them, and over the six years they have spent living and working together, protecting them and collapsing the days into a single moment as full and heavy as the earth, and as she feels this he watches her, and sees the flecks of sadness evaporate.

CHAPTER FOUR

He leaves her wrapped in a blanket in the kitchen, eating a piece of bread, and walks along the gravel path. He passes Greyfriars and Christ Church, dodges a cart on Newgate Street, and is soon on Paternoster Row. This is the home of the makers of books, printers, binders, booksellers, inkmakers and type-founders – though many master printers make their own type – but not home to the carpenters who make the presses. And not papermakers, who all live overseas. This is why he must buy his paper from the Stationers' Company, the guild that governs and controls printing and the making of books in England and Wales. He is a member of this guild, though he is not active in it, having no taste either for the ceremony or the internal conflicts that most makers of books seem to relish. But he is obliged to work with the Company, not least because it imports the paper that printers must use. So he walks to Ludgate Hill, turns up Ave Maria Lane and enters Abergavenny House, where the Stationers have kept their hall for half a century, and finds a clerk who will sell him some paper. Eagle's coins are heavy in his pocket. He has missed this security. He will miss it again when he parts with it, though he knows the return will be good. Eagle is vain enough to pay the right price.

Later he stands outside Abergavenny House holding two reams of paper. This is not a light burden. Yet he still wants to delay his return, because the building opens onto Paul's church-yard, and he wants to visit St Paul's. He has some business with God.

He kneels in a pew near the back, the paper beside him. He doesn't need to look at the prayer book; he doesn't need the minister to speak for him. He needs God to listen. What is the use of all of these words, what is the use of speaking your faith, if there is no listening? He looks into his heart, but he has been deep inside his heart since the previous morning, and he knows all that lies there. He has tried to be a good man, through some hard times, but she is better. She is so much better, it is her nature. She must live. Jeremiah was taken. Cannot she be spared? He would willingly lay down his own life. He knows that's not how it works. But if it could. He would not hesitate. He would not ask why he had been forsaken or discarded. He would bear it without flinching. Because she is so good. And she has suffered so much.

This is his prayer, the covenant he offers.

The space of St Paul's is quiet in a distinctive way, as though the breath and flowing blood of those it harbours reverberate within it. It is never really quiet. It has a quiet that is oppressive to the ears, and makes you wish for some noise to break it. He looks up at the windows, follows the coloured light onto the stone. He admires the men who made this, the men who made the plans, the men who built it, the real makers, the masons who cut the stone and carried it so high, the glassmakers and carpenters. How much more overwhelming the conception of this than the making of a book. Not the words, but the material, particular, substantial book. Theirs was a vision of great scale and minute detail and astonishing craft. It humbles him, it chastises him, tells him not to expect too much.

He pauses, and lets the silence take hold and grow. Silence must be broken by listening as much as by speaking. How long must he wait? When he thinks that he has waited long enough, he prays more conventionally, for his family, his friends, his neighbours and all whose lives are in peril, for all of the living and the dead. Then he stands and leaves the church without bowing to the altar.

Outside he stands on the steps and looks along Ludgate Hill towards the Fleet. He is high, looking down on the city, with his back protected by the church. He stands in the new portico, rebuilt by the famous Inigo Jones. It is an impressive piece of work, but not in keeping with the rest of the building. Most of the cathedral is covered in wooden scaffolding, to allow building work but also just to keep it upright. The spire collapsed when it was struck by lightning a century ago, and it has not been rebuilt. Jones's ambition extended to a pleasant doorway, but his talents do not stretch to a whole building. Parts have been amended in the past few years, but it is a crumbling gothic ruin. Magnificent, awe-inspiring from the river, tyrannising over the landscape, the still heart of the city, but nonetheless mouldering, a testament to insufficiency in the face of history, a ruin.

Looking down towards the Fleet, there lies a different London, the London of judges and the law, parliament and the court. They could be different cities, though they rub up against each other. And for a time, while the wars raged, they were even more different and distant than now. Westminster, which has now been relocated to Oxford on account of the plague, had a different complexion, in conflict with the king, always seeking to argue with him. During the wars and in the time of parliament and then of Cromwell that followed, the law courts were more than the instruments of the royal will. The court was empty, the palaces used by Westminster. He read it in the newspapers, learned about it from his neighbours, heard the gossip among the stationers. He could barely conceive it, much less understand it.

His London is different. It is the city of merchants, and the city where people make things, a city connected by water to the whole of the world. His trade relies on a German invention, a Dutch approach to buying and selling, Dutch type, Italian and French paper, writing from all over the world, and the knowledge imparted by many who come from even further, from the east, and the Mediterranean. And yet he lives in a quiet street where he helps his neighbours, knows the boundary of his parish, keeps the law, takes his water and bakes his bread. It is where he feels at home, though not because he is disconnected from the world.

He walks there now. Along the path, through the wall and ditch, back to his shop, carrying the heavy paper. Once there, he unwraps it on the big table, checks it for a second time. It is good.

For a moment he is lost in the wild linen fibres as they weave and dive into each other. They hold the light in a way that nothing else does; until they have been through the press, and their otherworldly glow is tarnished ever so subtly. He holds a sheet up to the window, and murmurs, 'Ellie.'

★ ★ ★

He finds her still in the kitchen. She has more colour in her face, not just her neck. Again he feels, despite the distraction of the birds in his chest, that she is what he understands as the meaning of beauty. Whatever poets might say, English or Italian.

'How are you?'

'About the same. A bit better. Did you get the paper?'

He nods, concerned.

'How was it? What did you see?'

He says that the paper was heavy, that it is good, clean and bright, and he tells her about standing on the steps of St Paul's, looking west. He does not mention praying inside the church, nor how he tried to bargain, make a covenant with God.

'The streets were quiet. I heard no cries,' he adds, 'I saw nothing amiss. No signs of death. Nothing. It would have been as it was before, except the streets are so quiet.'

'It's gone away?'

'It may be. It's going.'

'The streets are quiet because people have fled?'

'And because many have died. And others are hiding in their houses with their stores of food. Everything together. It makes a peaceful walk, full of hidden fear.'

She groans lightly. 'We will print, then?'

'Are you well enough?'

'I'll help.' When she stands, though, she regrets her haste. 'Give me a moment.'

She breathes, and he holds his breath, then when she regains herself he breathes, deep down into his belly, and he remembers the morning.

40

'I'm fine,' she says. 'Let's dampen the paper.'

This he does. It prepares the paper to receive the impression of the type and the ink. He checks the forme, the tightly-framed pages of type that lie on the press. He sees nothing faulty; it's all flat. He takes the top sheet of paper and secures it within the open frame of the press. As he does so, Ellie uses two pads of cloth with wooden handles to soak up ink and spread it evenly across the surface of the type. She rolls and dabs it, and looks at the shine of the oil on lead in the light through the window. When she thinks the ink is even, she nods to him. He folds down the frame with the paper and slides it between the bed of type and the heavy iron platen. Then he turns the handle, and the platen descends, pressing the paper, secured in place by the frame, down against the inked type. The soft paper takes the contours of the type as well as the black ink. He pulls hard, with his weight, then releases. A turn of the handle takes away all pressure, and he slides out the frame and frees the sheet of paper. He holds it up for Ellie to see.

She nods. 'Let's read it then.'

And he pegs it onto a string hanging across the room, so they can read it together as it dries. They read two upright pages, then he turns it and they read the other two. He can read upside down, but she cannot. She turns to him and smiles.

'There are no errors.'

'I've not forgotten how.' She affectionately prods him.

'Of course you haven't.'

They gaze upon it for a while, the beauty of black shining on near-white. Sometimes it looks as though particles of sand glisten in the black. All the letters are in good order, straight and true. There are no marks from pieces of type or wooden furniture that stand proud of the surface. It is all expertly completed. Now they can print this side of the sheet, five hundred and sixteen copies, perhaps with some losses.

And when they have done so, James will take apart the forme of type and its four pages, removing first the quoins and wooden wedges, and then the pieces of lead, one by one, and he will redistribute each element to its original place in the separate compartments of the cases of type, and then they will begin the whole process again in order to print the other sides of the same sheets of paper.

★ ★ ★

Before this, they have to repeat the printing of this side of the sheet five hundred and fifteen times. At first they grow faster with practice. Then they slow down, because it is tedious and repetitive. Then they slow down further through weariness. Inking type is hard work, though it looks easy, because each letter across the whole sheet must be evenly covered, and this is best achieved by a firm motion. Ellie quickly becomes tired. They are only half way through the run when she says: 'I need to pause'. He is now angry with John Smith for abandoning them when they needed him. He has been watching her wane with growing despondency. He has seen the increasing effort as she daubs and rubs the type with the ink pads, her forehead damp. She is strong and not easily spent. He can see how frustrated she is with herself as the inking wears her down until she gives up trying to seem well. She tries not to let it show – she thinks it does not – but it does. He has seen something like this before, once.

'Ellie, you must rest. I can do this alone.'

'It always takes two.'

'I can do it alone. It'll just be slower. You can start again when you feel better.'

He walks to the other side of the press and wraps his hands around her belly, pulling her to him.

'I'll rest for just a while.'

Holding her belly he finds himself wondering. He tries to shut the thoughts out, but they won't leave. Has he misread the signs? Has he misunderstood providence? It is a little shameful if he has. In his hands he feels for something, for some promise of change. There is nothing there, but how would he know? He holds her tight, and does not know how long he has been holding her. Long enough to bring them back here.

She sits by the fireplace, which opens behind onto the kitchen hearth, wrapped again in a blanket. She is the same, it is the same for her. She goes away, in her mind, she comes back. She watches him go, and puts her arms around him to bring him back, and he comes back and again they are in the same place. She sees and feels the same drifting away, but has no words for it.

'Aren't you cold?' she asks. He shakes his head. 'It's the work, I suppose. Keeps you warm.'

He nods. 'Have they started?'

She looks at him blankly. 'What?'

'Your flows.'

'No.' She shakes her head as though she doesn't know why he's asking.

'I thought perhaps …'

'Oh. I don't know. I don't think so.'

He loads the paper in the frame. Then he walks around to the other side of the press, loads the ink pads with ink from the tray, and inks the type meticulously. He is out of practice. He puts the pads back in the tray, walks back around the press. He folds the frame down, slides it into the press, between the bed of type and the iron platen, and pulls the lever. The damp paper receives the impression. He releases the lever, frees the frame from the press, and extracts the sheet. He holds it up. There are some blemishes, a smear of ink on the outer edge, and some faint patches where the paper hasn't taken all the ink. He is less expert at inking than Ellie. He doesn't show it to her, but hangs the sheet up to dry. They are already running low on space. He will have to collect the dryer sheets from their earlier work and pile them up out of the way. There is never enough space in the printing shop. It must always be orderly.

She is dozing off.

'Why don't you rest in bed?' he asks, though he will miss her company. In response she only moans, no words. Somnolent. She is more deeply asleep than he had realised. 'Shall I carry you up?'

She sighs and nods, and he helps her up the stairs, half carrying and half walking with her, supporting her weight and guiding her. He puts her in bed and places the blankets over her, tucking them in to make sure the cold air doesn't touch her. She smiles at him when he tells her that he loves her, and says that she loves him, but it's as though she isn't really there.

* * *

He resumes the printing. It is slow and he soon grows frustrated. He breathes to quell the frustration. It is already growing dark when he completes the run. He checks on her twice. She is resting, half awake, half not. When the run is done, he gathers all the nearly-dry sheets into a single pile. This affords him a sense of accomplishment. The rest lie drying around the workshop, still a little too wet to risk touching.

He faces a dilemma. Should he break up the forme of type now, and redistribute the letters into their trays, or should he leave it until the morning? If he does it now, then he can start to set the reverse of the first sheet in the morning when he wakes. He risks, however, inattentively throwing the wrong type into the wrong compartment, which then leads to errors when he next uses the type, and thus to more corrections while the work is being printed. If he leaves it, then the early hours of the day when he is most alert will be spent breaking up a page rather than putting a new one together. And he is much quicker at composing type when he is alert. He decides to try to break up the page. He puts the forme beside the table with the half-empty cases of type. He unties the string, removes the frame, the wooden wedges, the quoins, puts them in their proper places, and then begins to pick up the pieces of type one by one, and throw them gently into their respective compartments. He takes two tallow candles to make sure there is enough light, one on each side of the type table. He should not be working this late, he knows.

When he is done it is much too late. But the printing room is tidy, and he will be able to start afresh as soon as he is ready in the morning. It has been an adequate day's work, better than he had feared at several moments during it. He will worry about Eagle in the morning.

He treads as lightly as he can up the stairs, carrying some broth and a piece of cold meat.

'Ellie?'

'Mmmm,' she answers.

He checks the shutters are tightly closed.

He sits on the bed beside her, and feels her forehead. It is clammy. He weighs things in the light of a single candle, perched in the dim bedroom that contains fully half of his life, the possibilities of endings and beginnings. He is not alone in his shakenness, this tumbling disquiet. Everyone in the city has been so stretched by fear, attenuated by the concern that they or the ones they love would catch the plague, that they can no longer distinguish between hope and terror, and easily find each in the other. He thinks of a child, and he is filled with despair; he thinks of death and he imagines the ease, almost wants the release. Until everything topples from the balance, the scales crack, and all tumbles into anxiety. Everything is swallowed by a bad end.

He breathes. Not now. Tomorrow he will rise at a good time, and will set pages three, two, seven and six. She will help him if she can, but if she is still unwell then he will do it himself, and she will be well soon.

He takes off his clothes and climbs in, trying not to disturb her. Yet he cannot resist sliding over. She is facing him, and he takes her hand. She holds his. He feels her breath on his face, tucks the blanket down. He slides his free hand along her arm. He doesn't mean to at first, but he moves it to her armpit and tucks his thumb under; then over her shoulder to her neck, and caresses there, and then down over her breast with its proud nipple, her belly, navel, hair, and to the side of her pubic mound, where he slips a finger deep into the hot and damp creased skin. He finds nothing. So he edges closer and puts his hand over her belly, and tries to sleep.

CHAPTER FIVE

He stands outside the shop. It is Wednesday. He calculates, for the eighth or ninth time, whether it is possible for him to finish Eagle's pamphlet by Monday, and whether it is likely that he will do so. He does not expect that he can. Perhaps if John Smith reappeared, they might complete the work together. But otherwise, surely, he cannot. He will have to inform Eagle that it will be delayed by a day or two. He would do this today, but he doesn't know if it will be one day or two. Or three or four. Wrapped in his blanket, he watches the sun lift over Aldersgate. He is thirsty. Nothing seems right, but he can find nothing wrong. Ellie has slept heavily again. She is mending.

September is approaching, bringing cold air with it, and the light will soon change with the dawns. August has three more of its pink skies, and he savours the first of these. It has been still and dry too, and September will bring rain and winds. He breathes. The air smells of the river, of birds, cold stone, and of slaughtered lamb, though also of human excrement and putrefying flesh, sweet and distant. He breathes, he needs more air.

He will not seek out Eagle. Instead he will set and start to print the second forme. He doubts that he will complete the printing of this today unless he has Ellie working with him. Printing is a job for two people, working opposite each other and together. Theirs is a kind of dance, moving alternately, making something singular through their togetherness. He fits the paper, she inks the type; he pulls the press while she inks the pads; he removes the sheet and they pause. Nonetheless, he will make progress, and as long as he does then the work will be done, sooner or later. He does not expect that Ellie will be working with him. Whatever is amiss, she slept through the usual hour when they wake and pray, and she did not rise with him this morning.

Though if she had, he would still be standing here unaccompanied. This moment is his alone. This is when he daily plants his feet in the place where he lives, and says: this is mine, this is me. This is the life we have made, over six good, hard years. It may not be far from Smithfield, only a short walk, but it is not the life I was born to, and it is a good life. And this is my place, and this the life I live. For Ellie, he knows, it is different: for her this is the end of a journey that might have taken a dozen different turns and ended up, as it began, far away. Her journey started in the mountains in Wales, near an English castle, a town with a bridge over a river, where no one spoke English. It rained every day, and she fled the rain. If she needs to feel the ground beneath her, she will stand in the shop, surrounded by the printing presses, the type, the books she has made, the walls that are hers. Standing there, she knows that she has found the end of the journey, that she is no longer in service, can read, and can speak her mind. He, though, needs to know that London is his, and that he will not be dislodged. The same sentiment is brought by different things, fifteen feet apart.

He will take her the last of the bread and some beer, and talk to her. The dawn has lost his attention, and he keenly feels her absence. When he feels that she is too far away there is something missing in him, and he loses all ability to take hold of and inhabit the moment. He wonders how she is, he imagines what she is doing, he conjectures how she feels, and so he forgets himself. The lack is inside, not out. Now he pictures her lying awake and wondering where he is, wondering if he has gone into the city, troubled that she might be alone, needing something, so he turns his back on the dawn, forgets his morning prayers, and goes back into the house.

★ ★ ★

She is moaning, in pain. Still in bed, not completely still, but turning and shifting with the pain. She doesn't see him enter.

48

'Ellie?' He feels he has been in this same moment too many times, as though he is waiting for something. It is not terror that touches him, but something building towards terror. The feeling he sometimes had as a child, awake in the night, alone and uncertain. Fearing not one thing, but many nameless things that might or might not be. Together they are more than any one thing could ever be, because his child self cannot concentrate on the one and tell himself it is not so, that there is nothing there. The plurality of uncertainties conspires against him, then and now. There is something unkind in this feeling that is not terror, cruel because it overwhelms him with a buzzing swarm, on all sides, within and without. It grows louder, more unfocussed.

'James. It hurts. I'm aching. Everywhere.'

He hands her the small beer. 'Here, drink this.'

She lifts herself up on the bolster, and he sees that her neck is pink, pinker than before. The skin there is rough.

'Your neck.'

She drinks. 'What's wrong?'

He doesn't know what to say. He climbs in beside her, wraps his arms around her, holds as much of her as he can. He wants to cover and protect all of her, body and soul.

'I'm frightened,' she says.

'Not yet.'

'Everything aches.'

'It did before. Do you feel sick?'

'Yes, a little.'

He remembers how it was before. It began with her finding it hard to get out of bed. She would never snap awake like he did, but she always made herself rise at dawn, and prepare herself for work. Then one morning she called out that she was going to be sick, and she was. She lay back down and they began to hope. It was over a month since her last monthly flows, she thought. The sickness passed, but it was back the next morning. He offered to find a midwife, but she said it was too soon, and they waited. Another few weeks, and then she agreed to see the midwife. And she had confirmed it. She was pregnant. They would, all being well, have a child. James was not sure how the midwife knew, but he accepted her judgement because he was so eager for her to be right that he could not imagine her wrong. And she was not wrong. Two months later and Ellie began to show. Those were good times for their printing house, and she was not as thin as she sometimes was, there was no scope to conceal the bulge of a child; and they were good times to get pregnant, as she was not so thin that her flows stopped. And she began to grow round, and James was even more fascinated by her body. He wondered if it was right and proper, if it was godly, so compelled he was.

★ ★ ★

He had always been compelled by her body. He thought her very beautiful, but beyond that, something about her nakedness unnerved and beguiled him. He wanted to nestle under her skin, he wanted to protect her under his own skin, he wanted to swap skins to make a being that was neither and both.

He remembered the first time he had seen her naked, when he removed her clothes, every layer, piece by piece. It was St David's Day in the year 1661, five and a half years ago. They were standing by the big bed, and he saw her form in the light that broke through the shutter's crack.

She was not shy or awkward. She had been married before. He had been married before, but this was different. Years of labour and regret and sadness and loneliness were suddenly resolved. He had seen the virtue and kindness shine through the features of her face. Now he saw them in her body, together with her sexual appetite, hitherto entirely hidden. She was tall, broad, round. Her skin was smooth, fine and soft. Something about the proportions he saw, the surfaces he touched: he knew he was lost. He quickly undressed and wrapped his arms around her, pulling her shoulder to his, her breasts into his chest. This was where he was meant to be, how he was meant to be. He had been looking for this. He would never let go. This was both end and beginning.

They had lain down on the bed, and had fitted together.

Their size and shape matched like the pieces of a master carpenter's mortise and tenon joint. Now he was in her arms, and she held him as he had never been held before, not by his first wife, not by his sisters or mother. There was something in this that was about more than sex or making children. It was about learning that he was a particle of something else, a larger entity. He was not made to be whole without her.

The appetite was also sexual, however, and mutual, and they made love constantly. But she did not become pregnant. They worried and they talked and they prayed, and they wondered if God had chosen not to bless them. Ellie had been listening to a Baptist preacher named William Kiffin, who held his services not in a church but in a private meeting house, and she began to take his view that the baptism of children was a misuse of the sacraments. So she was baptised again, as a fully-consenting adult. This did not change her unfertile condition, but she was lighter in spirit. Only after more than two years of marriage did they learn that she was pregnant, first revealed by the morning sickness, and they had been married almost three years when Jeremiah was born.

The pregnancy did not abate their appetite for making love. The child was his, and it was hers, and both he and the child were under her skin, and he was folded around hers.

★ ★ ★

'I feel sick, but it feels different from before,' she says. He is holding her, wishing he could hold her tighter.

'You don't feel as hot as you did. In the night you were burning up. And you slept again.'

'That's good.'

And he slips his arms, stealthily, down to her groin. He accidentally touches her labia, and she responds, she gives a little shudder and looks quickly up at him, with a smile. Her lips are damp. He slides his fingers, and then the heel of his palm, along them. But, again, he cannot help himself, cannot stop the impulse.

He feels in the folds of skin to the side. There is nothing. She is clear. Then he slides his hands up again, playfully over her labia, up to her belly. His palm rests there.

'You're crazy,' she says, but she pushes herself back into his groin. He wishes to hold this moment, to live for a while entirely in it, and he breathes her in and out again as his hand feels for signs of hope. A spark of life reaching to his fingertips. There is nothing. But her breathing is steady, deep. While he holds her like this he feels he can hold onto her, that she cannot go anywhere, that she is safe. The moment is theirs and it will last.

Until he breaks it. He cannot stop himself from checking, hearing in his mind a hundred conversations held since the plague came to London, spreading rumour and news of the symptoms, the preventatives, the cures, and he cannot keep them out so he loses that moment and his hand slides up from her belly, over her exquisite nipple, to her armpit.

She feels it before he does. She utters a little cry.

'Oh.' Her breath stalls with the pain.

'Ellie.' He feels a swelling there, small but certain.

'It hurts.'

She closes her eyes. He cannot see her face, but he knows she closes her eyes. He moves his hand back to her belly.

They lie for a time without speaking or moving. He does not know for how long. It ends when she begins gently to convulse. At first he thinks it is a fit – he has heard about fits in the advanced stages of the disease – but then he realises that she is sobbing.

'Ellie. You will recover.' She does not respond. 'We will see you through this. I will feed you and you can rest, and you will get better. People recover these days.'

She does not respond.

She doubts what he says, and she cries not for her death but for everything that will now never be. Her thoughts have lost all anchor, and they are so wayward and unruly she wonders if they are someone else's thoughts. She stands and watches them overwhelm her, without being able to subdue or influence them.

She cries for one thing then another. Then she feels a fire rising within, and as she grows hot she becomes drowsy, and the thoughts become ever more disjointed but at least she is relieved by sleep.

James lies with her a while, but when she is fully asleep he gently rises, folds the blanket around her, and goes downstairs. He is full of love, fear, sadness, self-pity, despair, anger at God, and these feelings pile one on top of another until he doesn't know which is which. He is sick with grief and rage. He has to shut the doors on all this, or it will overthrow him. He decides to work on Eagle's pamphlet.

★ ★ ★

Composing type is dull but requires close attention, and it helps him still his nerves and his guts. He starts to set the second forme, starting with page three, because page two, the back of the title page, is blank. Eagle is writing about the closure of the theatres, closed again as they had been during the war, because they spread the plague. Can you not see, he asks, that the plague was also a judgement on them?

He tries to ignore Eagle's meanings, just to see the words. By the end of the third line he realises that when he had broken down the page the night before he had not been as attentive as he should. He has found three letters in the wrong compartments. This gives him something else to concentrate on. He makes the page, line by line, loading them onto the bed. With every line he thinks about how he is approaching the end of the page, reckoning the progress. Words impale him with associations that he must keep at bay. Surprised, unprovided, distemper, shows, judgement, fire. He pushes them away, and will not let them touch him. They are only words, mere buzzing.

Halfway through the page he is in his measure, breathing as profoundly as the tightness in his chest will permit, and he has shut out the contagion of the world. He starts page seven, and then page six. The forme is almost done.

He pauses, eats some bread and cheese. He checks on Ellie, who is asleep, moaning softly. He inspects the store of ink: there is enough. He has wasted no paper from the two reams. He is tired of his work, bored, cannot feel that there is any point in continuing, except for fear of doing nothing. He is good at this work, but no longer cares. He does not want to read. He sweeps the floor in the workshop and the kitchen, dusts the hearth. He makes some dough and leaves it to rise in the hearth.

Then he completes page six and the forme. He secures the type and places it on the bed on the press. He collects the printed sheets of the first forme that are still hung out around the room. He is ready to print. But first he takes the end of the bread and the cheese to Ellie. She is still asleep, so he leaves it by the bed for her. He takes the dough to the bakehouse.

It is only as he walks back that he realises that he is meant to be walled up within the house. Ellie has the plague, and the house should be secured. No one knows about her, though, so he is free to walk as he chooses, restricted only by his conscience. He risks spreading the plague to others through his perambulations. He resolves to be silent about the sickness, and hope that, if she deteriorates, her cries do not attract the attention of a neighbour.

He may be carrying it with him; he may even be infected. He is contaminated, an outcast. He hurries back to Ellie, who has eaten the bread and cheese and fallen asleep.

He begins to print the second forme on the back of the already-printed sheets. He takes the first pressing, hangs it, and proof-reads it for errors. There are five. He unties the block of type, releases some of the quoins, and changes the five erroneous letters for the correct ones. He then re-secures the type, and takes a second impression. He reads this, and identifies a single additional error. He corrects this too. Then he prints a third sheet, but this one he does not check. There will be two copies that will be different from the others, but he will put them in the middle of the run, so Eagle doesn't notice them. He prints. Progress is slow, as for every sheet he walks around the press to ink the type, then back again to pull the lever to drop the platen. But soon the sun is setting, and he remembers the bread.

Again, he walks to the bakehouse to collect it. He worries that someone will see his condition, see into him, and call out that he is a pariah. He knows that this cannot be, that you can only see the symptoms, not the disease as it lies waiting, but nonetheless the thought intrudes upon him. He walks tall, but with his eyes down.

It is getting dark when he returns home. He cooks a stew, eats some, takes some for Ellie, but she is asleep. He cleans the kitchen, tidies the workshop. He has made perhaps a hundred copies, all of which now lie drying. He will gather them in the morning. He takes a tallow candle up the stairs. The day is almost over, another day.

* * *

He climbs in beside Ellie, and she is her normal temperature. He knows that he should not be here, that he should sleep in John Smith's bed, that he risks contracting the plague. Yet he has long decided, if it could be called a decision, that he does not care. He will not be parted from her. He has resigned himself to providence, and he will stick with this resignation, even though it means giving nature every opportunity to strike him down. This is not how they will live. And besides, she will recover.

She stirs when he presses up against her. She takes his hand, and holds it against her breast. He thinks he should sleep, they should sleep, but she seems to be awake, he can sense this, and he knows he cannot sleep yet. He caresses her nipple, and she responds, pressing herself against him, teasing him. He turns her over, and he kisses her. Her breath is stale, but they kiss, and then she is touching him, and he is touching her, and they are fully naked and inside each other. They make love, and he is careful not to lean too heavily on her, or to touch her armpits. They make no mention of this, though it lies between them. When she climbs on top of him, as she usually does, he can see by tallow-light that she does so gingerly, that it hurts her to do so. They both feel a weight upon them, a burden, but they don't speak of it. He cannot not love her this way. He thinks she feels the same. The plague cannot change that, and there are things he fears much more than death.

When they are done, both satisfied, she rolls away from him, and they hold hands. He breathes, he breathes, he needs the air.

CHAPTER SIX

He is in the street again, watching the sky change. These are his cobbles, his ruts running along them. He woke in the night and prayed, and now he feels that he has done what he can to accept whatever obstacles fortune has thrown in his way. He has embraced his wife, followed resolutely the path that he set out on six years ago, one he will not be diverted from.

He thinks of it as fortune, though he knows that it is God's will, the implacable forces of a Creation that is good, even though it doesn't always appear that way. But he is beneath God's notice, so fortune is as valid a name as any for the forces that operate subordinate to His will, the regular but inexplicably complicated motion of the clock. He won't scrutinise the motion, looking for patterns. He will accept the judgement of fortune. Fortuna to the Romans, he remembers from his brief schooling, was a goddess, carrying a wheel, the wheel of fortune, representing luck. The wheel turned and sometimes you had good luck and sometimes bad. Like the thieves next to Jesus on the cross: one was saved, the other damned. Jesus was the fulcrum, the wheel's axis, on which the world turned, which meant that one thief went up, the other down. There is no way for him to know how the wheel of his fortune is turning, but he stands braced.

He is surprised when he feels her arms around him.

'You're up.'

'I feel better this morning,' she says.

As they stand facing east, the air loses some of its crispness. Streaks of grey traverse the pink horizon with random architecture, as though reflecting the city's streets. She sees it too.

'There's another city up there,' she says. They think like this, he knows. Sometimes he is transparent to her, sometimes she to him.

'Another world. Do you think they suffer with the plague?' He regrets it immediately, and says, 'I think it will be warmer today.'

'I'm going to help you print.'

'You've recovered enough for that?'

'I think so. Perhaps it was the night physic.'

He laughs as she squeezes him with her full strength, which appears to have been restored. He catches his breath when she releases him.

'We should go back in for some more of the same medicine, then?' he asks.

'After we've made a start on the work. A reward.'

The street is empty, but he wonders how they would be seen, by a neighbour or a passing stranger, as they embrace here like young newly-weds, amorous and silly, rather than a six-year couple in their middle years.

He thinks of the pinkness of her neck, and decides they had better go in, in case a neighbour looks at them through a half-open shutter and asks a question. But then he turns, and sees that her neck is not so discoloured this morning. The city in the sky is changing too as the pink there deepens and the clouds are momentarily blue.

'Let's start work then,' he says, and she leads him in.

* * *

They print: she inks, he operates the press. The sheets are cleaner as she is more diligent in her inking than he was yesterday. As he gathered the dried sheets into a stack, he saw that they showed signs of weariness or haste, patches of faint letters, black smudges where there should be white space. Ink out of place. No matter, though, they were good enough for the purpose.

Her hands grip the ink pads tightly, the fingers pale and the knuckles red, a little raw, the sinews on the back prominent. She wipes them on a rag after each application, because she does not want to mark the printed sheets before hanging them to dry. It's hard on her hands, he thinks. He wants to hold them, to feel them on him again.

The wet sheets around the workshop grow in number, the heap of sheets with only the first side printed shrinks, until they are halfway to completion. She does not weary. Until she says, 'My head isn't right. It hurts.'

'Then you should stop.'

And she takes a seat in the corner, by the hearth.

'I'm sorry.'

'Don't be. You're getting better.'

'It doesn't feel that way now.'

'But compare with yesterday. You hardly moved. Today you're up.'

'They hurt. The buboes. They really hurt,' and she begins to cry.

He kneels and puts his arms around her waist, laying his head against her breasts. 'Should I find a physician? Or a plague nurse?'

'No,' she says immediately. 'Then we'd be trapped here. And you won't finish Eagle's little book. And how would we eat? And doctors bring as much danger as relief. No, let it take its course.' She kisses his head on the thinning hair. 'You'll take care of me.'

'More night physic?'

She laughs, 'Later. I'll rest a bit and watch you.'

He prints, slower now, and tires, and the printed sheets are less orderly. Once again there is dark where there should be light, and light where there should be dark. The ink rebels against him.

She watches him contentedly, admiring the way he moves. Then she falls asleep in the chair, wrapped in a blanket.

It's warmer today, he thinks; she doesn't need a fire. He stands over her for a while, feeling the ache in his arms from inking the type and pulling the press. He watches her sleeping face. There are no lines when she sleeps. He eats some bread and cheese. It's not enough, so he takes some honey and hazelnuts too. The sweetness is consoling, touches the emptiness. She is still asleep, mending.

He is making little headway with the book, though, and decides that he should inform Eagle that it will take longer to complete than he had predicted. He knows that Eagle is preaching today, at two hours past midday, at a house on Bread Street Hill, and decides he will go to listen, and speak to him afterwards.

He says to Ellie, 'I'm going into the city, to speak to Eagle, and tell him his book will be delayed. I'll make up a reason, perhaps blame it on John's leaving. I'll listen to his sermon first though, before telling him. It'll make him less annoyed.'

She sleeps while he speaks, and he leaves her curled up in the chair.

★ ★ ★

The gravel path through the ditch and small gate leads him to Yule Lane, across Paternoster Row, to Paul's Alley and the churchyard, past Paul's Cross. He walks to the east side of this, then along Watling Street. Here he leaves the ward of Farringdon Within the Wall and enters Bread Street Ward. He hears bells. Where Watling and Bread intersect he sees Bow church to his left, and these are the bells he hears, but instead he turns right and walks along Bread Street until it terminates at Knightrider Street. Two carts bearing goods into the city slowly pass west, then he crosses and heads up Bread Street Hill towards Thames Street. He has been told to look for the sign of the compass, but he has not gone far when he hears Eagle's voice, echoing off wood and plaster walls.

'And the Lord put forth his hand, and touched my mouth. And the Lord said unto me, Behold, I have put my words in thy mouth.' He pauses. 'And how shall we know this? How shall we know it is the Lord's doing? Shall we know the prophet by his words, by his deeds, or by other signs?'

'By the spirit in the words,' cries out one in the unseen audience. Eagle's voice comes from an empty baker's shop, to which the door stands open, the downstairs shutters wide. James enters, and sees the man standing on a box, a congregation of thirty or more men and women before him, crowded around.

'By all of these, if you read them rightly,' the preacher says emphatically, his voice scouring the flagstones. He is already deep into his exposition, but James listens for over an hour to Eagle's sermon. It concerns the nature of true prophecy, the marks of the true prophet, his sense of vocation. The prophet sees the future, but he also, and here Eagle notes that he will come back to the question of women prophets in a future sermon, sees things that are far off, not only in time, but also in place and in truth. Because the prophet sees meanings that are remote or hidden. Why does the Lord need such men? Because the blind and the ignorant and the worldly cannot read the signs. The prophet is a channel, because His messages need glossing for those rendered senseless by sin. Because He is kind.

And then he turns to the next verse of this chapter of the Book of Jeremiah, which will make the second half of today's preaching. 'See, I have this day set thee over the nations and over the kingdoms, to root out, and to pull down, and to destroy, and to throw down, to build, and to plant.' This will take some parsing he says, and he picks out his themes, leaving them hanging.

After another half an hour James is tired. Eagle has beaten him into agreeing with every sentence even before he weighs what it means. A destruction is necessary before a rebuilding. Remove the roots and the cut tree will not grow again. All flesh is grass. This plague could be a great levelling, striking down so many people, before a new righteous law, and a newly righteous people, spring up. They would cut down the weeds, burn the stubble, raze the nations and the kingdoms as a careful husband-man tends the fields. And these people, their eyes cleared by a true prophet, looking upon the pastimes of former generations, singing and dancing and revels, would see them as the devil's works and permanently forsake them.

James is troubled by the talk of levelling and destroying nations and kingdoms. It sounds like radical politics, as though Eagle is hinting at the levelling of kingship, the uprooting of monarchy. This is a notion that cannot be so much as whispered safely on the streets of London these days. The civil wars, parliament and Commonwealth and Cromwell's Protectorate are not far behind, still raw in memory. The new king has spies and informants on the streets, and if you are caught speaking or even listening to sedition then you will find yourself apprehended and imprisoned, or just beaten unconscious by a gang hired by someone working for the secretary of state or the licenser of the press. He will not be allowed to keep his printing press if he is found in the wrong place, and his reputation is not untarnished, he is sure. He frequented too many conventicles in his earlier years, and printed works for Simmons and, worse, Giles Calvert, in the days before the return of monarchy. It would not take much to paint him as a radical, he fears. He would not want to be dragged to a courtroom to discuss select passages of Eagle's sermon.

He remembers the days when there had still been some hope for toleration, just after the king's restoration, and then he remembers St Bartholomew the Less, and the flowers, the blue wildflowers with which Ellie had speckled the church, and the white, yellow and gold flowers she held in her hand. Did she preserve any, did she press them between the pages of a book, did she hold onto them as signs of promises?

The preacher has reached his peroration, his voice is raised and the pitch more varied. There is a judgement coming, he interprets for us, and the plague is uprooting, pulling down, destroying, and then there will be a throwing down, a throwing down by a means that he cannot yet disclose, so tightly wrapped has God kept His plans, buried in His heart of hearts, and only then will there be a building and planting.

He is sweating, his forehead shining. The gaunt, grey-haired man, his face more lined than ever, pale and fierce, steps down from his box. His hearers murmur their approval, then speak up and praise him. There is one family, in sombre clothing, who look like good puritans from head to toe, the man wearing a hat, the woman covered. There is a man with coarse, red skin who may be drunk, perhaps looking for entertainment. There are three old women, dignified and unbending, who speak their praise noisily.

He speaks the truth, he is a Jeremy, they say. There are various apprentices, some smelling of bread, some of fish, some with blackened hands. James scans them to see if any look like candidates for an informer or spy. None seems likely, though any might be. Then he scans to see if anyone looks like him. Are these people like him, or people quite different from him?

Who, he asks himself, is free to be here; who can afford to be here on a Thursday in the height of the afternoon? Is the business of the city so dwindled that they don't have work or duties to attend to? How many gatherings like this are taking place around London at this very moment? He is here, admittedly, but he has his reasons. He wonders if Eagle will be understanding, since he is, at this very moment, neglecting his own work to listen to a sermon.

Looking at the faces, none much like his own, and remembering that all flesh is grass, he is troubled. He has forgotten again. He might bear the infection with him. He might be the scythe that cuts the grass. Every face in this room, man, woman and child, all might die because he is here with them, brings with him the plague. He might fulfil Eagle's prophecy. They could all be dead within a week or two. All flesh is grass. He should be at home, and instead he is the mower.

The room empties, until Eagle spies him.

'White. I'm humbled that you came.'

'It was inspired, Solomon Eagle. Your sermon. It made me examine myself.'

'Thank you, White. Come again.'

'I will, God willing.'

'Ay,' says Eagle, and takes his arm. 'We should not presume.'

'Though,' James adds circumspectly, checking the faces still leaving the room, 'I would be loathe for your words about the levelling and uprooting of nations and kingdoms to be misunderstood.'

'They're the prophet's words, not mine.'

'And, as you said, you are their conduit, Eagle. Can you

speak them again without repeating them as yours? Without owning them in some way? And besides, you offered to interpret the words.'

'Well, I said that to interpret was the prophet's work, so I'm grateful that you take me for a prophet. But in any case, White, I think we are among friends here, among people who would not interpret these words unsympathetically.'

'I hope so.'

'And besides, the meeting itself is contrary to the law. I was imprisoned for attending one like this a year ago.'

James nods. He had almost forgotten. He should not be here, with Ellie sick at home.

'And my little book?'

'Is being printed. That's the reason I stayed after your sermon, much though I wanted to go straight to the printing press and make more progress. I'm afraid we lost John Smith, my apprentice.'

Eagle looks startled.

'No, not to plague. He fled the city. A friend of his died of the plague, Fowls, the family locked up, and he was startled and left the city. Over-hastily.'

Eagle relaxes a little, and appears to reflect upon their souls.

'And my little book?'

'Not Monday, as I said it would be. I hope Tuesday, but certainly Wednesday. And I've read the proofs and it is sound. You will be happy with it.'

'And the ink?'

'Is good and black.'

Eagle is satisfied.

'I will come on Wednesday, then. But if it is ready earlier then send for me. I live near to the Hart in Spitalfields, just on the far side of the market. Ask for me there.'

James agrees, though he doubts he will be walking as far as Spitalfields next week, even if he prints the book on time. Which he will, he resolves. He will do it with his own hands, and forsake sleep.

'Thank you for the sermon,' he says as they leave the baker's shop. They leave it unoccupied. He realises that he does not know to whom it belongs. It may be abandoned, left during the exodus of the summer before, or since then. Many, particularly those who were not poor, left their properties in the hands of friends or relatives. They sought refuge with friends in the country. If the baker was one of these, then the shop has become a temporary church, with or without their knowledge.

'Come again, White. Come again next Thursday. I will speak of the true women prophets.' He turns north up Bread Street Hill, but James halts. 'Come, I walk towards Bishopsgate, and you to Aldersgate, I think. We can walk to Cheapside together.'

'Another time, Solomon Eagle. Right now I must go to the river.'

They say goodbye and he walks to Queenhithe harbour, where he stands at the water's edge. The Thames is cold and brown, the tide in, hurried. Two boatmen cross the river, opposite ways, both with passengers. There is a boat docked here; he thinks it may be an eel boat. Rats scurry. Two men pass, speaking in a language he does not understand. He thinks they may be Dutch, despite the war. No, the war is over, trade restored. That is why they are here. He stares into the water, full of secrets, full of bodies, rolling by. And he thinks: I must get home, to Ellie, before I lose myself.

CHAPTER SEVEN

He walks west, following the river, following the sun that glances off it, now hurrying because he is thinking of Ellie, now slowing because he is tired. The air is fetid, and he cannot breathe enough of it. He passes St Mary Somerset and is approaching the place where he must leave the river and turn right to pass Paul's, the boundary between Queenhithe Ward and Castle Baynard Ward, where the tight alleys open and look down to Paul's Wharf, when he sees, running to him from the river, a dog. Once this would have been less remarkable, but two things stop him now. First, this dog runs to him, as though he is its master, as though it recognises or wants something from him. Secondly, there are fewer dogs than there were, roaming the streets freely. The dog stops before him, shakes, and water flies everywhere. James steps back. It has swum in the river, then, and just climbed out. It wags its tail, as though at him.

He tries to remember the breed. A Chien-gris, a Dun hound, he thinks, a big-shouldered dog, with rough, dark grey hair, turning to black along its spine. Not a river dog, but a hunting dog. Not a poor man's dog. It could be from Burley House or Baynard's Castle, both on the river near here. He stoops and rubs its head, running his thumb between the eyes. The dog closes them for a second and sits, tamed.

'Where are you from then? Whose are you? Where's your master?'

It has intelligent, tired eyes, and he imagines it saying that it has no master, that it belongs to nobody. He looks to the river, for an owner, but sees no one. It is not ill-fed. There are plenty of fish cast aside for a stray dog on the quays here.

Then he thinks: I might have the plague on me, from Ellie.

I could give it to this dog. He lifts his hand.

'You should go. Find your master, your home.' He speaks aloud, not in his mind. The dog does not move. 'Go, run away. Swim home.' No response. Now he fears drawing attention to himself. He should be discreet. 'I have nothing to give you. I can't feed you. I can barely feed my wife or myself.' The dog stares at him, with steadfast eyes. 'Go away,' he insists.

He turns and walks, more frustrated and angry than seems fair, and he cannot explain why. When he looks over his shoulder the dog is there, on his heels.

'Go,' he shouts.

No sooner has he turned into Bennet's Hill than he sees a ghost, a memory, and hears it too, so he knows it is real. It is a cart, coming down the Hill towards Thames Street, bearing corpses. He hasn't seen one in weeks, months, because he avoids them, and usually they come at night. His stomach churns in anticipation, and he prepares to squeeze against the wall as it passes, and look to his feet.

But then the dog barks.

He looks again. No, this is a smaller cart. He stares, wondering if it's the afternoon light that impairs his eyes.

One man rides the cart, another walks with the horse that pulls it. Something about them he dislikes, it makes him sick, as they seem to feed on death, hunched like human birds of prey. He doesn't understand why the response is so strong and so quick. He has had a surfeit of death. The men are not calling out for the dead, but move steadily and stealthily. They are watching.

The light changes and behind the man on the cart he sees not a pile of shrouds or winding sheets, nor even the pale skin of bodies that have had their clothes ripped from them, but something else, mottled fur and black eyes. They are dogs. They are not covered, but their carcasses lie naked on the cart. Flies bristle over smears of blood.

The dog barks again. The man leading the horse has seen him. He carries a noose.

James remembers. The dog catchers. The rakers. He saw a

cart once, but that was a year ago. He thought they had stopped this, that all vagrant dogs had been slaughtered. People said that they had killed thousands, perhaps tens of thousands of dogs from all over the city. They had taken not only stray creatures who lived on the streets, but animals in homes, kept for companionship. They feared that canine fur carried fluxes and effluvia bearing the plague, and all policy is shaped by terror. The dogs are to blame, so the Lord Mayor instructs poor men to find and massacre them.

He looks at these men as they approach, though, and he finds no sympathy for their poverty. They have blood over their shoes, up to their knees. They have seen and instigated so much death that their own eyes are now dead. And still they pursue more killing. They are paid by the corpse, once they reach the burial pit. A clerk will write out the number of dead in a ledger, and the men will be handed some pennies, and then they will tip the dogs into the hole, using a shovel to move the bodies at the bottom that will not fall. Am I unreasonable? he asks himself. He feels anger at these men, for their contribution and tribute to the empire of death.

'When will it be enough?' he mutters, as the noose-bearer approaches him.

'Good day to you,' the noose-bearer says. His mouth moves excessively as he speaks, showing black and yellow teeth. His voice is harsh, and his greeting sounds like an accusation. James looks at the man sitting on the cart, who has a club laid next to him. He can see how this works. The man stares back implacably, with the same eyes.

'Good day. A good day for you, but not for the dogs.'

Nothing. A sharp, superior, contemptuous gaze. The inheritance, James speculates, of the power of death over life.

How it works: the man with the noose will talk sweetly to the dog, in a whispered, false-friend voice, and then slip the noose over its head. The dog will pull away, and he will hold the rope tight, and once it has weakened with the tightening of the noose, the man with the club will jump down from the cart and dispatch the dog with a blow to the head, or likely multiple blows. The skull will crack, perhaps the brains will spill, blood will issue onto the cobbles. Between them the men will toss the body onto the growing pile on the cart. And then they will move on, looking for the next.

'Is that your dog?' the man on the cart asks.

James looks down. The grey dog is sitting by his side.

He looks up again. 'I thought this was over. The dog killing. The dog rakers.'

He does not know if this name he has given them is understood to be a hard word, a rebuke.

Still no response from the noose-man, and as he meets his stare he thinks, you shall know them by their eyes.

The cart man answers. 'We've started again. We stopped when the dogs were gone, and the plague abated. Now they're back.'

'I did not read the Lord Mayor's order.'

They ignore this. 'Nonetheless. The dog is yours?'

Still, there is something like a hesitation in the reiteration of this question. He takes a breath. The mayor's order. He read it when it was printed and posted in the summer of the year before. He read it pasted on the walls of Aldersgate. It shouldn't matter if this dog was his or not. All dogs were to be killed. They even killed the cats, and think about how many thousands and tens of thousands of cats there are around London. Or were, before the slaughter. House dogs were no different from stray dogs. Master or no should not matter.

The orders also specified that a dog catcher who intentionally showed favour to a dog and let it live, despite the royal orders, would himself be imprisoned. The dogs of the wealthy, or a fine-looking dog such as this one, were not to be spared. Though, as is always the case with the wealthy, they would escape the law, or the consequences of the law, with impunity. Money buys advantage, even for a dog.

He sees that they are furtively asking him for a bribe, that is it. He need only offer them more than the fee they would be paid for killing the dog, and this dog will live. Trying to guess what this fee is – perhaps a farthing – is useless, though, for he does not have a farthing on him. He cannot offer to bribe them.

And he cannot flee the city, where their jurisdiction ends, because he is too far from the city's walls and a gate, and they would catch him or call out to the watch if he ran. And he cannot resist them, because they are two, and armed. And besides, this is all madness, because he needs to get home to care for Ellie.

Then he sees it. Their hesitation. They are not assured of the law, or of their authority, or their jurisdiction. Perhaps that's another reason why they would prefer a bribe, because they are not confident that they can take his dog. Which is not his dog. And he is risking his safety in order to save a dog that is not his.

He snatches this opportunity. 'You have your licence?'

They prickle and rise. He has established that he can read, and now that they are a little discomfited he sees how to proceed.

'I have not read the Lord Mayor's order because there is none.'

'It was last year.'

'And it was revoked last year.'

'It was revived.'

'And so you can show me the order, and your commission.'

The moment the noose-bearer turns back to look at the cart man, James sees that he has read them correctly.

'Or perhaps you can write it out for me, so when I speak to the magistrates they will confirm that you have just such a commission.'

'We were indeed commissioned to collect all the dogs.' This is the noose-bearer, brazen.

'I don't think your warrant extends to this,' he says. And the fact that they have hesitated for so long now proves their uncertainty. They have shown favour to this dog, which the law expressly forbade, by not taking it immediately. And he is certain that they cannot read.

'I don't think you can tell us what our warrant says.'

'Not if you won't show it to me. If it even exists.'

'And what do you know about the law?'

They are armed, he thinks. He looks at his hands. They are

clean from ink. And he wore his best jacket to meet Eagle. Again, he resigns himself to the workings of providence.

'I am a lawyer. And you are *contra legem*.' He knows a handful of legal terms and Latin tags from printing, always set in italics.

They eye him. They look at his clothes. They make their calculations, half-informed, half speculative. Their passions play a role too. He stands firm. The longer he waits the safer the dog becomes.

'And now, I have business.'

The cart-man's mouth is hard, bunched. He has made his pennies for the day, and will not risk them.

'Stand aside. You can keep your dog.'

He nods, and the man with the noose takes the horse and leads it on. The cart passes him, and he holds his breath. The stench is foul and he cannot bear to look at it. So many dead, and he can find no meaning in it, none at all.

He walks up Bennet's Hill, with the prospect of St Paul's ahead of him, and a grey dog behind.

'Are you still here?'

★ ★ ★

He walks to the other side of St Paul's. He carries a fear within him he cannot see clearly, and certainly cannot name. In the churchyard he stops. The dog stands beside him.

'You're mine now?'

He is talking to a dog in Paul's churchyard. He wonders at himself. Something has possessed him. These are days of fever and madness everywhere he looks, and he is not entirely himself. He looks at himself as from an angle, worrying about his wife, concealing her plague, concealing the infection in his printing shop, walking around London, listening to a brimstone preacher, speaking with a dog.

'Fine. I'll call you Tobias.'

They walk on together, and when he sees Christ Church and the hospital he begins to feel safer and less fearful.

He arrives home, and calls out, 'Ellie?'

There is no reply. Straightaway the ache in his head returns. He goes upstairs. Tobias is already asleep before the hearth in the printing room.

She is there, she is half awake, she is in pain. Sometimes she whimpers. He gives her a drink, and holds her, careful of the buboes under her arms, and whispers in her ear that he loves her. She takes his hand and lies down. He tells her the story of Tobias.

'I'd like to see him,' she says.

He helps her downstairs, a blanket over her shoulders. When she sits on a chair beside the hearth, Tobias wakes, rises and nuzzles her while she strokes his head. Then he lies at her feet.

'You should dry out properly,' she says. His coarse coat is still damp.

'Will you sit there?' he asks.

'I ache wherever I am. Sometimes the cramps are terrible. Not all the time.'

'Shall I print?'

'Yes, I'd like to watch you.'

So, though it is late to be starting this, he returns to the printing he left off earlier in the day. As the last of the sun is spent he completes the run of the second forme, so that each sheet is now printed on both sides, and eventually the pamphlet is half done. His legs ache from walking, to the Thames and from one side of the printing press and back again as he inks and pulls the press, and his arms ache from the labour, but the pamphlet is half done, and the sheets lie drying around the shop. He warms a bowl of pottage, pulls up a chair beside Ellie, and feeds her and then himself. The city is quiet. He is glad for Tobias' breathing, hoarse in his dreams. He dreams of running, of swimming, of a warm hearth.

He leads her upstairs; she leans heavily on him.

★ ★ ★

He wonders if he should leave her alone, to rest and recover. But six good years, five and a half married, and she is too much alive inside him. He kisses her face, her neck, she pushes him down to her breasts. She moans, and it is not all pleasure. He rises and looks at her with alarm, with a question, and she nods. He licks her thighs, checking, and there is no rash, no pain, no sign of more buboes, only a musty taste of salt, and he licks around her thighs until she pulls him up, and he enters her. But this night she does not climb on top of him.

CHAPTER EIGHT

O n Friday morning, the last day of summer, there are clouds. Dawn is sluggish. It picks listlessly at the clouds. He stands in the street, smelling her on him, their enveloped smells, their smells winding one around the other. He is tired of worrying, he wants to hold onto the worry. Everything ahead of him is blank, as empty as his next ream of paper. The moment is a smudge. He does not have the materials within himself, no ink, no paper, no type, no machine. It takes the stones to bring him back. The sky, reticent, unrevealing, will not give him what he needs this morning.

He slept and he prayed in a feverish manner. He said the prayers he knew he had to: for his neighbours, his family, his friends, for Ellie and for himself. He hoped they were not insincere because the words followed a formula, because they were too self-interested, he hoped that they were sincere enough to be listened to. Ellie did not rise to pray, but he heard her murmuring along with him as she lay in bed, and he thought she might have been petitioning with him. He slept again and woke wet with sweat. Ellie was still asleep. He went down and Tobias was waiting for him at the foot of the stairs, tail wagging. He ruffled his coarse, dry fur.

'You already know not to come upstairs,' he said, an observation rather than a question. Tobias followed him around, but stopped when he stepped out of the front door.

Sunrise is over, but the difference is disappointing. He is aching. He thinks it is because he did not sleep well, and the printing sits upon him. He grows old. Perhaps this is how it will be. Or, and now he thinks of his prayers in St Paul's, perhaps his covenant has been accepted. Ellie seemed a little better yesterday. Now it is his turn. He aches.

He breathes, takes the air deep into his stomach. His animal spirits speak back in undertones. He no longer needs to utter his morning orisons, because he has become one with the world to which he will return, in which his flesh will dissolve, that is the message of the obstinate dawn.

He returns inside and Tobias greets him. He wonders why people speak so ill of them, why they compare lazy people to dogs, why sinful or immoral people are like dogs, why someone should say as greedy as a dog. This is what it means to have a dog. It is always there, and always lets you know it is there. It is never pointedly absent, you never have to scrutinize it for hidden meanings.

He must go to the butcher for offal and bones, back to Smithfield this morning, back to the gambles of the past. It will not touch him, because he has too much else on his mind.

He finds Ellie food and drink, and tosses Tobias a crust. The dog retreats to the hearth. A bone would be better than bread.

Ellie seems a little better. She sits up in bed, and they kiss.

'More night physic,' he says. 'You're getting better.' Again he does not mention his prayers in St Paul's, the offer he made. He thinks he had best keep this to himself.

'How's Tobias?' she asks.

She remembered, he thinks. She's recovering.

'Full of love and adoration. And hungry. I'll go to Smithfield, get some bones and offal. The pain?'

'Is bearable. I slept. I heard you pray, and I prayed too. The dreams were hard.'

'Hard?'

'Full of echoing spaces. Hard walls, burning sounds.'

'The buboes?'

'I can't touch them. It's agony. But if I'm careful. And there are no more.'

He sighs. He does not want to read the signs with too much haste, but he does, and he re-reads and re-reads them.

'I'll go to Smithfield now. Then I'll start the next sheet. Tobias will be here to stand guard over you.'

'Good,' and she squeezes his hand.

★ ★ ★

He turns right and walks to Little Britain, past St Bartholomew the Less, and into the open market of Smithfield. It savours of lambs and pigs and slaughter. His shoes feel dirty already.

Smith, a butcher who serves the farmers from the north east, leads a pig across the grass. 'White,' he calls and nods, and James nods back, because he feels he has to. How does he know Smith? he wonders. Did they play together as children? He digs in his memory, but finds nothing. He can't recall anything before the casual acquaintance of exchanging greetings in the market. He realises too late that he should have asked Smith for bones. It was already in his mind to call on Williams, because he imagines that Tobias will like cow bones more than pig or sheep, though he cannot say how he has decided this, and also because he should ask after Jane Williams, who, by chance, is Ellie's cousin. He has often tried to fathom why the world should be so small that his childhood friend and he should both marry girls from Brecknock, and that the two should be cousins. If there were some other connection, if they had known each other before, or if they had worked in a similar employment or trade, then it could be explained, but there are no such reasons to be found, and so it must only be an unlikely chance.

He crosses the grass towards Williams's shop, and there it is, the old house. He won't let it touch him, he tells himself. Not the black shutters with heavy eyes, not the decayed roof, nor the fact that it's not been whitewashed in years. He does not know why it has been allowed to fall into this decline. He will not let himself be dragged back in. He won't remember his late sister Mary, and he will not recall Margaret, who put them all behind her when she married a Catholic gentleman with a small farm in Lancashire that was his own, found for her by the delicate mediation of their mother, and he will certainly not think about their mother. Though it is already a little late for that.

During his brief schooling, the other boys would complain about the heavy or hard hands of their fathers. They would show

77.

off their bruises for entertainment, competing with one another for the widest or darkest. His friend John once displayed a black eye the size of an apple that was more purple than black or blue, though at least one classmate said it followed from falling out of an apple tree. In contrast, John White, his father, had light hands, though often caked in blood. James did not fear him. His brothers, John and Thomas, were more likely to beat him, because he did not pull his weight, or because he did. Because he was not good, or was. Or for no reason, beyond that they were boys. His father was mild, weighed down by flesh and blood. Every day except Sunday there was butchering, and on those Sundays when he took Communion he rolled his eyes when the minister said the wine was blood, though he meant nothing impious by it. James's mother did not take Communion, except when she had to for appearance's sake, once or twice a year.

It was not his father that James feared. And it was not hard or heavy hands. It was hell and the devil. It was questions that were too hard for him as a child to grasp. Now when he looks back he wonders that he didn't know the answers, and he finds it easy to imagine what he would say to her, if she weren't already long in her grave and food for worms. But it is his adult being that he pictures replying to her, and he was a child then. He finds it hard to reach that child, because it is lost there and detached from him now.

The grass of Smithfield is gone from under his feet. Now he's back in the house. She is sewing, darning the children's clothes. Margaret is there too. Not Thomas, he thinks, though he may be. He doesn't see Thomas. Young Mary, Jane and John are elsewhere, working, John learning to wield the butcher's cleaver. The room is dark and closed, wrapped around them. In another world it would be comforting and safe, but here it is airless and without light. Their mother is telling them that their English church is lost, that it was invented by Luther, and that before Luther it was nowhere and because of this it cannot be the true church. The true church stretches out over an unbroken line of days, like a long succession of candles, illuminating the darkness. Unbroken and unstained.

He is trying to learn to sew, though he knows that it is women's work. Margaret is much better than him at it. Her stitches are close and even, while his stumble from point to point. His fingers are rebellious, bungling. She is two years younger than he is, though he isn't sure how old he is in this memory. Thomas is three years older than him. These are certainties that families tell you.

And because of this he is damned, because the Lutherans and the Calvinists and the neither fish-nor-fowl spawn of the church in England are no true church. But she cannot tell them this, because it is a secret.

But she tells them this because she loves them, and does not want to see them burn.

'But what about father?' he asks, and the look that she shoots at him leaves him shaking. She will see him saved, because she wants him to be saved, and because it is in his power to see that he is. It is in his power to disavow the breed of Satan, though he must speak with and receive the ministrations of a true priest too.

She tells them that Luther soiled his body. He soiled his body with nuns, and then married one of them, thus soiling the priesthood. He has no idea what this means. She tells them about purgatory. It is a place full of pain, she tells them, torture, righteous pain, inflicted to purify and purge the foul matter of mortality. Because we cannot be pure enough for heaven without the refiner's fire. And in heaven we are light and white and without the weight of bodies.

And then she tells them about the pain of childbirth, of the three infants who died when she gave birth to them, and so went to their graves full of sin. And the pain was great, and the blood was great. And yet she knew happiness. Just as those who enjoy the pain of purgatory know happiness, because they know they have been spared an eternity of hell and are working their way up to heaven. They console themselves with that thought, and cry tears of joy as they pass through the refiner's fire. And you two, she says, have the blessing of knowing this when you are children, and so can spare yourselves hell and a long, long duration of torment in purgatory. She will see them saved.

And she pulls them to her chest, and he twists in discomfort.

He has, during this dance of memory, arrived at the butcher's shop. Williams is inside. James enters and they stand at an awkward distance. Londoners no longer know how close to stand to each other. Last year they stood as far away as possible, but then the plague receded over the winter and this caution was relaxed. Now it is back and they are more careful, but it has been so long, and besides, Williams is his friend.

'How are you, Roger?'

Roger Williams tells him about Jane, who is well, and James lies about Ellie. They will find out soon enough, he thinks. But then he thinks they won't, because Ellie will recover and no one will know. Plague doesn't leave the same marks as smallpox. Williams is in good sorts. He has a cheerful disposition; he has survived the decay of trade that almost destroyed London last year and the relief has turned to confidence. Jane has news which Williams passes on, of home, of Brecknock, of two marriages in Crickhowell and, to her relief, the absence of plague. Ellie's family are also, she thinks, all well.

He buys some shank, a modest cut, and Williams gives him a bag of bones.

'A dog, in these days!' He shakes his head, laughing. 'You were never one to make it easy for yourself. I'm sure he'll be a content dog.'

'He chose me. You can't turn your back on something like that.'

'True enough. An angel at the door and all that, as they say.'

He thanks him for the bones, and leaves. For a moment he feels lighter because of the connection they've renewed, then he remembers. Has he endangered a friend's life?

He is back on the grass of Smithfield, familiar grass. If they paved it, as they have done Whitechapel in part, and the Exchange, it would be harder to clean. The grass drinks up the blood. But they will pave it sooner or later, and when they do they will have to wash and scrub almost every day. And there will be narrow gutters running with blood in the mornings.

And there is his mother, watching the heavens drip with blood, the blood of our Lord running down the firmament, a sign, a warning, a promise. But you have to listen. She takes his hands in that warm, gloomy room, holds his palms up roughly, studies them, shows them to him.

'Can you keep them clean? I don't think so. But you can pray and repent and do penance. That's the nearest thing. I'll teach you. See who can learn quicker, you or Margaret.'

It will be Margaret, he thinks. His consignment to purgatory will be longer.

She has a prayer book that she shows them, though she can read neither Latin nor English. She keeps it concealed beneath a board in that room. They know her secret, she tells them, and they have to keep it, because otherwise the book will be taken away, and it is her soul's defence. The bulwark of her salvation. They both nod solemnly. He isn't certain of either of those words.

Again she pulls them to her, binds them with a tight embrace, tells them that they are her pearls, that they mustn't speak of this to the others, that this is for them alone. We are her favourites, he thinks. That's the secret. They mustn't know this, because she doesn't want them to. Mary, Jane, John and Thomas, the older ones, she hasn't chosen them to know what she knows. This, he assumes, must be God's work.

She tells them about Mary, after whom she was named, after whom his eldest sister was named, though he wonders if his sister was after the virgin Mary, the second mother of mankind, or Mary their mother. She tells him that she is the path to God, to heaven, the pure intercessor, who is infinite in her kindness and softness. When he hears the word intercessor he doesn't understand what it means. He thinks it sounds like something his father does with his knife, his sharp, longest knife, that takes apart the joints with precision, the joints that won't come apart and should not be shattered with a cleaver. Is this what Mary does, to separate those who know secrets from those who don't, break apart joints into the good and the

81

bad, choose who shall be listened to? He does not want to be consigned to silence. Is Mary the butcher of humankind, kind like his father, and so a butcher, taking the goodness from the foul?

He has sworn not to dwell on things, not to go back, not to see into that room. The room brings fear, and, though he doesn't believe in those things, the spirits that lurk in its corners and shadows, in the cracks in the wood, that doesn't stop him fearing them, with an ugly unnamed fear, as though his thoughts themselves might take on the shape of his fears and bring them to him, make them present and real. He has sworn not to go back there, but as he crosses the market and sees the house, he is there again, in that room, warm and dark and sealed to the unredeemed, the doomed, the unforgiven, those without grace. He is with Margaret and with his mother and her finger is pointing, pointing in love and in compassion, pointing only because there is a message that she must convey.

He has been with another boy. He thinks it might be Roger Williams, but it could be anybody, even the disregarded Smith. They have been running wild, running north of St John's of Jerusalem, and into Clerken Well and over a wall they should not have scaled, and up a pear tree. And he has climbed the tree, and perched in a fork of its branches and leaned to reach the pears, and he has gathered them and thrown them down to his friend, so far below that he is unidentifiable, many pears, more than they can possibly eat, and his friend has caught them, most of them, while they laughed, and his friend has gathered them in an apron, a butcher's apron taken from his father's shop, and so they have scrumped a lifetime of pears, until he sees the gentleman coming. And he knows then that they are in trouble, and so he climbs down the tree, quicker than he should, but at some point in the descent he realises he fears the gentleman more than he fears falling, and so he hastens and jumps from the last or next-to-last branch and regrets it, but he is down, and he runs with his friend, whom he still can't identify, they run to the wall while they hear the voice of the gentleman call and shout after them, and as they run his friend wraps the pears up in the apron and ties it, and throws it over the wall before climbing after it, and he climbs too, though more slowly, and they drop and are safe, but for the voice of the gentleman, who tells them fiercely not to come back again, not to come back again or they will be for it. And they run home, safe.

But they were not safe. He doesn't know if it is because the other boy's parents have seen the half-haul of pears, and asked the right questions, or because the gentleman knew who they were and where they lived, but he is now before the judge, jury and executioner that is his mother and her firm belief in truth, justice and not stealing pears, and she is speaking to him of damnation. She tells him that this is how damnation begins, this is what it looks like, that she had had high hopes for him until now. And he thinks, but you never told me it was wrong to climb over a wall to harvest some pears from a tree that was just over the wall. But apparently she did not have to tell him, because the rules are so numerous that they can't be explained one by one. He should know them without being specifically informed. He feels his own little Luther arising within him, and this agrees with his mother. He is not good.

And perhaps that is the moment, or perhaps it is another time, but at some time he finds himself shut out of that dark, gloomy, airless room of salvation, and he does not know whether it is because he is too old and has to work or because Mary, one of the Marys, has lost all of her hopes for him, but his mother stops holding him tight and speaking to him of how he can avoid the torments of purgatory. She treats him as she did before when outside that room, but now there is no inside. And now her chiding smarts more. When she tells him that he has not cleaned the kitchen properly, it means something different. When he drops a pot and it shatters she beats him, but now there is no redemption in that beating.

His schoolfriends feared the beatings of their fathers, but he did not fear his father, nor the blood under his nails and on his hands.

Now, as he heads home, away from Williams' shop, the prospect of St Bartholomew the Less before him is a promise of safety, an escape from a noisome past, one that smells of carcasses and offal, and the evisceration of the body in search of meat and of the soul, an escape into making books, and, in good time, into six good years.

CHAPTER NINE

As he walks home he is possessed by a notion. He feels at home outside his shop, knowing that Ellie is there, touching his feet on Farringdon ground, on the cobbles. There he is planted in the soil, there he belongs. It is because he is part of the city, the city outside the walls. And just as he leans against the city to know that he is real, so the city leans on him. They support and are props for each other, they depend on each other. That's it, that's all; but the notion possesses him, and won't leave him alone. It contains a kind of truth, one that he can't easily express or justify, but he knows that it's so and that it won't be shaken.

When he arrives at the shop Tobias greets him. This is what it means to have a dog, he thinks, as Tobias presses against his knee and wags his tail. He puts the cut of shank in the cool larder and gives Tobias one of the bones. Friendship is rewarded, and the dog retreats to the hearth to lie licking the marrow.

'Ellie?'

She sits up a little.

'James?'

He embraces her, and then lies next to her. 'How are you feeling?'

'Too hot. Maybe a little better.'

He tells her the news he heard from Williams: her family are said to be well, there have been two marriages in the town, there is no plague in Crickhowell.

'I hope it's true. How is Eagle's pamphlet?'

He had almost forgotten about it.

'I'll set the third forme today, and start printing it. I'll have to work on Sunday, though we mustn't tell him. He'll think it will besmear his truths with our sin.'

She smiles a little. She doesn't think that printing or sin work like that.

'I'll try to help.'

'You should rest. You look better.'

'The buboes – they're harder, and I think they may be leaking, or perhaps I'm sweating. It's a good sign if they do?'

'I shouldn't touch?'

She flinches. 'No, don't.'

'And no new ones?'

'No, just the armpits. And I will try to help with the presswork. If only a little. I'd like to help.'

They kiss, and he sees that she is uncomfortable, distracted, but he feels her need too, and not only that she does not want to let go, but also that she wants to hold onto him in life and death, and that she wants to make love with him in life and death and in the extremity that lies between.

She comes downstairs with him and prepares some food in the kitchen. He can hear her shuffling in there as he prepares the table to set the type. He glances at Eagle's manuscript. Shapes are distracting to the mind of the reader and their spirit; the inner light is cast into shadow. Only repentance will clear this. All the words seem familiar: perhaps they mean more when read in sequence, but he will not read them again. He wonders why he has forgotten Eagle's sense so soon, as usually it's harder to ignore the meaning of the passages he sets once he has read the book, but this time he's forgotten it entirely. He will pick up type without thinking about what the letters contribute to saying. They will be pieces of lead shot, and they will make him and Ellie less poor. They will make it through these times, and afterwards they will prosper.

He sets the first line, then the page, followed by the next page, and the one after, and soon the forme is almost complete. He stops to eat, then Ellie sits by the fireplace to keep him company. He finishes the final page, surrounds all four with a frame, inserts the quoins and wedges, ties them tight, and puts them on the bed of the press ready to print.

Ellie inks the type and he operates the press. His heart is full, because this is who they are. And all is well for a while, before she begins to puff and slow down. They both ignore this, and pretend for a while that the other has not seen it, but then it is too obvious, and they look at each other and admit defeat. They accede without words. She leans on him, head on his shoulder, weight sagging into him, hot and damp, and she whispers, 'I'll rest a bit.'

She goes upstairs, and he tries not to find anything ominous in it. She's tired, she's getting better, she was better today than yesterday, she was working hard. He continues to print by himself, moving from one side of the press to the other. He is determined to print a hundred copies of this side of the sheet today. Then tomorrow, Saturday, he will finish the run. He pictures in his mind's eye the shop full of wet sheets hanging to dry, and to imagine it helps him fight against the ache in his limbs, which grows until it is more than discomfort or uneasiness and becomes a real affliction. Purgatorial, he thinks, and almost laughs. Thank the heavens that Ellie helped him climb out of that slough. If you spend so many years in a marsh, despairing, convinced that you don't merit any better, then you can't escape without a lot of help.

* * *

Upstairs, Ellie has bound herself in a blanket, because she likes to be covered when she rests, covered from head to foot, with only her mouth, and sometimes not even her mouth, above the blanket or coverlet. Her feet need to be warm, but there's some-thing about the weight of the covering over the rest of her, especially her shoulders, that helps her relax, helps her push away the bad things of the world. The problem today, and since Wednesday morning, though it may have been Tuesday night, is that when she covers herself she brings her arms in towards her body, and when she does that she puts pressure on the buboes, and the pain stops her from sleeping. Sleep for her has become a flitting between a light slumber and a drowsy wakefulness, and it's never enough. If her arms are spread open she is not comfortable, and she feels that she isn't really covered. She has to push her elbows out and pull the covers towards her, without twisting her arms too much at the shoulders.

And sometimes she is too hot, and sometimes too cold, and it is hard to know what to do with the blankets when this changes. And sometimes it's hard to sleep because she is thinking about her discomfort and how best to avoid it.

She is bound in the blanket, and the buboes feel easier, and she has checked again for more, but there are none, and she is feeling hot, even her feet, and she can feel that gentle pull that rises before she is overcome by sleep.

It's good to know that James is downstairs, and that Tobias is watching over him, and that Tobias will be a sentinel, because the world and its ways cannot always be predicted. Some of the fire in her is released with this reflection, leaving the pattern of its absence etched inside her and her thoughts. And then, not for the first time in these past few days, she is on the bridge over the Usk, and she is dreaming in another language. She looks down at the river and her brother says something, and the sounds reach with ease from the abrasive to the sing-song. In the dream she visits the fort on the hill, and she says, this is our fort, this is our hill, and she knows that she means that the castle, which is also ruined, is not their castle. But though the castle, which is nearly an hour's walk to the south, stands much lower than the fort, she knows as she says it that this is bravado. So she trudges home, towards the castle, ruined by her ancestor Glyn Dŵr, who she is certain is her ancestor. She arrives home and her father is printing a book about Glyn Dŵr. He asks her to proofread a sheet, but she has forgotten how to read. So instead she devises a means to harness the sheep he farms to the press so James doesn't have to pull it. But just as the engine begins to work, her first husband, Matthew, walks into the printing shop and declares that because he is not drowned she must not help James to find new ways of printing, and he sits in her father's chair and calls for a plate of food. At which point she doesn't know whom to serve or listen to.

They are of the line of Glyn Dŵr. His sons returned to the people and became farmers, awaiting the right occasion to restore just rule. These are the stories her father was told by his father and so on.

At which point she realises that she is awake again, or not dreaming. She tries to slip back into that dream, and pictures herself leaving her father's farmhouse, which has become her own printing shop, and imagines walking out onto the lane, passing the crossroads, recalling how far she has to walk before she is at the cross in Crickhowell, and which road leads to the river. She sees a badger on the outskirts of the town, but in her mind it is a ground pig, a *mochyn daear*, which is the proper name for a badger. She is a little frightened of badgers, though she likes to watch them from a distance. They are funny, persistent creatures, but with a worse temper and fiercer than a dog.

Why would she dream of her father printing a book? she wonders. He owned no books and she never saw him read. Nor was he like James; perhaps he was a little more like Matthew. Certainly he liked Matthew, who was younger, her age, and a soldier. A man of ambition. For all that the people of Crickhowell and the neighbouring mountains spoke of Glyn Dŵr and home, for all that they thought people from elsewhere lacked that true sense of belonging to a place that they themselves had, they nonetheless dreamed of travelling elsewhere, of making a better world elsewhere. And Matthew, her first husband, had travelled to England to fight in a war with Richard Vaughan on the side of the king, and when that did not kill him they met and she married him, with the encouragement of her father. Her mother, having died with William's birth, had not been there to advise against it. Or to tell her about married life. He took her to London. She has no happy memories of those days. If she looks for unhappy memories she will find them, but that was sixteen years ago. And five years later he was dead, and his body lost somewhere in the Barbados, where he had been lured by Cromwell's Hispaniola expedition. He was a typical son of Crickhowell, she thinks, dead on a faraway island, longing for the home he chose to leave.

And who is she to think this, she wonders, as she lies wrapped just so in a bed in Farringdon, barely able to speak her own language, and wavering between extreme hot and cold? But she doesn't find it hard to resent Matthew Rice, which some pronounce Rhys, who may not have been honest with her once in their five years together, and certainly not in the wedding vows that began them.

★ ★ ★

Tobias growls at the door. James pauses. He fears it is the watch, come to ask about Ellie's sickness. He carefully places the wet sheet down in an empty space on the floor and goes to the door. There is no one there. Tobias stands at his feet. They smell the warm, dry air. Tobias growls.

'What is it Tobias?' He smells again, and realises that he is short of air. There isn't enough air in him, nor enough out there. 'Do you smell something too?' He can't put his finger on it, can't locate it exactly, but something in the evening air oppresses him. 'It'll be dark soon, come on.' Tobias growls again before turning his back on the city walls.

He looks at the sheet he has just printed, now on the floor. It is satisfactory, though there is a pale patch in one area where there should be rich letters. Then he looks at what is left of the ream of paper he has to print, and he feels even more tired. He has not got very far.

He takes Ellie some food. She moans, apparently dreaming. He studies her face for a while, and reminds himself of his good fortune. Then he goes downstairs and eats. The shank is good, and perhaps it is because he is eating decent meat that he feels hot and full, as though his stomach is warming him for the first time in days. He feels so hot he needs to rest a bit, so he sits by the hearth and Tobias lies against the chair leg. His attention comes and goes for a while, and when he is present he thinks of Ellie lying upstairs, and when he is not he sees only the lever turning the press, and the movement of pads inking the type.

★ ★ ★

They had been married nearly five years when Matthew told her that he had enlisted for the expedition to attack Spanish colonies in the West Indies, led by William Penn and Robert Venables, under whom Matthew was to serve. She asked him the apposite questions, but he didn't stay long before leaving. She didn't have to think of many questions. It seemed he couldn't wait to leave. Perhaps there was some other woman in the city he needed to say goodbye to, perhaps he thought that he would find a woman in the Barbados. Then he departed, leaving her alone in a strange country, in this city that was like no other place she'd seen, so teeming, so dirty, so populous, so disorderly and full of human life.

She entered service, which was what she did in Brecknock before she'd been given to Matthew Rice, and it was fortunate that she'd learned enough English to work here. The family, though English, were kind to her: David and Sarah Cooper, and their children, Sarah, William and John. They didn't tease her for her accent, though they did make her say things in Welsh for their entertainment. They lived near Charterhouse Lane, right on the furthest reaches of Farringdon, and they could have chosen to go to either Bartholomew the Great or the Less, but they decided to attend the Less as their church because they liked the minister Thomas Bishop. She did not much like him, as he was too fond of unnecessary ceremony in the church, but she grew used to him.

She waited for Matthew to return. She asked David Cooper to read aloud the newspaper, *Mercurius Politicus*, when it contained news of the Hispaniola expedition. She suspected that the news-writer did not reveal all that the government knew, and that he made the adversities and defeats sound less disastrous than they were. But there was no concealing that the whole business was a failure. She thought he might come limping home. In the summer of 1656 she petitioned the Council's office for news of her husband, to find that he was over a year dead. They gave her a sum of money to compensate her widowhood. She kept it under her bed.

Then, one September, she was leaving the church after one of Bishop's series of sermons on the four last things, and speaking her criticism to no real purpose in the churchyard, when a foreign voice intruded, and joined the conversation in her head, and the voice stayed there and never went away, and though she had sworn never to remarry, when he asked her to marry him she agreed. The widow's money had gone to buy printing equipment. James said that the shop was as much hers as it was his, that they were not to be separated in mind, body or property, by the devil or the law. This was something new to her.

She is digging all this up, running through it as a way of subduing the pain. Piece by piece she puts the events together in sequence as they happened. But the coldness in her bones begins to fade again, and she grows hot inside, and as she boils memory becomes dream once more. She is dreaming of the fort, Crug Hywel, and she is following with teetering footsteps the ditch, the work of ancient giants, and she is a burning beacon in the Black Mountains, lighting the way home.

CHAPTER TEN

Downstairs James is inking the type and doing the presswork and he is so tired that he seems to be standing beside himself, not quite in his own body, observing his own tiredness. This is not right. He should not be so tired, he tells himself, though he knows he has been working hard, doing hard, physical work, ever since Eagle appeared on Monday morning. He is getting old. He did not think that this would happen so soon. He has always been vigorous in body, not easily tired. He does not know why operating the press from both sides should be so much more difficult. But switching back and forth drains him in both mind and muscle, as if it is two jobs together, rather than one followed by another. Perhaps there is less rest between: that must be it. He mops the sweat from his forehead.

In front of him the type runs back and forth, as though it is a page of ants. It seems a long time ago, years ago, that he stood in Williams' shop and heard news of Crickhowell, and a lifetime ago, before this lifetime, that he sat in the warm shadows and heard news of purgatory. Sometimes too many things crowd in upon him, and he doesn't know what to do with them, as though he's an ant lost in that crowded page. Much as he wants to forget this, he wonders when he last saw his mother. It was when he was apprenticed, he thinks, but he can't be sure. It seems strange that he's not sure. Why does he have to fit lots of pieces together in order to try and remember when things happened? Why don't they stand alone, so he can recall the things he wants to without all of the things he does not? He should be able to cross Smith-field without going back into shadows and involuntarily meeting ghosts. He is disappointed with himself. He thinks this as he observes himself from a slight distance, from the other side of a crack that has opened up within and without him.

He swirls the pads in the tray of ink until they slip and slide freely. He lifts and shakes them. Then he rubs them over the type, until all of the proud surface has been covered. The light is failing, though it might be his eyes. He thinks it has been covered. He tilts his head to see the glint. He wipes his hands. Then he places a clean sheet of paper within the frame. He has lost count. Once secured he folds the frame and slides it over the type. He pulls the lever to drop the platen. The platen makes contact with the lead type, with only a skein of linen paper between the two.

And he feels as though he is cracking inside. He knows he has to pull harder, and just a little longer, for the ink to transfer to the paper, but the pain is riotous, unnatural. His body wants to spring back, but his mind, his will keeps it in place. He holds the explosion back, while his head seems opened and bared to the heaven above him, with fire and brimstone his only thoughts, until he releases the lever, and the platen springs back slightly through natural force.

It is some time before he can push the lever back, to lift the platen and free the frame and paper. He has no idea how long that time is, or what passed through his mind during it. The moment is completely lost. Unsure of himself, disjointed, he hangs the sheet up to dry. He thinks that he cannot try to press another sheet. He thinks that he cannot stop now. He wonders what time it is, and he listens for church bells. It seems to be early in the evening, but his eyes do not feel right. He sticks his head out of the front door. Perhaps it is growing dark after all. His eyes feel dry. He should sit down.

He drinks a cup of small beer, and then another cup. He sits down by the hearth. Tobias, he had forgotten about Tobias, comes to his knees for affection. He rubs his head and back and belly. Tobias shines with gratitude. He can give affection to another, that is easy; it is himself that he is shut off from. Where is he? One moment he thinks his brain is exposed to heaven, the top of his skull shorn off so that a man might look inside and see his thoughts and feelings, the next he thinks he cannot think or feel them himself, that if he looked inside his own head it would be without meaning, unreachable. What is this person who is pushing me aside? he asks.

He aches, but that proves to him that he is real, not merely an illusion. Pain is immediate, and, if it doesn't ground him, at least it shows that he is not somewhere else. He breathes and it does not help, because there isn't enough air in this room. He should step outside, but that's too far away. He grips the chair and waits for this dizziness, which is more than dizziness, a dizziness of the spirit as well as of the eyes and mind, to abate.

He tries to remember whether he has taken food to Ellie. He thinks he has. And he thinks he has eaten. He should keep his strength up, he knows, but even if he hasn't eaten, he couldn't now. The pain is making him nauseous. It is, he thinks, still at a distance from himself, a pain rather than merely an ache from his labours. It spreads beyond the muscles, into his nerves, his organs, his head. He has been overly ambitious. He could have told Eagle Wednesday or Thursday, and he is sure that Eagle would have accepted this, given the times they're living through. Though there are a hundred or more printers still working, fewer than there were a year or two ago, but still a good number hungry for work and for bread, and he should be grateful, he is grateful, for the commission. But things go wrong. And this can be foreseen, though the particular things that go wrong can't be predicted. And so perhaps Eagle would have forgiven him, or he would have found another printer, and he has lost track of his reasoning.

He thinks of lighting a fire. Black ants now swirl around the hearth. A fire might take the edge off the heat. There are no glowing embers, though, so lighting one would mean moving. And the black ants are congealing to a solid mass, and he doesn't know what they will be doing next. The purple light is closing in around them with the death of the day, so the nest floats on a purple lake, shimmering and twisting with the turning of the earth. He needs to hold onto them, hold them with his gaze, or he won't know what they'll do or where they'll go. He breathes deep, and this steadies his eyes, but as soon as his breathing pauses the pain grows worse. Perhaps it would be best to just sit with the pain, and not fight it, until it goes away. Perhaps this pushing it back is just playing with it, allowing it to live longer and grow stronger. Perhaps it would be refined by fire, the suffering made temporary, and he would emerge from the flames cooler and healed.

He must heal soon, to care for Ellie, or she will not grow well again, and she must and will grow well. He looks through the swimming ant-mass, and as in a mirror he sees the will of God, and it tells him that she will grow well. At this news he relaxes a little, and as he embraces the pain it diminishes. Then the ants disperse into moving letters again, their purpose completed. He shouldn't question.

That still leaves the problem, however, of whether he has fed Ellie. He dredges his memories from the day. They are jumbled, not in order of time. There was the dawn, Tobias, and Smithfield market, the grass, Ellie's sweating buboes, the typesetting, finishing the forme, and printing, some with Ellie, some not, printing alone and the pain. He thinks that is the correct order, but he isn't sure. And the shank, of course, buying the shank from Williams, and he thinks that he cooked and gave some to Ellie in the afternoon, or evening, so she will have eaten, though he cannot remember whether she ate with him, or if he left it by their bedside while she slept. Their big bed, wide as her arms, wide as the world.

He begins to cry. This is strange. It's been a long time since he cried. Two years, he remembers that, he remembers the occasion, but it's too much for now, not now, he thinks. It is strange, after the passages of his tears have so long been blocked. Something inside of him is releasing, cleared perhaps by the purifying heat, crystalline structures long since formed, now thawing and discharging out into the world, through the medium of his tears. He hopes that it is not obstinacy or contumely that he feels this way, but it feels good. It is a relief, a relaxation of something that has for too long been too dense, too compact. For a brief moment, a short turning of the hourglass, the him that is doing the observing shifts closer to the him that is being observed. As he is undone, he begins to find the weight of his emotions, his agitations, his feelings, his passions.

Last night's lovemaking comes to him, and the tears fall harder. When he is inside her, and she holds him, and they breathe together and move together, they become one creature. That creature is more him than he is himself. He cannot lose that creature, cease being that creature. She feels this way too; he knows this by the way she held him through her pain last night, pain that was worse than that which he feels now. It is about more than pleasure, comfort or sensuality, more than the flesh. The pain and the pleasure cannot be weighed against each other, as they inhabit different universes. He remembers the elastic resilience of her skin as he touched her back, the muscles taut, then her face. He is burning up with desire and fear of loss.

What his mother said about purgatory comes back to him. Not about the suffering or the refining, but about the foolishness of those who would not let go of the world. What is a pear, she asked, to ten years of the breaking of bones, to a hundred years of being nailed to a bed, or the carrying of an insufferable burden over sharp cobbles? What is a hundred pears? He was a child, and so he must learn, as adults had, to let go. 'How do I let go?' he asked. She shrugged, and did not answer. But then every time he broke one of her unwritten rules, she would grab him by the arm, take him aside and say, 'That is not letting go. Just that.'

He has let go for near half a century now. He wants to stop.

He is no longer crying, as the fire has dried him up inside. He can print no more. He should try to go upstairs. He can hardly see. He tries to rise from the chair. It is an unconscionable effort, but he does so. He lights a tallow candle. Tobias stirs and worries his bone.

'Goodnight Tobias,' he says. Tobias stares at him as he shuffles away, then returns, in the shadows, to his bone.

The stairs are a mountain, but he conquers them, one by one. Ellie is asleep, though she murmurs wordlessly as he enters. Her face is no more red or chafed. He puts the candle on the bedside table, and removes some of his clothes, then gives up. He climbs into bed beside her. Lying down he says his silent prayers. He thanks God as best he can, and asks that Ellie be spared, because she is good and kind. He turns his head and blows out the candle. He doesn't have enough air. He breathes. He needs to lie on his side to sleep, but he doesn't have the will or energy to roll over. Instead, he slips his hand over to touch her. She's there, firm, material. He thinks perhaps she's not as hot as she has been. If the buboes are seeping, and she's still here, and she's cooler, then that's a good sign. He remembers his prayer to God in St Paul's. He would lay his life down for her, and he would not complain, and he would not recriminate with his maker, but bear it patiently because it is she for whom he lives, and he would die for her too. He slides his hand down to her groin. Her skin is wet. Her groin and thighs are clear. There are no buboes.

He can sleep now. He only needs to roll onto his side. Then he will face her, and he will place his hand on her hips, her round hips, and fall asleep, connected.

He breathes and rolls over, and lets out a cry. There is a blackness in the middle of his forehead, a blackness made by a nail entering. The self that stands beside him looking at him disappears entirely. He is not there. It is in his arms too, a searing pain that dismembers him, so he is not a body but a pile of dirty matter.

His cry did not waken Ellie, and he must let her sleep. He breathes. He will be silent. He lifts his hand, his right hand, and feels towards his left shoulder. His touch is measurelessly tentative as he slides it towards his armpit, and finds there, brittle to the skin of his fingers no matter how gently he touches it, a patch of bubbles on the flesh, delicate but definite, discreet but an unmistakable sign, and he knows that if he presses them any harder they will roar with pain and tell him the message that he has been hiding from.

His first thought is: I cannot die, I must care for Ellie, I must not die, not yet. Then he thinks, and what a relief to die, if she were to die. Then he thinks, my prayer was heard, this is what I petitioned for, and I will bear it with good grace and even joy. Then he thinks, I must not die, because I have to take care of Ellie. And these thoughts circle around and around, and he cannot break the circle. He breathes to ease the pain, and because there is not enough air in the room, or in him.

He thinks: I must sleep. I must hold all of this together. I must finish the pamphlet, provide for her, I must be able to get through tomorrow and the day after. I must sleep because if I don't then tomorrow I will be nailed to this bed, and will be of no use to anyone. I must sleep to get by and do whatever has to come next. I will resign myself to this, but not yet.

And he breathes, and he itemises in his mind all of the good things that he has to be grateful for. Six good years. The time he first heard her voice in St Bartholomew the Less churchyard, their walk to the Thames, their courtship through the winter, naming the trees as they walked beyond Charterhouse, naming the birds, by appearance and song, as they passed west of Westminster into a place neither had seen before, buying the ring, his asking her to marry him on the bridge, and the very ponderous way in which she had finally agreed, the purchase of the shop, their wedding, her pregnancy. Then it unravels. But there is more, and with the utmost effort he locates it. A thousand conversations. A hundred thousand ordinary things. The way she tucks her skirts and ties ribbons in her hair. The time they walked to Spitalfields to look at silks and laces, and they spoke to a Dutchman. Her compassion, her kindness when she told him to put aside his mother's words. Her enthusiasm for Kiffin and for her baptism. Their first book together, a book they made, teaching her to read and her joy in that, her reading to him and him reading to her by turns, printing together, on opposite sides of the press, drinking a dish of coffee in a room in an inn, going to see a play, the time they walked over the frozen Thames, always slipping but staying upright. He lines them up like candles, and they light the way.

CHAPTER ELEVEN

He wakes and it is like any other morning, though everything has changed. He is feverish and his mind is cloudy, but his body responds to his will. He observes himself lifting himself from the bed, not putting too much pressure on his armpits, not squeezing them together, and leaning over Ellie as she sleeps and kissing her firmly on the mouth. He relieves himself into the chamber pot and goes downstairs to find Tobias waiting.

This morning Tobias follows him over the threshold. They stand outside the front door, him wrapped in a blanket despite the fever, because he fears the cold more. He is burning, inside and out. Tobias senses this, and rests against his leg. He looks into the dawn to the east, over Aldersgate, over the city, and over all its church towers, to Spitalfields and Portsoken Ward and to the river and beyond, and he knows that the city rises with him, and prays to the dawn. The city has arteries and veins and a pulse; the city has lungs and breathes and gasps because there is not enough air. The city watches the sun and stirs into life, it stands and watches and waits.

One thing the plague has shown is that walls don't matter, they don't stop the plague and they don't mark the boundaries of the city. Farringdon Without and Farringdon Within the Wall stand next to each other, hold the same people, have the same houses, and you can walk from one to the other in minutes, through Aldersgate, wall and ditch, Newgate, Ludgate, or by water, the Fleet or Thames. This city lies within and without its walls. Even the massive city walls are permeable. And his skin too is permeable, as he exhales sweat and inhales the city's fumes through his pores. He is the city.

He is the city. It inhabits him and he embodies it. He lives and dies in the city, and it lives and dies in him. The burning in his head has opened him to this prophecy, like a seraph, whose name means burning with love, it connects him with his maker, above, in a wordless and perfect communication. An invisible pillar of fire explodes from his skull and reaches heaven. He is listening.

A wind blows from the east, but it cannot shake this flame. The love he feels for Ellie consumes everything around it, everything in his path, and it is the same as the love of God, and it is more powerful because it is here and it extends to the flesh and carnal knowing, and the city knows this and he is the city. He stands faintly to the side of himself, dislocated and unattached, blurred in his own eyes, and he looks upon himself as a prophet, one who sees things far off in time and space. He drinks his small beer and it will not cool him. He is aflame, and he will walk that short and narrow path that God has laid out for him.

He thinks back to the walk from St Bartholomew the Less to the Hand and Shears on the first day of March in 1661. She wore a dress that she made herself, with Sarah Cooper's help, with French lace and silk ribbons. Despite her age, and though it was her second marriage, the brown fabric was so pale that it was approaching white, the colour of youth and hope. The ribbons were shining gold, the lace the colour of rich cream. The street froze around them as they processed, arms enfolded, the people watching her, tall and glorious, ribbons in her abundant brown hair, turning the viscous air around her to spring. He'd never felt so blessed. And when they entered the tavern and saw the table laid out with a cloth and a pie and the sugar-iced cake, the surprise and then the smile on her face left him breathless and mute with a rising superabundance of joy.

Then they processed one more time, out of the Hand and Shears, between St Bartholomew the Great and St Botolph, across Little Britain, past St Bartholomew the Less, with the afternoon sun shimmering in her hair, and he was again overwhelmed with his good fortune, and felt that he didn't deserve anyone as good or as beautiful as her. He felt proud to walk with her and at the same time fearful she would be taken away, just like that, unforeseen. As though angels might swoop down on stout wings and steal her. Because she merited so much better. He tried to push such thoughts away on their wedding day.

His worries were again buried, or dispelled by bright light, when she saw the shop. He had more or less kept it secret from her. She knew his old, cramped premises north of here, near Long Lane. Their new shop, where they would live, was so much more spacious and bright, with more light and air. He could see in her eyes the anticipation of the books they would make here, books full of light and air. He pushed open the door and she stepped inside. Her face dazzled, even when she saw the dust. She kissed him again. He opened the shutters. Then she found a broom and swept. She looked around the downstairs, found a pot and put the flowers there, in the light.

He stood behind her, hardly daring to touch her, so flawless and immaculate she appeared in her dress. They had embraced and kissed before, often, and he had covered her with flowers, but now he hesitated, because the promise was too great, her broad shoulders and hips, the belly he knew would be fertile, acres of skin he had yet to uncover, now wrapped in untouchable calico. He looked, astonished and stupefied, at her hair, her shoulders, the ribbon and lace, and was frozen while wide rivers of desire flowed unseen. Her back was the most beautiful thing. He felt redundant. But then she breathed out, and he slipped his arms around her, first her belly and then her breasts, and she pressed against him. She turned, he led her upstairs – or did she lead him? – into their bedroom, with its spacious bed. She opened the shutters a little, so that shards of light illuminated the dress. Hesitantly he unwrapped her, not wanting to forget a second of it or weaken any of the sensations he felt as the fabric fell away and her nakedness was revealed.

He stands there and reiterates in his mind every moment, every aspect that his calcineous thoughts will let him repossess. There are pieces that won't come to him. He does not know what they are, but he can tell that there are impressions, emotions, glimpses of flesh missing. He is agitated, inflamed. He must go inside and ask her what she remembers. But his thoughts twist and are deflected even as he formulates them. It is because of the heat that rises from his brain to heaven, which creates a fierce wind, that his thoughts are swept away. Made for an English spring, they cannot withstand these burning currents.

No one sees him. The streets are empty still. The sky has woken him. He goes inside, bringing the city with him and within him, Tobias faithfully at his heels.

* * *

She's awake in bed, and he hands her the cup. She is thirsty. He fetches another cup for her. He climbs in beside her, and they wrap their arms around each other, awkwardly and tentatively, for fear of finding pain. Once they have discovered a comfortable, entangled position they hold there, at once relaxed and in a tight grip.

'I am dead,' he says.

It takes her a while to work out what he means, as she is holding him and he is very much alive. She can feel the pounding of his heart, the heat of his limbs, his breath upon her neck. Then she can hardly bring herself to ask the question.

'You've caught it?'

'I have.'

'You caught it from me. I've killed you?'

'No.' Though he can't clearly justify why he rejects that idea. 'I resigned myself to whatever would happen. I chose to do that. I was ready for that. It could have happened or not happened, it could have happened anyway, without yours. Then I would have given it to you.'

'No, you would have run away and hidden to protect me.'

He wants to tell her that she is now safe, but he doesn't, because she mustn't know about the covenant he has made.

He tells her about his pain, and she tells him about hers. They describe the symptoms, the sense that they are not truly themselves, that they observe themselves from a small distance, to one side within the person. That right now they are watching themselves together, from above the bed. The hot and cold, the rushing of the blood, the sore eyelids, the trembling, the aching in the head, the fluttering in the heart and stomach as though a creature is dying there.

Then he says, 'I've had a sudden understanding. I am the city. It came to me as I was standing outside, looking at the dawn and the sky over the walls. It was like a premonition. The city lives in me as much as I live in it. Just as Farringdon stands within the city walls and without, so the city is alive in me. As though I feel everything in it within my own body. I can see every person walking along Thames Street and on Cable Street, I can hear the guards within the Tower, in Baynard's Castle, hear the talk in Leadenhall Market. They ripple in my ears, my eyes, over my skin, not as though I'm looking at them or hearing them directly, but because they're all around me, there somewhere just on the edges of the senses.'

She says nothing. She thinks it is his fever or hers but she cannot fathom what he means.

'I think it means something, Ellie. I think it's a sign.'

'The plague,' she says finally, 'it doesn't only make your head hurt. It gets inside your head and changes it, mixes things up. You don't see right. Your thoughts get stuck, just go around and around. You can't get to the end of anything.'

'There's a column of fire burning out of me, reaching up to heaven. I think He's listening to me, speaking to me. I just can't understand the words yet, because they're not human words but something above and beyond us. But He's answering. I prayed to Him and asked for an answer, when I was at St Paul's. This is His response. He heard me.'

'I hope it's true. But you're feverish. You should rest.'

'Are you feeling better?' He knows the answer.

'Yes, a little.'

'It's a sign.'

'It's a sign that resting is good. We'll recover. Do we have food for a while?'

'A week, perhaps.'

'Then we can stay here and rest. Get some sleep.'

And he does feel the heat soothing his core, and then lulling him to sleep.

She leans over him, whispering.

'James, you're not dead. You're more full of life than anyone I've ever known. The way you manage to get on with doing the work, and caring for me, even when everything is awful. You always do. The way you bear adversity, forgive everyone. The way that Jeremiah ripped you apart, and you just carried it, and worried about me when I lay there unable to move, as if it wasn't about you too. You can't die. Not before me.'

He does not hear her.

★ ★ ★

He wakes, and it is the middle of the day, and he is disconcerted, without any bearings. South could be east, north could be west, up could be anywhere. Ellie is next to him, and he has been dreaming about her.

He reaches for the dream. It's hard waking up so suddenly, because you lose that chance to snatch your dream back before it entirely disappears. Nonetheless, he leans back and reaches for it, and there's a little there, just enough to catch hold of. A building, a large empty building with glassless windows. Outside, he doesn't know, it seems empty, desolate. The life is inside the building. He's there with Ellie, and they're exploring the building; no, they're searching. From room to room, among broken pillars. The building is ruined. And they're searching …

He cannot tease out any more than that. The dream seems familiar and he thinks he may have dreamed it before. Some people, magicians and wise men but also probably fools, think that dreams have secret meanings, that they contain concealed knowledge, either because they're magical, or because they're another way that God speaks to you, opening your head. In either case, they're supernatural, something beyond nature, magic or divinity, and they are something you read, like a poem with the light and the darkness mixed together. But school did not teach him how to read dreams, so all he is left with is an empty echoing building, with Ellie, searching through the ruins. There's dust coming in through the windows instead of light, and there are other people too, strangers, but they do not speak to them. He does not want the two of them to be noticed; they are furtive, he thinks, though perhaps just not wanting to be seen. He doesn't understand where the light is coming from. It's a dull, orange light, a wintry light rather than a summer's. There are no shadows, though plenty of things he can't see properly. The little he sees is all he understands. Though he also feels a sadness.

She is asleep, he is awake now, and how long he has been asleep for he doesn't know. He is fully alert but it still takes a deliberate act to bring into his conscious mind what has happened. The buboes, sleep, the vision at dawn, the understanding, the memories of their wedding, then speaking to Ellie and telling her that he is condemned, then sleep. And what next?

He goes downstairs, and finds Tobias.

'I understand,' he says. 'You've been sent to look after her for me. When I'm gone.'

Tobias tilts his head, looking at him quizzically, and James would swear an oath that he sees a sign of comprehension in his expression.

'You know.'

He walks around the abandoned press, observing it from both sides. He should have wiped the ink off the bed of type before it dried and left a fine crust that will clog the next sheet. He should have cleaned the leather inking pads. He should have tidied the shop. An abandoned press is a lonely, half-living thing. He looks at the stack of unprinted sheets, which is taller than he remembered, and much taller than he had planned yesterday morning. He looks around the shop at the hanging sheets, now fully dry, and there are fewer than he had hoped. He begins to gather them into a pile, but he soon loses interest. He cannot even concentrate on this. The pain in his head bears a message.

He puts them on the table. Four printed sheets, with fair crafts-manship, though nothing he should be proud of. He wonders: did I remember to take a proof? He thinks, and he cannot remember. There are breaches in his memory of the day before, and this disturbs him. Did he check for errors? He doesn't know.

But once again he has lost interest in the question, and his mind passes back to something else: the pain, the message, the prayer in Paul's, his pact. What is he hearing about the city, what is the message here, the one that shoots in a flame from his head? Though, he reflects, if it is a message then the flame does not ascend from his head, but instead descends from heaven into his wide-open brain. He knows his body has been opened to the city, that he has become one with the city, that the life force that rolls through the city's ways now surges through his veins. Every gift comes with a responsibility, so is there something he needs to do? What are God's instructions, delivered straight to his living, scalding, susceptible skull? He listens. He breathes deep, and listens for voices, or a voice. A voice within the city, within or without the walls, a hidden, occult voice that is intended only for him, though whispered within Broad Street Ward or Cheap.

Does he hear it there, within one of the markets, surrounded by other voices, talking about money or meat or the fineness of the yarn, a voice saying, walk with us, beside us, take the same path? Does he hear it in a tavern, a preacher's voice, saying, there is no path but the one chosen for us? Does he hear this voice in a heated argument in a remote kitchen in Tower Street, where a woman cries, if you can't bear it on your shoulders, if you won't willingly face the burden, then how will you look your judge in the eye when the final judgement comes, how will you be numbered among the righteous, how will you be saved?

More to the point, he asks himself, is the question how will she be saved?

He listens again. Does he hear it by Cheapside Cross where a drunk man whispers to his cat about how well they will eat and drink tonight, in the George Inn, and then perhaps no more? Does he hear it in the croaking voice of a waterman, approaching the mooring at the Steelyard, saying that he's glad that the trade is picking up there, that they have been lean times, that the men of northern Germany always seem to know so much about the world? Does he hear it in the voices of Billingsgate fishwives, who say that their husbands don't leave them enough to feed the mouths at the table, and what do they expect them to do about this, do they expect them to beg or steal? There is the voice of a child, rapt and attentive and a little joyful as she says, I will miss him, but little Joshua is going to heaven, and I will join him there one day: does he hear it there? Or perhaps he hears it in the voice of a bunched-up woman, warming herself over a stove, croaking to herself that, yes, it was a good life, and yes, there were disappointments, and yes, her first husband harmed her in both body and spirit and crushed her, but his end was no more than he deserved, and yes, the second was a good man, a kind man with soft hands, and yes, who would have thought that the business with the house should have turned out so well, yes, and the children were boundless comfort, and yes, the plentiful harvests outnumbered the meagre, and yes, there was a time to leave things though they had been ever so good, yes, when the time was full and unresisting. Then things go a little more quiet, and, yes, he hears a voice whispering near a fireplace, a voice full of age and weariness and wisdom and regret for the world, saying that one of the thieves was saved and the other damned, and the saved thief was promised that he would be with Christ in paradise that very day, but that the price of paradise was a sacrifice, and only a sacrifice would save paradise for the world, which was otherwise damned.

And then the pain is too severe for him to hear any voices. He crouches and strokes Tobias.

'I hear,' he says, 'I hear you.' And he puts on his boots.

CHAPTER TWELVE

He stands in the doorway and looks to the city, over and beyond the walls, but this afternoon, unlike this morning and every other morning, it is not in order to feel grounded, because he is the ground. He is the city, its skyline, the streets, the houses and warehouses, the parts that jut over the river, piers and docks. He is everything that is not earth, sky and water. He is the city. He is the spirit to its body, an extension of its material being. He is the medium that interprets its senses, because the city has senses. The city is not merely a machine, an engine for activity and busyness, but also a living, breathing thing. Every turn in a corner, every worn edge of a casement, every window-pane, every cobble, every shutter, every taper, every emptied chamber pot, every sewer dry of water or wine, every bell in a tower, every tower, every pew, empty or full, every market stall, every tap, every gallery in an inn, every nook in an alehouse, every washbasin, every printing press, every loom, every furnace, every oven and kiln, all the bakehouses, every shelf of folded sheets, every shop on London Bridge, every shelf of archives in all the Inns of Court, every dock in every courtroom, all the halls of the noble guilds, the kitchen table in every poor person's home, the fishermen's quays, every mooring and solid cleat, every winch, all the ironwork at the docks, the roof tiles and chimneys, the stoves and scuttles, the fire irons and tongs, all the china and every book, so many books, every fiddle and lute, every flag-stone, every arch and column and colonnade, all the fonts in all the churches, all the spires, all the barrels in every cellar, the taps and mugs and bottles and mirrors, the graffiti, all of it, painted on whitewash and scratched in stone walls, the holes in the road, the graveyards, the burial pits, the buried broken glass, the bright tiles and half-height bricks, the wooden boards and plaster ceilings, the wattle and daub walls, every playhouse and bearpit, every chapel and secret place where people go to pray, all the rooms of government, every privy and palace, every prison and leper house, every crypt and conference room, every green field, every hovel and doorway and ruined porch, every leaded pane and cracked frame, every joint and joist, every vault and every dome, every fallen wall and brick and gable, every garden, closed and open, every street, lane, hill, row, alley, way, road, avenue, shambles, court, and gate, every bar and barrel in every victualling house, be it tavern, inn, alehouse, brewhouse, all the clothworkers' shops, the curriers' workshops, the glaziers' and goldsmiths' workshops, the mercers' and pewterers' shops, the vintners' and chandlers' shops, the weavers' and plasterers' shops, the cutlers' shops and the drapers' shops, every hoard of silver locked up in a church, every lock and key, every weather-cock, every tomb and gravestone, every bone and all the interred gold, all the broken and mended things, the cracks in all the stones that let in shreds of light, these are all part of him and who he is, and there is none of this that is not him.

Something brushes his ankles.

'No Tobias, this isn't for you. You have to stay and watch over Ellie.'

Tobias stares long and hard, with his bright brown eyes, before he turns and enters the house.

His head is burning as he steps out into the city. He had thought he would proceed directly to St Paul's, the heart of the city, and from there eastward, towards its head and belly. But instead he finds himself turning around to St Botolph without Aldgate, an old church built by friars. He likes its compact scale, without unnecessary aspirations. He then follows Little Britain. He does not turn to St Bartholomew the Less, because he already carries every stone of it upon his shoulders. And when he reaches the green of Smithfield he beats its boundaries with his feet, and he knows that he is undertaking a kind of magic, that he will rewrite the history of Smithfield by ritual, that he will confine and possess it.

There is his mother, and he is running to her, eight or nine, he guesses, with a corn dolly he has made. It has a hat, a belt and shoes. He has named it Mary, for her. He goes into the dark room, breathes in its obscurity, feeds on the shadows. There is a small fire, and the room is warm. Margaret is by the window seat, with a book in her hands. He thinks: she cannot read yet. But then he wonders how much he really knows. It is bound in red velvet and has a brass clasp. How does she come by such a book? He imagines the touch of the velvet on his fingertips as he strokes it, soft with a suggestion of bristles. And hears the creak, the crackle of the pages, because the spine is tight for such a small, thick volume. He has seen them at the bookstalls, at Robert Allott's stall in Paul's churchyard, and Allot has permitted him to touch them. He has smelled the pages, which have the fresh smell of cut hay, or something like it, because nothing is quite like newly-printed paper. This room does not have that smell. Instead there is pitch and smoke, and the decayed and putrefied warmth of his mother. He thinks about her clasping him to her breasts, and the smell of soured milk. It is disappointing.

'Mother,' he says, 'I brought you this.'

Young Margaret looks up at him. Her wide blue eyes are cold and appraising. She is only six or seven, he reckons. She has her mother's eyes, old and unforgiving. His mother is younger than he is now, he thinks, only forty or so. To be older than one's parents is hard, confounding. She looks down again.

'What is it?' Margaret speaks, not his mother.

He looks to his mother. She is sitting in the chair by the fire, a sewing basket beside her and a needle in her hand. She is darning a shirt. The shirt is pale brown, the thread is the colour of an autumn sunset, an early redcurrant, and the stitches, however neat, pick out the wound.

She looks at him, smiles, and looks to Margaret. Her face is wrinkled, he sees, her eyes sunken. Are these the marks of death creeping outward? The purple around her eyes makes him think of fruit, but autumn fruit, blackberries. There are overflowing crops of blackberries to be found surrounding Charterhouse too.

And mulberries. But the mulberries stain his hands, so when he steals them, if it is theft, he has to visit his father's shop and wash his hands in blood to conceal the stain.

Blackberries leave a lesser stain and can be forgiven.

His tongue clogs. Margaret stares. There is something he needs to say, a question to be answered. How does he explain the corn dolly? The answer to the question seems to involve an account of why he made it, how he made it, the angle of the sun, creeping illicitly over farmer Marsh's fence, the moment when he lay down in the corn and felt the prickles on his skin, which made him think of the shoes, and the moment when he named it, which he did aloud, in full view of the circling crows. He thought he would like a black feather to put in the dolly's hat, but none appeared. There is too much to describe and explain, and his tongue trips up over every intended syllable. He says nothing.

'Why don't you answer your sister, James?'

She is looking at him again. He searches those eyes for love or compassion. They are mottled. Also blue. His are grey.

Because his answer is too long, and they won't hear it. Is there a shorter answer? What is the answer they expect?

His mother turns to stoke the fire. Sparks rise, then she looks at him again.

'It needs another log, don't you think?'

He thinks about this. His mother knows the answer, so why is she asking him? Is she testing his knowledge of fires, of keeping fires alive? Is this something he must learn to be a good Christian? Do angels have to learn how to stoke the fires in purgatory? Or do those fires never burn low? Does this fire need air or fuel?

'James!' She looks towards the pile of logs on the other side of the fireplace. They are neatly stacked, and all cut to a close length. Which of his brothers did this, he wonders, such a neat job? And laid them up so tidily, to please their mother? They took the side branches off too, to form kindling, which now lies in a pail by the logs.

'James?'

He understands. He fetches a log and places it carefully, so as not to make sparks or ashes that might fly into the room, in the flames. By the fire he feels a different, fevered heat. He stands back, and looks to his mother for her approval. She looks to the fire, prods it with her iron poker, watches with satisfaction the sparks fly up the chimney. She turns to him and nods.

Then she looks again at Margaret. They exchange an understanding.

'What is it?'

Now he speaks without thinking. The words jump out of his mouth, and he doesn't even think they're his.

'A corn dolly,' he says.

Margaret smiles.

Because there is only two years between them, he played often with Margaret when they were young. This has only recently been interrupted, since his father started calling on him to spend more time with the boys, cleaving meat and hewing bone and scrubbing the ceaseless, unstoppable effluence of blood. He does not know which is worse, his knees on the floor with a brush, or his hand in the air grasping a cleaver. The blood leaves his knees black. Margaret will never do this, but instead will learn to sew and cook. She was always better at sewing anyway. They no longer play together, and the gulf between them has grown. But there is more than this. She is their mother's. She lives in the marrow of this room, narrow, closed, oily and ruthless. He doesn't understand how she has grown to be so distant, so foreign.

'For me?' she asks, and he thinks, though he is not sure, that her expression is joyful. He wants to feel close to her, but doesn't.

'It's ...'

And he halts because he knows that there is more happening and more at stake here than he can fathom.

'I was thinking ...'

The silence is worse than anything, because his words fall into it, and he can hear them falling as into the deepest well. They don't stop falling.

'When I made it ...' He stumbles again. That is not what

he meant. 'I thought. It's because of the ...' Though perhaps he should not draw attention to the clever way he has given the dolly a hat that actually looks like a hat. His mother might think it too conceited.

He has not had time to register what is happening when Margaret bounds across the room and snatches it from him.

'Thank you, James.' She bounces back to the window seat.

His mother looks down at her sewing. Has she seen or not? Has she understood?

He looks between the two of them, while neither looks back, and he wishes he were back at the butcher's block, listening to his father's knife. But there is no such relief. The door is there, but he wonders how much of a defeat it would be for him to walk out now, with no further words said. He should say something. His mother should know, or at least choose to refuse to know. He hesitates and is trapped there.

'What's its name?'

Once again, fear of not speaking makes the word jump out, almost involuntarily, before he has a chance to wrestle the word down with reason.

'Mary.'

Margaret utters a short laugh. She holds the doll aloft, and calls, 'Mummy!' His mother looks over. Now events happen too quickly for him to register them.

'Mary, indeed!' says his mother, asperity in her voice.

There is no pulling it back now.

'But why does it wear a belt and a hat?' asks Margaret.

'It looks like a man,' states his mother.

'It's meant to be Mary.'

'You should have given it a man's name, not the Virgin's.'

'Nor your mother's,' his mother adds. 'When did you see me in a belt and hat?'

He knows that they're right, but he cannot explain his decision. He also knows that there was a reason, but his anxious mind won't retrieve it. He has to find something else to say.

'I thought you would want ...' No, not that. 'Do you like it?'

'It's funny,' Margaret says. 'I do like it.' She lies in the window seat and the dolly does a little dance on her stomach while she hums.

'Let's not burn it then,' says his mother. But why would she burn it? 'Thank you, James.' Again he is trapped in the middle of the room, far from the door, from the window, from his mother and sister. 'Have you no work to attend to?' She is already looking at the darning in her hands, probing the cloth with a needle, pricking the loose threads. He doesn't move. She looks up at him. 'You've washed the blood from your hands!' she says, and laughs.

He flees, and he hears Margaret laughing as he closes the door behind him, to keep the warmth in.

And then a few years later, perhaps seven years, he is in that same room again, still warm and gloomy and tightly closed around its inhabitants, but now it has become the room where she lies convalescing, her mind and body full of troubles, full of inflammation and dropsy. She has called him in to give him her blessing. She is stretched out on the makeshift bed, lying on her back, covered with blankets. This, he thinks at the time, is how he will remember her. She pulls a blanket up to her chin as he stands by her bed.

'James, child.' Her voice is hoarse and she will punctuate it with coughs. 'Closer. Every word is a struggle.' He wonders in what sense, what kind of struggle. In her lungs, in her heart, in her conscience? Or all of these together? He leans in.

'Yes mother?'

'I didn't think you would grow so tall. I named you after James the less, not James the great.'

'Father says I take after his father.'

She grunts her disapproval of this notion.

'Only in that respect, I hope.'

Without a more specific accusation he does not know how to defend his grandfather.

'My father was more inclined to the church,' she says, 'but there's still time for that. And you've given up your father's trade?' He knew she didn't approve of butchering, because of the mess and the lingering raw, musty smell. He hoped she would be pleased. His wife, when he found a wife, would not have to see the caked blood trapped under his nails.

'Father will buy me an apprenticeship. Next year. It has been agreed. As a printer. With a man named Simmons in Moorgate.' He thinks she knows this already, but he must say it anyway.

'A printer?'

'Yes.'

'Of books?'

'And pamphlets. And little jobs too, handbills and paper.'

'And you are happy to do this?'

'I am, mother.'

She looks out of the window. Her eyes have a kind of shell over them, a transparent yet thick film. She sighs. For a moment he thinks he sees her soul fly through the window into the autumn skies. But she is still here. 'I suppose there are some good books,' she says.

'I thought your book ...'

She silences him with a look that clogs his insides, his heart, his lungs, his bowels. 'There are some good books. Will you be printing any of them?'

'I don't think that Simmons is that sort of a printer.'

'I wonder if the goodness might have rubbed off on you. Like soot, but pure.' Now she looks at him properly for the first time, as though she is weighing him in her scales. 'Perhaps it's too late, and you no longer care anyway.'

He does not know what to say to this, because it is in a sense true. He wants her to hurry with her benediction.

'Give me your hand.' He extends it. She takes it and pulls it under the blankets, into the sudorific heat, and places it on her bare stomach. He is frightened. When did she last touch him? Has she touched him since the uncomfortable, almost painful times she clasped him and Margaret to her breast while warning them of hellfire? He can't remember. Was there a kiss sometimes when he went away? He remembers none. He touches her open pores, and feels a hard lump there, distending the chafed surface of her

118

skin. She winces. 'Gently.' She will not let his hand go. 'See?' He nods. She keeps his hand there until he is ready to pull it back with force, and then she releases him.

'You feel it?' He nods. 'What do you think?'

'I don't know what to think.'

'I'll tell you. I'm not going to be here with you for long. Soon I'll go to meet with my maker.' He pictures her idea of her maker, in white robes and flowing locks, speaking Latin. Her maker shows whom He loves and whom He condemns forthrightly, because He has no need to conceal it, because He sees everything and He is absolutely good.

'I'm sorry mother.' He sees that there is no other way but asking. She will not be forthcoming, and he must pay the requisite price. 'I have come to ask for your blessing.'

'For what, James?' Surely this is a convention; does he really need to specify the bargain? 'For my apprenticeship. For my future happiness. For my marriage when I find a wife.'

Her attention comes and goes from the window to him and the hand that now hangs by his side, but for a moment she fixes his eye directly.

'You think you'll find someone willing to have you? You'll have to prosper in your book-making if you hope for that. You'll need riches. Don't go expecting a dowry.'

Her dropsy or tumour or whatever it is has rendered her even less diffident, he thinks.

'Nonetheless,' he says, 'For the future, work or marriage or health.'

'Yes, yes, of course.'

Margaret has appeared at his shoulder, unheard. He smells her before any other sense tells him of her presence. She smells of soap and lavender.

'Don't tire her,' she says, and goes to the window seat. She smiles at their mother, who smiles back at her daughter. With the light behind her, and her mass of curls, Margaret looks like a picture of virtue in a church. No wonder her mother smiles when she sees her.

'I'll take that then, thank you mother,' he says.

'I'm sure you will.' There is a weary resentment in her voice; resentment, he thinks, that she wants to leave this life, but still wants to live, that she will not see another summer, that her husband may marry another, that her children will outlive her and perhaps one day forget her, that she will no longer be the instrument of judgement, because she is going to a place where that role belongs to another.

He nods and shuffles backwards towards the door, fearful of turning his back on her.

'You don't think of the pain, James. You don't understand the suffering this causes. Like childbirth, but ending only in death. No joy in life. I shall be happy to go and meet my maker soon.'

'In Purgatory?' he asks, and flees.

And now he walks the bounds of Smithfield and that history is trapped, confined within a jar, possessed and written anew. The old house and what weighs upon him there are razed, he thinks, though perhaps there is more. More to be unearthed. If there is, then he will find that too, and stop it in his jar.

And his head still burns as he walks the market's bounds, with an undiminished flame, and it sparks and the sky coruscates with him as he turns into Chick Lane and heads west, towards the Fleet River.

CHAPTER THIRTEEN

The Fleet smells impossibly, unconscionably bad. Every kind of rottenness is there. The stench of organic matter, sweet and salty, that compresses the head; the vapor of citrus which cuts through everything and catches the back of the throat; the reek of human flesh, which brings antipathy and fear together. There must be bodies here.

He has heard of this, though he's never seen it himself. People who caught the plague and who weren't shut up in their houses, or who were shut up and managed to escape the watchmen who guarded the doors, some of these lost their minds. He doesn't know whether it was the pain or some other effect of the disease, the lack of air in the lungs, or something else invisible within the body, a swelling of the brain or other organs, but they lost all sense of themselves and became quite mad. Last year there were many stories of this. They walked through the streets, trembling or moaning, they ran howling, not responsive to anyone trying to speak to them or usher them back to their houses. Though very few would try to speak to someone so visibly dying of the plague. Some of these plague sufferers would speak, he heard, and their sentences would be broken, fragments of sense, not about death and salvation but instead about the ordinary bits of their lives, the morning, their sister, windows and doors, chair legs, broken pots. But as the pain intensified or spread, they would become insensate, and forget about heaven and hell and do the natural thing, which was to throw themselves into the river. Perhaps they thought the water would soothe the pain, would ease their sores, or perhaps they wanted to drown. Bodies washed up on the Isle of Dogs, at Greenwich, all the way to Gravesend. Bodies clogged the docks at St Katherine's.

He thinks that this is the smell he now encounters. The smell of desperate corpses creeping along the Fleet below the surface water, twisting and writhing with the current as they seek the outlet to the Thames and the North Sea, where the chill will end their burning. As they putrefy, the waters will bubble near the banks, as the gas rushes to be released into London's miasma. He can't see any bubbles, but he imagines the bodies there, conjured by an undeniable stench. He is happy that his sense of smell is a little impaired with the fever.

Will that be how I will end? he wonders. Running mad and desperate. Seeking relief in oblivion. He knows, though, that he must see it through to the end, that pushing through to the end that God ordains for him is part of his covenant, the bargain they have struck, and he must not seek to hasten or abridge the final minutes. He will not think that he is forsaken. Rather he will know that his purpose and desire have been fulfilled. He will not lose his mind, then, but he will hold onto it like a newborn child.

This thought does not offer him much solace.

He breathes, and chokes. He walks south along the Fleet, with the city on his left. He walks on the far side, the Bridewell side, having crossed at Cow Bridge, he doesn't know why. Now he walks through fields, fields with cows, and he is away from the city that is also him. He is at some distance from himself, from the ground, he is displaced, and he hurries back to himself, Ely Place and its gardens to his right, St Andrew Holborn ahead of him. It is a new church, younger than he is, though constructed on the site of a much older building. Is this always the case? Do we always make new things in places where there is already something, and is that because we seldom do anything really new, or is it because the places are truly holy? If he asks the city, if he looks within himself, there will surely be an answer. He looks at the stones of St Andrew, and knows that good people pray there, people who keep secrets close to their heart, who seek the light, and that people who are less good pray there too, people who wish to think themselves better than others, people who believe themselves entitled to places, both in this life and the next. He looks at the graves. There are no fresh graves. There are too many bodies to bury. He feels their bones within him.

If he were to carry on down Shoe Lane, he'd arrive at Bridewell, the prison for scandal. Instead he crosses back over the Fleet at Holborn Bridge, and heads along the other bank of the river to the Fleet Prison, the prison for debt. Of course, he thinks, other people are put in both prisons, as a way of insulting them. He senses his way among the rooms of the prison with their crowded beds, iron gates, damp walls. How could anyone survive the plague here? As he walks along Fleet Lane, past the prison, he rubs his hands over the wall and prays for the lives of the inmates, prays through the channel that burns from his brain directly to heaven, and he thinks they will be saved, most of them. When the Lane meets Fleet Street he turns left and ahead of him is the hill that leads up to Ludgate.

These streets are the next step in his rewriting of history, but here it is the people without the walls of the city that he sets free, free from the city magistrates, the aldermen and mayor, free from Westminster and Whitehall, free from the bishops. The prisoners will have to wait. He frees them from fear and poverty, and he tells them that it is easier for a camel to pass through the eye of a needle than it is for a rich man to enter the kingdom. He has never seen a camel, or even a picture of one, but he takes this as no obstacle. As he walks, the pride of the mighty is torn down.

But as he approaches the wall, there are other people whose supplications he feels. He feels them there, in the ditch that burns in his skin like a tattoo, the ditch that runs along the outside of the wall, from here to the other side of the city, where the Tower stands. Once a river ran there, though that's scarcely discernible now. The riverbed, the ditch, has been filled in with the city's discarded stuff, years of waste, and then the magistrates ordered that it be covered with soil, and gardens planted, and a mud wall has been built in places to keep the citizens from throwing more waste in there. But everything that has been cast there over the centuries leaves a trace, and he feels every remnant and residue

123

rise inside him, and the story of the city unfolds in sprigs, cuttings, leaves and oddments of the unwanted.

This much he can bear. It's the bodies that hurt him, make his eyeballs graze the rough sockets of his skull. The ditch moves up and down, respires gently, season by season, as it digests the bodies, and they turn from flesh to worm to loam and back again. You would have to watch for months, but you could see it with your own eyes. There are bodies here, of plague victims, of people without homes who died in the street, of infants, of maids who died in childbirth, of murdered women, all discarded. But there is another sort among the dead that arrests him here. The cats and the dogs. Hundreds of thousands of cats and dogs, not buried but cast into the waters of the ditch. Though the ditch enters the Fleet there is little or no current for most of its length, and so the bodies, human, canine and feline, drift away at the slowest pace. In the east, between Bishopsgate and Aldgate, the ditch is known as Houndsditch, because of the bodies that clog its way. People only pretend to care, he thinks. They expect the love of their dog, and then they say things like, he who lies with a dog must expect to wake with fleas. They fuss their dog when alive, then toss it in still waters to rot when it dies. Or they throw it in a plague pit. He doesn't wonder at this so much as why they pretend to love their dog in the first place. He shakes his head as he feels the whimpers of a hundred thousand and more cats and dogs beneath his feet, all left to decay just outside the city's walls.

He walks up the hill, across the ditch, and passes through Ludgate as though the city is his, which, in a sense, it is. And there is St Paul's. But that is not where the city leads him now, as he turns not right into Creed Lane, which would lead him to St Andrews Hill and a view of the river, where he would wonder why all the streets give a different name to what must be the same hill, but instead he turns left, up Ave Maria Lane, past the Stationers' Hall, and past the stalls of many booksellers. And this is not his destination, he thinks, but he must stop here, and he defers another reckoning that awaits him at Amen Corner, and instead his route remembers and conjures to his view, both in his eyes and with his mind, in the present and through all the history embedded in the stones of this city, the printers and booksellers and all manner of makers, carriers and vendors of books.

He feels in the docks of the city where William Caxton stepped when he first came back from Bruges to make a London book. And from then it had been a falling off, as men who used print seldom carried such learning and letters within them. And with Luther and Calvin and Melanchthon, the matter of books was no longer poetry but instead controversy and religion. And then it was news, and for all that he wanted news to be printed, it was not the highest use of the art, which was in any case no longer truly an art but merely a trade, and he himself had wanted to be a Caxton but he is no better than any other printer of cheap and profitable jobs. And here he has to reckon with himself: what is the point of learning, what is the point of letters, what is the point of the mysterious craft of printing books, if the end is only enter-tainment and news that people forget from one year to the next?

He steps to one stall, kept by William Miller, for whom he did a piece of work years ago. There are books on Julius Caesar, Alexander the Great, Hannibal, Pompey, lives of the great men, written into the length of a pamphlet. There are books about Germany and the Netherlands. Copies are laid out, stitched but not bound, with their title pages in full view. He runs his fingers over the linen-fibre page, and feels its journey from the south of France, over roads across mountains, through Paris, by boat across the narrow channel between their countries, and along the Thames, to here. The soft fibres whisper movement. Here they become something different, transformed. The shirt worn by a peasant near the Pyrenees becomes the life of an ancient Roman in London. He smells the linen, still fresh, the savour of the ink. All it lacks is a calfskin binding to sit on a doctor's or lawyer's or preacher's shelf. And next to this is another, titled *A Practical Exposition of the Historical Prophesy of Jonah: Delivering sundry brief Notes in a Cursory way concerning the mind of the Holy Ghost in the several Passages*. It is not published by Miller but printed by his brother, who sometimes sells, on others' stalls, copies of the books he has made for other publishers. The book promises, the title page says, both to exercise him and nourish him. He is beyond such needs, as his maker has already written large the future of both his body and mind, but, while Miller assesses him from behind the stall, he picks it up.

It is a heavy book. Miller has sewn it into a plain blue paper wrapping. The paper crackles, like kindling flames. Here is a passage about ministers crying exhortations to sinful people and places. Here he reads that God will not in vain wear out his rods of affliction against sinners. Here he reads … and he tarries. 'Consider, as stout as thou art, upon a great fit of sickness or some other stinging cross, thou mayest be brought to fear exceedingly in spite of thy heart,' and here the writer turns to the book of Jeremiah. There is no escaping the name. Eagle's sermon, this book on Miller's stall by an unheard-of writer. The boy is all over the city, like a cataract over his eyes, inscribed in its abandoned bakers, the cracked churches, blocked water-ways, the ringing of its bells, in its hushings, in the echoes in its conversations. He tries to obstruct the thoughts, but they will intrude. He pushes them, and pushes them. They come back. The boy's eyes in particular, blue as a kingfisher, black as coal. It is only by looking at the page, constraining the letters into focus, and making out the words, that he can stop the thoughts from puncturing and stinging and leaving a sore distress under his skin. Or, he wonders, is that the plague, that same plague he is now spreading among the booksellers of St Paul's? Has he run mad?

He reads. Jeremiah chapter twenty tells of Pashur, a governor and the son of a priest, who strikes Jeremiah and puts him in the stocks, but then sets him free and the Lord tells him, through his prophet, that he will live in terror and his friends will be destroyed. The mighty will be cast down, always. And James thinks of another verse from that chapter when Jeremiah is dejected and curses the man that brought his father news of his birth, 'because he slew me not from the womb; or that my mother might have been my grave, and her womb to be always great with me.' He thinks about those words often. Jeremiah cursed his own birth and the messenger who brought the news. But that is not what this writer means: he is thinking of how the powerful are overthrown and prostrated when they cross God. He reads: 'A hard-hearted sinner thou art, but hast not the strength of steel or stones.' Like Eagle, this man thinks that he is a prophet, that he can tell the reader about his or her own sin. And yet he probably never met the reader. The prophet will say that he sees things far off, beyond the reach of human eyes. Eyes that are stronger than steel or stones, a gaze that will cut through and bend and break and melt even the hardest things. Even this city, this mighty city, could be opened up and levelled by the prophet's eyes. And he reads on: 'Beware, when conscience awakes, and sin is set in order before thee, all thy hardiness will prove but as stubble when it is put to the fire.' And he feels the fire that is burning through him, consuming the stubble within him, and he wonders if this stubble is his sins, and if so then what his sins are, if they're pride or covetousness, if he has taken too much in this life for granted, if he has not been charitable enough to the poor, if he was greedy, if he craved worldly comforts without working hard enough for them, if his thoughts were too selfish or angry, or even if he has felt excessive love and desire for his wife. Is this what must be burned to the soil before a new crop can be planted?

Now he has read enough, and he flicks through the pages of the book, and from every page the same words leap out at him: God, man, mercy, just, will, prophecy, danger, sin, Jonah, pestilence, fire. He puts it down.

'Are you well, White?' asks Miller.

'Well enough. And you, your family?'

'All well, God be thanked.' And he enumerates the printers, booksellers, typefounders, carpenters and inkmakers and their families who have died in the past year and more. As he does so, James watches his knuckles whiten. The tragedies haven't released him, they won't release him, he sees.

'And people are buying your books?'

'Anything about the plague and religion,' he says, 'History not so much. People have had enough of history. They just want news and divine judgement. Are you working?'

'A little,' he says. 'Just now a book by Solomon Eagle about sin and destruction.'

Miller nods knowingly. 'For the man himself?' Now it is James's turn to nod and smile. 'What brings you here?' Miller asks.

It is a good question, and one he cannot answer. Walking the streets is always a risk, and people no longer do it to take the air, even if they have the leisure.

'To see the books,' he replies. 'To walk the streets, to remember their history, to listen to what they have to say.' Miller's gaze is severe. Does he seem quite mad? If he had a mirror, and were he to look into it, would he see a person he recognises? Or would he see someone who has become someone else?

He should leave.

'Good day,' he concludes, and walks on. He feels uncomfortable, but doesn't know if this is because of the way Miller studies him, or if it is because of his own fears, of madness or of being discovered, the way his mind is tricking him, or if it is because he knows that the fire burning inside him bears witness to a message that he has not brought into the world, or is telling him that he must walk the streets to uncover something unseen to human eyes, something unseen within himself, because he is the city, and the city breathes through him.

He continues along Ave Maria Lane until he reaches Amen Corner. He hears the ghosts of the ancient monks saying amen as they turn from Paternoster Row into Ave Maria Lane, the names of the places not expunged by the changes in religion, not erased in the words people use to chart their journeys in this new, reformed world. Under the stones the ghosts say amen. But that is not the purpose of his itinerary. Rather, he finds himself before a three storey, three gable square building, with an impressive arched doorway in the middle, and glazed windows all around. Big windows, plenty of glass, lots of light to read by, and no shortage of candles. Somewhere in here will be a library, and behind the wall to the left a pleasant courtyard with trees. This is where the College of Physicians meet. And here he stops, and another stage of his journey is done, and here he arrives at a letting go, his mind and ears and the past open.

CHAPTER FOURTEEN

Tobias rises, and meanders from the door to the bottom of the stairs. He listens. Nothing stirs. He walks around the printing shop, and then around the kitchen. It's safe. He returns to the door and curls up, his fore and back legs crossing, his nose to his knees, his spine a long crescent, his tail wrapped around.

Upstairs Ellie moans and wakes. She uses the chamber pot. It hurts her to move, not because of the swellings or the rash but because her limbs are so stiff. She wants to get up and go out and walk, but she knows she would not get far. She drains a cup of small beer and lies back down. She has been dreaming of Crug Hywel again, and the ditch, and running down and back up it with Iolo Morgan. She is uncertain of Iolo. He throws stones at cats. He tells her that one day he will make himself a coat of cat skins and never be cold again. It will take twenty cats, he says, and it will have many colours. But she likes running with him and he is almost as fast as her. He doesn't make fun of her for her height, perhaps because he knows she could wrestle him to the ground if she wanted. Even with the other boys he is quiet.

Now she is awake the boundary between dream and memory is uncertain. This is a memory, she thinks, not a dream, her mixed feelings about Iolo Morgan, and his talk of a coat of cats. They stand on Crug Hywel and imagine that they have a cannon that could strike the English castle from here. They describe a cannonball's flight, arching into the sky and down from Mynydd y Begwn to Crickhowell Castle so it topples and the stones roll down into the river Usk. The cannonball would at first be bigger than their heads, the circle of their arms, hands joined, but as it flew away, and burned in the air, now black now silver, it would shrink until it was an ant. An ant able to crush a stone wall two or three feet thick.

131

When they are done describing this they agree to race back to the village. It is downhill all the long way, and all grass and shrub, but will take them half an hour. And they will have to avoid the pen with the ram. And they will not stop to gather mushrooms, though she may, she thinks, pause to pick and eat blueberries, because her throat will be dry. If she races, and takes them in haste, her lips and her hands will drip with their blue, almost purple, the colour of her mother's eyes.

As she thinks this, Iolo steals an advantage and sets off. She does not worry, because it is a long run, and he has set off too fast, as he always does. He will tire, and she will tire less.

She runs. The mid-afternoon sun is on her face and in her eyes. She is careful to find her feet first, because running downhill demands concentration. You have to be careful to place your feet in the right place, or your legs tire more quickly. Once she's sure of her balance and the swiftness of her feet she runs faster, landing on her toes, almost falling, catching herself just in time. She avoids the giant mushrooms, and the larger piles of sheep droppings, every now and then looking up to check she is heading the straightest way back to the village.

Her legs are longer than Iolo's, and it isn't long before she passes him. He runs like a boy, labouring, swinging his arms back and forth rather than using them for balance. She laughs as she leaves him behind, and laughter while running is better than other laughter. She even stops for blueberries. She follows the edge of the stream for a few minutes, then crosses over it when it turns in front of her, splashing through at the shallowest point, effortlessly. Now it's all in her body, which knows how to do this, and the breath flows through her and she is almost flying, almost gliding like a gull over the hills, almost defying the earth, its pull, its dirt, its seams of time.

The finish line is Porthmawr, they know this by previous agreement. They touch the gate but never pass through it into the grounds of Cwrt-y-Carw, the mansion. The children of the village all fear this, with a nameless kind of fear around which they make up stories of the English taking children back to England, planting them in the soil as fertiliser, or using magic to stop them from speaking their own language. In their language Porthmawr Gate is just Porthmawr, and it has a meaning, and Cwrt-y-Carw has a meaning too. The house was built by the Herbert family, and a man named Herbert owns it now. He owns many things, houses he does not live in, a deer park. She has never seen him, and he is said to be a friend of the king.

She reaches her destination, at the edge of the village, and Iolo is out of sight. She knows he will have tried to catch up with her, failed, and then given up. He will slow down. When he arrives, if she waits for him, he will find some reason why he lost the contest, besides being slower. He will have seen someone, and had to speak, or he will have seen an open gate that he was obliged to close, or he will have tripped over some invisible obstacle. Something, anything other than the admission that the girl is the fastest.

She waits for him now, sweating, and wishes that she'd eaten more blueberries. She is parched. He must have resigned himself to losing early, and now is running slothfully towards the finish. Her breath returns, the flow of sweat abates, and she wonders whether he has gone straight home. That way he wouldn't have to face defeat. She is considering leaving the gate when she sees him, running towards her.

'Ellie,' he says, breathless, 'You must go home.'

There is something in his voice that stops her from taking pleasure in her victory and mocking him. Immediately she's tangled in a fit of fear.

She runs home, and this run she does not enjoy. The stones in the road hurt her feet. Now her shins ache as though they are bruised. Her arms are tired too. Everything that once flowed is awkward, and she is the tall girl again with swinging limbs.

She bursts through the front door.

How much, she asks herself now, again, is actually memory, how much a fevered dream, and how much does she imagine to fill the gaps in her memory? She cannot be sure. There is no one she can talk with to check, to see if their memories correspond. Instead she is alone in London, sick and suffering a pain that stops her from thinking and acting clearly. She is a single candle burning in a darkened room, and what she sees in the shadows is all she has to go by.

Betsi is there. She looks at Ellie, and her face is completely closed to enquiry, without answers or feelings, at least any feelings Ellie can recognise; she is frozen, ossified. Or is she bereft? thinks Ellie. Or am I just imagining?

'She's upstairs, Elinor,' Betsi says. She is seven years older than Ellie, and has become the head of the kitchen and the household in the later months of their mother's pregnancy. Their father is a farmhand and works indefinite hours for the farmer who holds the farm in tenancy from Herbert. The running of the house has to be delegated to a woman, and his wife is more able to count money and more provident of the future than he. So Betsi has been mothering Ellie, and has assumed the corresponding authority. Her words are both permission and instruction. Ellie removes her muddy shoes and hurries up the stairs, no longer light or swift on her feet.

For some reason, Betsi follows her. She flies into her parents' bedroom, and sees her mother lying there. A midwife stands near the window, a shadow.

Ellie remembers then the stillborn baby before. Two or so years earlier, she thinks. She does not have a calendar to measure these things by. It is one of her earliest memories, she thinks, though her memories from these times are not in order, but return to her pell-mell when she goes seeking them. That time, her mother had carried the baby to term, and the midwife, a different midwife, stood where this one now stands, a silhouette against the intruding light, and she too was frozen. Ellie stopped in the doorway, this same doorway.

'Mam?'

The light didn't help her see, but there was a smear of blood across her mother's chest and shoulders. Her breasts were bare, with their inflamed nipples. Below them, cradled in her arms was a baby. She walked forward. 'Mam?' She met a look full of surprise and grief. Her mother shook her head.

'She's perfect too,' she said. 'Come and sit with me.'

Ellie crawled into bed beside her mother, wrapped her arms around her neck, and rested her head on her shoulder. The baby was still, its eyes closed, one fist, clenched, stuck out from the carelessly enfolded swaddling cloth.

'It won't be restored,' said the midwife, not to anyone, perhaps to herself, and went downstairs.

She knew that this was not the first baby her mother had lost, but the other had not made it into the world, not like this one. This was why she only had one sister. Though her mam-gu said that the other reason was that her mother was too thin, that she wasn't fertile soil for babies because there was no flesh on her. Harvests had been poor, the farmer was mean, Herbert was mean, there was not always enough food. And her mother was always scrubbing the floors, baking and washing their clothes. Too bony for babies, mam-gu said.

Ellie cwtched up to her mother, her sharp, bony mother, and began to drift off.

When she woke the baby was still there, and her mother's face still full of grief and surprise. Her mother's shoulder was wet where her open mouth had been.

Betsi appeared and took her downstairs. She does not remember the burial. She can't remember now what happens to a child that dies before baptism, what happens here in this world or in the afterlife. Someone must have told her.

This time, bursting into her parents' room, Betsi almost on her heels, the midwife is there, frozen, and again she can't see so well, and again she halts in the threshold and looks to her mother.

'Mam?'

Her mother says nothing, and the midwife says nothing. She can't see the midwife's face. Only slowly does she see her mother's face, which is still and blank. Again, there is a streak of blood across her breasts and shoulder, and this is mirrored by the blood forming a wide ring on the sheet that only partly covers her. Once again, her arms are folded, and there, nestled below her breasts, lies a baby.

'Mam?'

She approaches the bed. Her mother doesn't respond, but gazes sorrowfully as though she doesn't notice her daughter.

Then she hears a cry. The baby turns its head and sobs. It raises its hand, fingers stretched, claws the air, and turns back again. It beats its hand on the blood-smeared breast.

'Mam, why don't you?'

She doesn't understand. The baby is healthy, even more perfect than the last. Her mother should be happy, her bony and fertile mother.

But it is the midwife who answers, in her quiet, respectful voice. 'She just left us, Elinor. Your mam. I'm sorry.'

Betsi tries to embrace her, tries to put her arms around her, but Ellie fiercely shrugs her off, and instead goes to the bed and climbs in beside her mother and the baby.

She wraps her arms around her mother's neck, still warm, and rests her head on her bony shoulder and closes her eyes.

★ ★ ★

Ellie wakes feverish, and realises that she has not been asleep, but that her waking thoughts are now more brightly coloured and unreal than her dreams. She needs to drink, and her cup is empty. She rises and sits on the edge of her bed. The action hurts, but she wonders if now it hurts a little less. Tentatively she touches the buboes under her left arm. The surface has hardened, and she thinks there is less liquid in there now, that they have drained a little. But she explores too boldly, presses too firmly, and lets out a howl. Her eyes weep. She does not want their neighbours to hear.

She rises and goes downstairs, carrying her empty cup. Tobias waits at the foot of the stairs watching her laborious progress. She ruffles his coat, where the black streak crosses his back. He releases a low, contented hum as she does this. It is an effort, and she gives up and goes to the kitchen. He follows her, as though she is his charge. She wonders what James has said to him. The spigot releases the small beer into her cup. She drinks it, then fills the cup again. Her senses aren't quite right. She feels as though she has aged, that everything is an effort, that she has to concentrate twice as hard just to perform the smallest tasks.

There is a bowl of clean water next to the sink in the kitchen. She has to reach to get a clean cloth, and she wonders if this is sensible, but it doesn't hurt too much. She soaks it in the water, pulls her smocks away, and holds the cloth over her sores. Suddenly there isn't much air and she sways, but then the air comes back, and it feels as though the soreness is eased. She then applies the cloth to the other armpit. It relieves. But the exertion is almost too much, and she drops the cloth on the table. She will wash it another time. She will change and wash her smocks another time too.

The relief doesn't last long. She needs to lie down again. She is tired. But she doesn't want any more dreams or memories. It doesn't feel like rest. She heads back up the stairs, holding her cup with strenuous care. Her legs ache, which is ridiculous she knows, because her legs are strong. She is tireless, a runner. But she looks back at the stairs behind her and sees with dismay the dust suspended in the light, sees the mess in the printing room. She hasn't cleaned the house in days. It worries her. The house has never before been this untidy, this dusty. It is a defeat, a sign that the disease is ruining her and everything around her. So pervasive, it won't leave even the buildings untouched. She is disappointed in herself. Perhaps she will put this right tomorrow. While James prints. She pictures him working there as she mops around him, shaking out the dust, cleaning the windows, letting the light in. This is who they are, she thinks. Not people dying with the plague, not that. Tomorrow will be different, once she has slept some more, and the fever has abated.

She approaches her bed, their big bed, but there is plentiful dust in the air, and a cobweb on the shutter's hinge, and she remembers how she would clean, because a printer's tools need to be clean and a house needs to be spotless too, and she remembers when she cleaned for weeks, though the house was already immaculate, cleaning every day with the skin on her knuckles chafed, and her knees sore, her hair matted, though up, as usual, in a bun, and the cleaning kept everything away from her, and kept her at a distance from herself and her thoughts, though she knew all the time that all the cleaning would not rub out the memories and the conceptions with which she attacked herself and that, one day, she would stop cleaning and it would all still be there.

She drinks, lies back on the bed, pulls up the coverlet, and he is there, bright, vivid and undying in her mind.

CHAPTER FIFTEEN

He stands before the house on Amen Corner and he thinks of physicians. His thoughts are not charitable. Many of the physicians abandoned the city the previous year, as the plague began to rage, and not all have returned. They followed prudence more than any oath to heal, and they accompanied their wealthier clients into the countryside. But that is not the reason. He despises physicians more for what they did not do than for what they have done.

He fishes for dates. They do not leap into his hand.

It was two and a half years ago. Ellie sat by the hearth, a fire warming her and lighting the side of her face. He cleaned the press. It was the end of a printing day. He wiped down the type, removing the traces of dried ink that would clog the letters the following day. He rubbed all smudges of ink from the frame, the platen, the lever, expunging his own fingerprints. He oiled and polished the joints, so they both turned freely and shone. He scraped and rubbed grease into the thread holding the platen. He did this most weeks, but that night he did it to stop worrying about other things.

He watched Ellie rub her stomach smooth. She was round, ripe, pendulous, sore. Her hips ached from the weight, and every few minutes she adjusted the cushions, because there was no comfortable position. She was ready, she muttered, she was ready. But she was also full of fear.

'How many copies?' she asked, for the second time, just to say something.

'About two hundred,' he replied. 'Slow.' Then: 'Are you …?'

She nodded.

'I'll get some.' He walked to the kitchen.

In the kitchen he had forgotten why he was there when she called his name.

Her face was disconcerted, surprised.

'There's a pain, here,' and she traced an arc under the curve of her belly.

Breathless, his heart thundering, he was full of excitement and terror. 'We should wait?'

'Yes, for now.'

He sat by the hearth and held her hand.

Half an hour later he was running for the midwife, Mistress Grey, with whom they made an agreement five months earlier. They had seen her in the street many times since she entered their house and they had that conversation, and each time she had reassured them that they must come to her, any hour of the day or night. He hoped she would be easy to wake. Soon he was running over cobbles with her, her skirt hitched high. She asked why he had not already set the water to boil.

★ ★ ★

She sees him there now, the colours more intense than the room around her. He makes tiny grunting noises as he seeks her nipple, but she guides him there and he quickly latches on and is quiet. His head is covered in a thick mucus, and Mistress Grey hands her a warm, damp cloth. Watching her wrap him in his blanket, far from her arms, was too long a wait, and she thought the sun might rise. But, no, she will watch his first sunrise with him, though she would like to sleep. The midwife has finally allowed James to climb in beside her. He too looks down on the soft crown and matted black hair of their son.

This time the streak of blood is on him, on his half-buttoned shirt, with its crumpled tails. She is used to seeing printer's ink there, black not red, and for a moment she imagines he has been printing in both black and red, a munificent, big book, their masterpiece. A book for aftertimes.

The baby drinks. It is a peculiar sensation, as she feels both his touch and the flow of milk. It is not at all like when James touches her, she thinks; it is more like when she makes water on a hot day.

She is thinking about a name.

★ ★ ★

He remembers them talking about names for the first time. It was Christmas, and the temperature unseasonably warm. The Thames would not freeze that year, rather he remembers them stealing time from the working day to walk by the river, though she was big with their child and her feet hurt. Nonetheless she wanted to walk. He loved feeling small beside her, with her height and her girth. When they lay in bed he was only a shadow. He thought of her as a goddess, creating new things. After years of fighting to be something, he was joyous to be nothing.

'It will be a girl,' she said. 'Mistress Grey says so, and she's seldom wrong.' She reeled off a list of times when the midwife was right.

'A girl will be perfect.'

'You don't want a boy?'

'I want ten boys and ten girls.'

She laughed, 'We're starting a bit late for that.'

'What shall we call her?'

And so began the talk of names, part exploratory, part playful, part teasing.

'Elisabeth,' she proposed.

'Of course, a good name,' he said, while wondering about her mother. But why not?

'Not Mary?'

He laughed, but there was a small wound there.

'Elinor!' he retorted.

'No,' she said. 'Something different, not the same.'

They talked through the Bible: Judith, Sarah, Rachel, Rebecca, Esther, Abigail, Deborah. All good names.

'What was the name of Pilate's wife?' he asked.

'Who told her husband not to condemn Jesus?'

They couldn't remember. They agreed that she was name-less, which seemed strange. It might have been a good name.

'Should we wait to see what she looks like?' he suggested.

'She will be beautiful.' She rubbed his chin.

'She will.'

'She will.'

'Like you.'

She groaned and gave him a push. He knew what it meant, that she wouldn't accept that she was beautiful, which was one of the reasons he had to remind her so often, though for him it was entirely obvious. He didn't understand why she wouldn't accept it, and part of him didn't want to understand.

'And if it's a boy?'

'I thought you said it would be a girl.'

'But if it isn't?'

'So Mistress Grey isn't always right?'

She shot him a look.

'For a boy ... not James,' he insisted. 'Nor John, Thomas. No disciples.'

'Prophets then?'

He laughed, 'Moses? Ezekiel? Daniel?'

'I like Daniel.'

'No, no prophets.'

'Well, what's left? I say James.'

He groaned.

★ ★ ★

She is thinking about what happened when the baby fell asleep, then woke.

They have been in and out of sleep too, with lots of dreams coming and going but none of them sticking. They slip away, leaving just a feeling, of time, colour or space, nothing tangible, no stories. But happiness, always this little surge of joy on waking.

He kisses her, but she cannot take her eyes off the baby. It is trite, she knows, a word worn out by overuse, a hackneyed phrase, but he's a miracle, a one made of two, as wonderful as anything in creation, and yet created by them. A paradox.

But also a boy, and so not Leah. Their deliberations have proved fruitless.

'What shall we call him?'

'He looks like you, so a James.'

'No,' and he kisses her on her forehead again, though she still cannot take her eyes off the sleeping baby, swollen lips pursed against her nipple.

And then the baby wakes and opens his eyes.

And she doesn't know how tired she is, and how soon the dawn will be, and whether her mind is still clouded by the pain, which was endless from the moment it started until the moment it ended, but she sees it immediately. His eyes see things, they are full of truth.

'He is a prophet,' she says.

He laughs aloud, so that Midwife Grey looks at him, a little scandalised at their intimacy.

'You see – his eyes?' she explains.

'I do. Not a James then?'

'You know what I mean.' They are azure and they cut right through her. She imagines how the world would look to an angel who stood on the doorstep of heaven and looked down. No clouds. This is how and what it would see, how its eyes would look.

'A prophet with eyes that saw us as well as the world away from us?' She pauses, already knowing what she is about to say, and knowing that when she says it he will see it too. 'Jeremiah,' she says.

It catches him unawares, and he is surprised by the very sound.

'Jeremiah.' He pauses. 'A hard life?'

She would shove him, but still she cannot look at him.

'Yes,' he consents. 'But not for what he says about women?'

'No. And you will stay with me and be faithful.'

'I will,' he says, 'till the kingdom come.'

They look at the baby and it seems settled.

★ ★ ★

Later, when Jeremiah had colic, he called on Mistress Grey again.

She pulled him into her house by his apron, even before he had a chance to explain. Then pushed him into a chair by his shoulders. She was used to doing things, and describing things too, with her hands.

'Do not even ask,' she ordered.

He drank from the cup she had handed him, without even asking.

'What?'

'It's the College. They won't let me practise. Though I've never had a mother die, nor a baby that wasn't sick already.'

He nodded at this, not wanting to think about it.

'The college?'

'Of Physicians.'

'Why not?'

'Because they are fearful that someone they've consigned to the grave will rise again, and it will all seem their bad faith.'

'I don't understand.'

'They talk of qualifications. Their degrees. Their reading. All the healthy babies mean nothing to them. I need a licence.'

'You need a licence from the College of Physicians?'

'No, I need a licence from the Church. And the College will report me to the church for not having one, they say.'

'And can't you get a licence?'

'That costs ten pounds. And how can I earn that? Even if I was allowed to work?'

'You could borrow? I could help. Others too, I'm sure.'

'And that sum would buy me an interview with a bishop or a priest, and the questions would not be about my work but about theirs.'

'They would question you about a priest's work?' She is too quick-witted, he thought.

'He wouldn't ask me about delivering babies, and aiding mothers. He would take the College's opinions on that, men who learned it all from books, some written by ancient Greeks who never saw a birth. He would ask me questions about religion. To discover whether I should be a midwife. To assess my views on salvation and perdition and the nature of the human soul. He would decide whether I should be permitted to continue to practise as a midwife. And, seeing you are kind enough not to ask, the answer would be no. Unless I found a way to evade or equivocate.'

He didn't know if she was of the old religion, or a Quaker, or, like his wife, a Baptist.

'So the College can report me to the church, and they can tell the church that I am not competent to practise. But they leave it to the church to deliver the blow, to refuse the licence. And they will ensure that I am arrested if I flout them. Which I would do if I answer your questions. The College is happy to use the dirty hands of the church.'

'But how could they know that you answered my questions?'

'I don't know. But I don't want to see the inside of Bridewell.'

'I'm sorry for this,' he said. 'Sorry to learn about the College. Is there nothing that can be done? I've never heard a word against you.'

She softened a little. Reputation is everything. Especially when you are about to grow suddenly poorer.

'Is there something wrong with Jeremiah?'

He explained, and she described the preparation of a tonic, to be rubbed on his gums before every feed. And for a while Jeremiah's colic disappeared.

But when Jeremiah was sick again he ran to mistress Grey's house, and she had gone. No one knew where she had moved.

* * *

Jeremiah coughs, especially at night, when she lays him down. Sometimes he wakes wheezing, struggling for breath. She feels that she is falling, trembling and vertiginous. She holds him till his breath returns, and she scarcely breathes when she does so. She sends James to Mistress Grey and she appears to have fled. Perhaps she is able to practise in the countryside, where the College of Physicians has fewer informants.

His eyes are still as bright, but now there is something else in them. If only he had some words she might be able to guess, but though he seems to understand much of what she says, in the high voice she has assumed only for him, he says nothing in return. She knows that his speaking is a long time ahead, but this does not stop her from wishing this were not so. She feels that there is something wrong, but how can she know? She asks her neighbours, the goodwives and gossips with children, but they tell her that it is nothing. She thinks this might not be true. Why? His distress, or that something in his eyes. He is happy, but for this.

His hair, which had fallen out after a few weeks, is now growing back, and he waves at her when she calls his name in her sing-song voice. He plays with the corn dolly his father made him, he makes it dance, and makes a noise that she thinks is the corn dolly talking.

Every night he sleeps in the cot his father made, next to their bed. Every night he holds Gelert tight. This is the toy she knitted for him, in his first few weeks. She thought that she wouldn't be able to remember how to knit, but with a little help from a neighbour, all the bodily memories of childhood knitting in Brecknock were restored, and she knitted neatly. At first when she turned at the end of a row there was a loose thread, but this didn't last long. She knitted him a dog, Gelert, from a Welsh legend, a dog that would look after him, that would lay down its life for him, a child-protecting, wolf-killing dog. She told the story to James and he laughed loudly, then kissed her and Jeremiah. The baby doesn't play with Gelert, but every night he hugs and cwtches it when he goes to sleep. And now, when he wakes in the night, breathless and gasping for air, clawing and struggling to stay in this world, his chest rasping as though the air is coarse iron, he is still holding Gelert securely to his ravaged chest.

★ ★ ★

He remembers, as she does not, how tired she was. Not only from looking after the baby every day, the constant stream of attentiveness, the feeding, the washing of the cloths, the buying of food and cooking when the money was scarcer than it had been, enough to weary her at any time, but also the nightly watching, the state of half-rest that she would permit herself when worried that the baby would wake, expecting and knowing he would. She was pale, and her speech was now fast, now slow, often disordered, words out of place, the wrong words in place. He took the baby in the afternoons so she could sleep, and at that time she slept properly. And then he would work late, printing by candle-light. She would tell him that he worked too hard, and he saw that, for her, all this wasn't work because this was what women did. And it was hard to argue with her, because they certainly needed the money, and, when Smith was away, presswork with one was slow and arduous.

He remembers, also, that he grew less tired then. With the baby he ignored the effort. He ached less. Though now he sees that he could have worked harder, he didn't have the plague.

And one morning he woke and he had difficulty waking. He had slept deeply. All his dreams went, and came back again, and then they went. He struggled to rise. It was light outside, he could see that through the shutters. The light bounced down, erratic on the floorboards. I have to wake, he thought, and breathed. Ellie was asleep beside him, snoring. When she slept, at the start or the end of the night, her breath would rattle, forming half words, half grunts, a kind of brute music. He would listen contentedly in the mornings when he woke before her, as he usually did. He listened now, hearing broken, inarticulate phrases of a language he didn't speak, a language before time. He was happy she was sleeping. He needed to rise, to attend to Jeremiah, to make breakfast.

He could place Jeremiah near her breast so perhaps she wouldn't wake while she fed him. And he would lie on the other side of the baby, and fold his arm over them both.

It was hard to wake, because he had been asleep for so long, longer than he had slept in months. The long stretch of night had allowed him to enter into a more profound sleep, under all the restless dreams, a proper restful sleep. He rose, despite the struggle, and sat on the edge of their bed. His arm slipped back to rest on her shoulder, without thinking, and not intending to wake her.

Jeremiah had slept through the night, the first time in weeks. Perhaps he has recovered from this sleep-breaking fit of breathlessness, of falling into broken waking.

He listens. There is nothing there. The barking of a dog in the street, that's all. And it is only now that he feels uneasy. Something is not right. He breathes, deep into his stomach. All thought of recovering dreams is now gone. Something else is stirring, nagging at the edges of everything he can hold onto in his head. He is slipping.

He stands and walks around to the other side of the big bed. In the cot Jeremiah is still, his bottom in the air, his head turned to the side, so James can see the profile under the wisps of now-blonde hair, heavy eyes, long black eyelashes, upturned nose. His skin is pale. James reaches his hand in and strokes his baby's forehead. He is cold.

★ ★ ★

Ellie remembers, in vivid colours. She is in the same room, barely changed, and the memory burns out what she sees now. The present is a shadow of the past. As she lies there, dying of the plague, the pressure inside her skull seeming to squeeze aside who she is, leaving her to look at her world asquint, she feels, she knows, that anything she feels and knows now, and especially anything she sees, will seem pale in the shadow of the concentrated and abundant fullness of those times, and especially of that moment. James is on his knees, hunched over the cot. He is sobbing.

CHAPTER SIXTEEN

He walks along Paternoster Row, barely able to see, though he doesn't know if this is the force of memory, or the plague dispossessing him of his eyes. A tree on the corner distracts him. He looks at the leaves, rattling in the breeze that has been rising all afternoon. He knows that, though the tree is not part of the city, if he wished to speak with it he could. There are angels there, burning with knowledge, dancing among the leaves, which turn crimson in the light. Not red, but cochineal he thinks, a word he learned from printing a book years ago, and a colour made from crushed insects. Cochineal, a dye for rich men's robes. So he is seeing, but what he sees lies beyond the natural forms of this world, and his fever reaches elsewhere. He wonders whether it is false or true. He fears to ask the angels there.

The same minister that christened their son buried him. This Bramhall he liked no more than Bishop, but it mattered not at all. He was scarcely there during the funeral, though he was bodily present, standing there, not ashamed to show his grief. He could feel Ellie there, beside him, and he could feel the small body in the coffin before them. The rest was noise, and he couldn't hear it. He remembers not a word that was spoken. He has pictures that come back to him, that flash into his mind when he is not looking and not guarded against them. The baby being put into the coffin. The coffin lowered into the ground. Ellie's white knuckles, crushing his hand red, as though it was full of insects. She has gone from being young to being tired, almost as old as him. Though there is no word for that age.

Time is jumbled without order. He cannot reassemble it. To do so would involve too much thinking, digging into its seams. Labour he doesn't want to do, because it brings up other stuff.

You can't control the layers of memory, and you don't know what feelings will return. There's so much buried there.

Ellie lay in bed for three days. Then the next day she was awake before him. He found her scrubbing the kitchen, on her knees, with a brush. Every surface was immaculate, the floor, the walls, the tables, the cupboards, the basin. And then the larder, which she put into a new order and cleaned until it was a new room. And then she moved on to the printing shop. The next day she cleaned the bedroom and washed the sheets. And then she started again. The house was scoured as though it had never been corrupted. All the while she didn't look him in the face, though sometimes she let him put his arms around her, and she pressed against him for a time. Then the connection would break again, for an indeterminate time. On the sixth day she told him that she was going to help him with the printing.

★ ★ ★

Before that, though, was the first day. She lay in his arms and cried and said it was her fault. She hadn't woken that night when he cried for air, because she was too tired. She hadn't sought help, hadn't looked for another midwife. She should have known what was wrong, she should have read the signs, she should have been able to interpret the look in his eyes, she should have been with him, holding him when he died.

She thought: he knew he was going to die, and he couldn't tell me, and I should have known.

James said what he thought were the right words, but, though he couldn't say them, he thought the same things too. Why couldn't he tell?

They cried in disbelief through the morning. Any thought of God was shut out: their grief was about this world, in the present, and no vision of the afterlife would save or soften it. He forgot about God so completely that he didn't even think to blame him.

They fell asleep, Ellie holding the baby in her arms, James

holding Ellie in his. They woke again an hour or two later with full knowledge and nothing had changed.

★ ★ ★

Still on the first day, Ellie stepped into the street, barefoot. The world was spinning, and she spun with it. She saw the neighbours' girl, Sarah, and asked her to call on all their neighbours, to invite them to come to their house and say goodbye to Jeremiah. They came that afternoon, as the sun was setting. He struggles now to remember exactly who was there. There were John and Jane Cock, the barber and his wife, and their little girl Agnes. And also Rachel, whose family name he doesn't know, who sometimes washed their linen for them when there was too much printing work to be done. Did Thomas Bramhall pass through? And Mary Glover, and Isaac Penn were there. And more children, who were just outlines in his memory. Daniel the brewer from the Hand and Shears brought some ale, as if it were a wake. Perhaps that's what it was, he thinks. He drank a cup and for a time it overwhelmed him, as though his reason were precariously balanced and easy to topple, though he sobered again as quickly. There were about twenty mourners, he thinks, surrounding the cot in the centre of the printing room, where Jeremiah lay swaddled.

Agnes looked into the cot, and said, 'Look at his tiny face. He's listening to the angels singing now.' Why, he wondered, are children so accepting of death? He'd rather have seen her rage.

Ellie sat by the fire, and if she raged it showed only in the brittle stone of her face. Until everyone left, and the stone crumbled. Her sobs heaved her whole body, as he wrapped himself around her, still sitting.

★ ★ ★

There is a smudge of time, of days. Jeremiah in a narrow coffin, with Gelert and the corn dolly. Or is it the cot? A procession of mourners, none with anything to say. Perhaps they did say

151

nothing at all. Or she has forgotten. It's bright but disconnected and all smeared at the same time. She tries to focus on any detail and it disappears. But there is a collective image of things present and not present and gaps between, and one person is much like another in this picture, and James cannot help her now. She is alone in this grief, and he will never understand it.

She should have found another midwife, when Grey disappeared. She should have known more. Was it the colic, was the colic a sign? She should not have slept so deeply. Did he wake and cry without her hearing him? Was he alone in those final moments, wondering where his mother was? Did he know what was happening? What can a baby know about death, what could he see? Was there an angel to comfort him, or was that responsibility left to her alone, and she failed?

Now she is back in this room, doubled to then and now, the present grey and the past blindingly bright. They have carried the cot upstairs and are sleeping, or not sleeping, one last night with their dead baby. She wonders if they should have him in the bed with them, but he is too cold.

The funeral will be tomorrow, she knows that. James has spoken with Bramhall. Perhaps she has lost some days somewhere. Perhaps this is not the first day.

* * *

The service was sombre. Bramhall acquitted himself well, he thinks. Some people respond better to tragedy than to ordinary things. It seemed as though the whole parish attended. Bramhall spoke about mortality and the community of saints, and while he said obvious things about Jesus suffering the children, irritating James, he also spoke of grief and loss, of Elijah's mantle and the healing of the waters. What of those who are left behind? he asked.

Jeremiah was lowered into the ground, with Gelert and the corn dolly. He cast soil onto the coffin. Ellie was beside him, but he could not, cannot see her.

Today, he thinks, now walking along Paternoster Row, he would be hard-pressed to find a coffin or a burial plot, because the dead are so many. He thinks of all the fathers who have lost children in the past year, whose sons and daughters have been cast into burial pits. No wonder so many parents have died. Death would have been a relief. And the poor, too, especially those who cannot find or afford a midwife.

It was a September day, much like this one, though cooler and with less wind, without the drought and parched earth. So, not much like this one, but two years ago, and the light was the same. Perhaps two years to the day. He can't think of dates now. All those bits and pieces that attach to memory, without being directly memory itself, elude him. Not that it matters where and how memories can be fixed. Memories are not butterflies to be pinned, but caterpillars, waiting for metamorphosis.

Ellie lay in bed for the next three days, and then she started cleaning.

★ ★ ★

Her hands were raw, she remembers, from the tar soap. He found her a pot of ewe's grease, which reminded her of the Black Mountains. Her mother had used it, for her hands and for sore nipples. She looks at the pot and this comes back to her. Then she closes her eyes and rubs it into her knuckles.

If there is any uncleanliness, she will expunge it. If there was something about the house that made his sickness worse, she will scrub it away. She will put everything in its right place, and she will not be taken by surprise again. She notices little signs of disorder everywhere, as though she has become omniscient, and is using a sense transcending eyesight. And every disturbance she perceives, she fixes.

The house is now perfect, and yet it is no better. There is no dust in the larder, nor on the bookshelves, there are no smears of grease on the press, no inkmarks on the table, no stains or creases on the bedclothes, everything is put on shelves, lined up, sorted according to size, all whitewashed, polished and burnished, darned, mended, repaired, made good. The dust, smears, inkmarks, stains and creases, disorder and disarray, tarnish, roughness, holes, brokenness are all inside her.

She doesn't know how many days she did this for. Even at the time she could not have been certain, and now it is just an intermission of grief and guilt and self-recrimination. The cleaning keeps her focussed on not thinking. It is when the recriminations stray elsewhere that this strategy fails. She experiences a flash of anger at God, and she is ashamed. She knows it is a weakness, she knows that it is inevitable. He is all good, but He is also all powerful and entirely to blame. She loses patience with those good men in the Bible who serenely suffer all kinds of wrong without blaming God. She can't be like them. And after a few thoughts such as these, the cleaning can't hold her attention, and so she decides that she needs to do something, to make something new, to push aside as much as she can the sense of being stuck, and so she tells James that she will print with him.

He seems surprised. What has been said between them over the past few days? She can't recall.

They print together, but the inking of the type is so much less strenuous than scrubbing floors and walls and sweeping dust that she finds herself with too much scope for thinking. And without the exhaustion she is so much more aware of what her body feels. There is something missing.

They print a thick volume, a book of medicine by an old physician. The letters are small, and the paragraphs are numbered, and so it's difficult to set, and she has to concentrate on the inking, because she doesn't want ink to sully the white margins. There is some poetry in it, a verse prophecy concerning the author, and that requires a lot of italic type. It is the longest book they have ever printed, by almost a thousand pages. John Smith sometimes helps James operate the press, and he hangs the sheets, and they print quickly. She's glad it's such a big job, because the endlessness and the weight do much to oppress her self-examination. Every time an unwelcome thought intrudes, she looks at the drying sheets spread across the room, and at the thick portion of the manuscript that remains to be set and printed. It is months of work, and James did well to come to an agreement with the man who wanted it printed.

But still the thoughts do intrude, and that pang of absence. It is not only that she is no longer constantly focussed on the baby, it is more than that, the suffering is bodily. It is six months since she carried him inside her, but she feels his absence inside, in her womb. There is a space, a void, a numb vacancy. She is made a desert. She feels where he should be, where he was, before she risked letting him enter this world. She should have protected him. Her nipples still hurt too, though her breasts are no longer engorged. But that is as nothing compared to the sense that he should be there inside her, and instead there is an emptiness.

She inks the type to make the emptiness go away, but it won't.

This is not the kind of emptiness you can fill, she thinks.

★ ★ ★

She was frozen, he sees. Trapped in that moment. She had given up hoping that there might be a way to persuade God to return the baby. There was no pact to be made, and no talk yet of having another baby, no exchange to be made.

While they had been printing she spoke to him as necessary for their work, and they had even, in the soft nadir of night, discussed their grief, its contours, though not the core that neither could turn into words. But now she stopped talking to him.

At first friends and neighbours had come to visit, and she took some solace in the fact that they thought of her, though she could not answer any of their questions. They would sit in front of the hearth in the kitchen and go through the motions of a conversation. Now, at around the same time, they had stopped coming so often and so the loss was more palpable. People remember your suffering at first, but then they forget, and it's not in the first few insensible days that you really need them. But the end of these conversations had other causes too.

He'd seen Alice visit, for one. Alice Goodall from Buckingham, who'd married William Taylor, who worked in a merchant's office and knew his numbers, a clever man, and so was his wife, clever with words. Alice had sat with Ellie and asked her how she was coping with things, whether she needed help with buying food, with money, with managing the household economy, with cooking, though she saw she did not have to ask about cleaning. Ellie was mute, and Alice prompted her again, then Ellie said, 'What household economy?'

Alice thought for a while, discernibly puzzled, then answered, 'I mean keeping the house, the accounts, the managing of such things, settling debts.'

'But we have no such things.'

James overheard this, and thought he should step in and say something. But he knew he must let Ellie make her own way at some stage, not overly protect her, and Alice was kind and considerate. Alice pondered.

'When you think about the money that is coming in, you know, money,' and she waved a halfpenny coin to illustrate this, 'and what you spend, in buying food,' and she pointed towards the larder. 'To avoid debts,' and here she paused to think about how to demonstrate a debt. Ellie shook her head.

'You keep the numbers?'

'Numbers?'

'One, two, three, four, to count things? Then to add and subtract.'

James worked in the next room, from time to time looking into the kitchen. Against his will he kept checking on Ellie, waiting to catch her as she fell. As though all of his own sadness had turned into concern for her. So long as he felt that, he could avoid contact with his own gnawing grief. He thought, it is hard to explain numbers. But that was not Ellie's problem. She knew about numbers.

Ellie said, 'There's no need.'

'But there is, there must be,' said Alice, shaking her head.

'No, it's all the same.'

156

Alice embraced her, not knowing what to say next.

But, James thought, she keeps a book of accounts in her head, and manages the numbers and the domestic economy. She is much better at that than I am.

'I wish I had some words in your Welsh,' Alice said.

That's not it, he thought, that's not it at all.

And again and again it happened. A visitor would speak to Ellie, and they would not understand each other. They would listen to her sing-song voice, now flattened in misery, and think that language was the problem. She could not understand English. They would speak louder and more slowly, then give up. But he knew it was something else.

The visits dwindled and ended, and those few who did visit her from time to time found little in their conversation, and so communication was whittled away to nothing. She was frozen in that moment, trapped.

★ ★ ★

She thinks, why did it stop there? Why didn't the sadness and all the things I thought I couldn't live through translate into change? Why wasn't there another child?

After half a year they had tried to make another, almost as ardently as they had before, but none came. She thinks it may be because they did not want it as much, that, despite the absence they felt, the absence she felt bodily, the memory of loss tinged any hope for the future with sadness. Perhaps they weren't steadfast enough. And now the outcome is that they do not have a child, and she is lying in their bed dying with the plague. At least the child was spared a dead mother.

CHAPTER SEVENTEEN

He walks along Paternoster Row, his eyes failing him, but through this failure he is roused to perceive the things his eyes won't permit him to, the hidden things within and beyond. He passes St Michael le Querne and enters Cheapside. He is sheltered by tall buildings, four or five floors high, but the warm wind whips along. The street has many shop fronts, mercers, goldsmiths, and alehouses too, and St Peters and Bow churches, and the ruins of Eleanor Cross if you know where to look, and Cheap Standard and the Great Conduit at the end.

Facing the goldsmiths' shops, and wares he could only dream of buying for Ellie, he would ordinarily have felt cowed, but today he is the city, and the city is him and the city is in him. He is the refining fire in the goldsmiths' workshops, he is the gold and silver, the mercers' warehouses, the cellars, barrels and taps, he is the flights of stairs leading to the top floors, the rooftops, he is the beating heart of the country, fed by trade, exchange and commerce. He is the walls that echo the hundred tongues, and the interchange and translation among them, that make commerce possible. Because this is so, and though his heart is cast down, he walks with his head up.

He will say goodbye to Cheapside, which is half of the very foundations and reason of the city, with this final perambulation. He will breathe in its dust, and leave himself here, his footprints, his thoughts and memories. He will not think about the traces of plague, not those particles, though he wonders if the plague is really spread by particles, he will not think about infecting others, about leaving that here. Even as his body burns up, and his brain spurts its flames to heaven, he will not consider whether his presence might spread the disease and kill the traders of Cheap Ward in their shops.

He reaches the corner where St Laurence Lane crosses Cheapside, a place where the Lord Mayor always stops in his ceremonial progress through the city, feted by all the guilds and citizens who like to wear their best. Here his Lordship is greeted by the haberdashers and drapers who occupy the street, here he makes a speech. Taffeta abounds, wool and some silk, and this depends on the weather. Today the light would make it shine, though it would fly like a bird in this wind. No one greets James. He looks down St Laurence Lane, standing where the Lord Mayor would stand, and sees at the end the spire of St Laurence Jewry, which sits in front of Guildhall, all his buildings, all him. And something inside pulls him and he has only taken a few steps into the lane before it comes upon him, a rush of cold overturning him like a wave, diminishing him, so that he is no longer embracing the whole city but is instead in a tailor's shop, next to Cow Face, where the leather goods are sold, and the tailor is agreeing to make him a shirt. It was the autumn of 1641, he had recently established his own shop, as modest as could be but still his own, just north of Little Britain; he was already obtaining ample commissions for pamphlets of news, and here he was buying a shirt for his wedding.

The tailor measured him. He was hesitant because, though he knew that this was a unique occasion, which is why he was having a shirt made, he had never had a shirt made by a proper tailor before, and he was troubled by the extravagance. After all, it was only a shirt. He didn't need fancy work, for which he would pay piece by piece, he simply needed a well-made, well-fitting shirt.

His sisters had sewn shirts for him, and he had preserved them carefully through his apprenticeship until they had worn out. Then he had bought two shirts from a washerwoman, who claimed that they had been left with her, unpaid for, and was given one, also well-worn, by Mary Simmons, his master's wife. And those were all the shirts he had ever had or needed.

Edna had pressed him to have a new shirt made, with ribbons and buttons. She was also to have a dress made, with silk ribbons and bright buttons, and when they stood at the altar at St Botolph's church they would look fine together. This is what she told him. He wondered whether she had ideas about him and about their future life that would lead to disappointment, but he saw no way to say this to her.

The tailor measured him, and talked. He talked about the parliament, no parliament for twelve years and then two in a single year, and its assault on the king, its imprisonment of his ministers, because these men were, the parliamentarians said, evil counsellors. And the rumours of more to come, of unrest around the country and not only in Scotland, where they had already mustered armies against the king. He talked and talked, and James lost track, because he didn't have the time to keep up with all this news, even though he saw the pamphlets that the Scots had printed in the Netherlands, then brought to London by packet boat and horse's pack. This tailor must talk and read and read and talk all day. I think, he said, there may be war.

His mother would have approved of Edna, he thought as the tailor measured him, and he wondered how that might have influenced him. These things come back in strange ways, he thought, you never entirely flee them. Edna's grandparents, all of them, were good northern Catholics, and her parents, as he under-stood it, were the cooler sort of Protestants. And her sisters and brother had ambitions such as his mother bred into Margaret. Edna was different, had grown up caring and unambitious, untouched by their worldly concerns. She spoke sceptically of their pride, their sense of superiority, was quick to point out their hypocrisy. He liked that about her. She was fresh and uncorrupted.

As of that morning, however, he had been shaken and begun to wonder. Edna had been very particular about the shirt, and how he should find a proper tailor, who cost this much. It wasn't the cost, really, nor the fact that she wanted him to look like a proper man in the church, but the way she had said it, as though he didn't quite understand what was right, but would know as soon as she said it. Which he had, and he fully saw why he needed to go to St Laurence Lane. But when walking to the city wall he saw that he didn't really understand, that she might have said this two weeks ago, and that she spoke to him as her family spoke to the maid. And she had criticised this way of speaking to the maid, and also criticised the maid for not protesting at it. She was sure, she had said, that she herself would answer with well-chosen words if she were spoken to in that way. And now he wondered why he hadn't.

The tailor measured him, and then took him to look at fabrics, a fine wool, a Calicut cloth, silks which he could not afford, linens. He admired the lace. He knew that this was what Edna would want for a collar, but it was far too extravagant. It didn't matter, because the shirt would be so well made. This tailor's sewing was precise and neat, even neater than Margaret's.

The tailor tried to persuade him that he needed a vest and jacket too. He rebuffed him, though cautiously. He didn't want to mention the cost, though both understood that this was the sticking point, and both knew that the other knew this.

'You are getting married?' the tailor asked again.

'I am.'

'Is she beautiful? Is she rich? Or is she both?' He winked.

James ignored him. 'When will it be done?'

'Thursday, in good time.'

James hadn't given him the date, but he was right.

He chose a fine linen, knowing it cost almost a week's work. Edna would approve.

In his memory he walks back to the printing shop, the old printing shop, but now, in this time of burning, he turns back to Cheapside and heads east towards Mercers' Hall. In front of the hall, at the point at which Cheapside forks into Poultry and Bucklersbury, stands the Great Conduit.

Fresh water reminds him again of those who threw themselves into the river to ease their sores, or perhaps to hasten their death. Then, as he is caught in this vein, he remembers Edna insisting that he speak to the aldermen about their neighbours and the well. She did not see, she said, why their neighbours should waste so much water from the communal well, because in their parish of Aldersgate they rely on a well that is supplied by pump from a spring north of the river, and, on the outskirts of the most densely-populated parts of the city, there is less water than there is further south. She mooted paying for a direct connection to the city's pipes, and it is true that a printer would benefit from a fresh water supply, but he is not that successful a printer. He regretted making this point as soon as he said it.

'Why can't you be a Robert Barker, then? Or a William Stansby, or a Henry Fetherstone?'

'The first two are dead, and Fetherstone is Master of the Company. I cannot become an officer of the company.'

'Why not?'

'Because I am not made of such stuff.'

She was silent, but in the look she gave him before she turned on her heels he heard all the things she could have said. You should be. Other men are. Why did you not tell me before? That you would never be a success?

He thought, yes, but, we were talking about water supply. And the neighbours' profligacy. How did it get to be about my printing?

And the following morning, just as dawn was breaking, he woke to her shaking his shoulders, and she said, 'Go quickly, then. If we have to share the water, then you must collect it first thing to make sure we have enough.' And he went, and as he filled the buckets he thought, it is not worth disagreeing with her, for there will always be a long time of repaying thereafter.

He is not tempted to throw himself into the waters of the conduit, but embraces the burning.

He walks along Poultry to St Mary Woolchurch, and there the road opens even wider and forks into Threadneedle Street and Cornhill, and so he finds himself facing the Royal Exchange, Sir Thomas Gresham's building, home of commerce, merchants and newsmongers. Here people find backers for projects, and speculate with money, buying and selling goods and crops that don't yet exist. Ingenious men devise ways of moving silver and gold by pieces of paper that pass back and forth between many cities and represent the value of a particular weight in gold in that place. All of which relies on a good deal of trust between men and women who may never even have met. And it relies on men and women who can move words from one tongue into another, translators who must also be trusted. And all of these men and women depend on the news, not only that heard in church, alehouse, marketplace and street corner, but the news that spreads around Europe in writing and in print, news that connects the scattered places and enables merchants to judge and predict where commodities are needed and how they can be safely and profitably moved. And, much more, news is the oil that keeps the printing press moving smoothly.

And as he looks at the Exchange he thinks of Edna, and her wanting to walk the upper gallery and buy the commodities that arrived there from all over the world. It is strange, because he never thinks of her, but on this walk she returns with a bitter taste. The Exchange is a magnificent building, he thinks, stately with its tall, vaulted lower galleries, where the great international merchants undertake their mysteries, and the delicate windows of the upper galleries, where more ordinary commodities are bought and sold, and where fashionable women see and are seen. Last year fires were lit at the north and south entrances, to ward off and purify the air from the plague. Similar fires were lit at the Custom House, at Billingsgate, Blackfriars, Bridewell, Guildhall, St Paul's and other places, but the Exchange had two. The clouds of smoke made it hard to breathe in the nearest arches. But the place was almost abandoned in any case, with all the foreign merchants renouncing England, and the London merchants having fled overseas, or taken to the country. Some trade contin- ued, but grass grew between the flags and cobbles.

This is not the case now. Commerce has returned. The merchants think the plague is past, that the falling numbers of deaths from plague published in the weekly Bills of Mortality indicate that they can return to their reckonings of profit, and that the future will be theirs. These men, who calculate the odds, and understand risk better than anyone, are taking their chances.

Unless it is simply greed, he thinks. That might explain it. And here he is, a fiery angel of death, bringing the plague in him, unable to flee it, unable to flee himself, and brought here by the flames in his head, but he was here already before he walked here, because even the Exchange is part of him, and he is the Exchange.

Where did the fiery angel of death come from, he wonders. Is he delirious? He feels his head and it is still burning.

If he had read the Bills of Mortality for the week of her death, he would have seen her numbered, nameless, within the category, 'Consumption and Tissick'. He didn't read it back then, though, so he never learned how many others died of consumption and tissick in the one hundred and thirty parishes that week. It was unlikely she was alone, perhaps not even in their parish.

It began with a mirror. The king was dead, convicted of treason and executed. He had printed many pamphlets that year, but they were beginning to dwindle in number, and, for the first time in some years, he was worried. For years the printing business had been good; what if the new government put an end to that? Nonetheless, he bought her the mirror she wanted from a Frenchman near Spitalfields. It wasn't the finest quality, not good enough for a queen, but she could see herself clearly in it. It had a plain wooden frame, highly polished. He might have bought a finer one at the Exchange. And the commonwealth continued its struggles, Cromwell defeated the Scottish army at Dunbar, and then the Scots crowned the king's son at Scone, naming him Charles II.

'It makes the room lighter too,' she said to him, as she looked at him over her own reflected shoulder. 'And I've never seen myself so plainly.'

Now in possession of a mirror, every day, after she dressed, before going downstairs, she stopped and examined herself, first standing at a distance, then near. She brushed her hair, straightened her folds, inspected the pranking of her pleats.

One morning she came downstairs to find him checking his stores of printing stuff, ink and paper, and said, 'James, I am wasting away.'

He was attentive to her speech, knowing that when she initiated a conversation with him there was usually something she wanted from him, though it often took her a while to get to the matter. She liked him to guess first. But something in her tone that morning told him that this was not the case, that there was a want of confidence here. She meant just as she said, and he looked at her and saw that she was pale.

'I'll buy some meat,' he said, and went to Smithfield.

He could see that something was troubling her, but it was only when she began to cough that he worried that the problem was more than the thinness of their diet. She stood before the mirror and said, 'Look James, I can see my bones.'

He looked, and wanted to reassure her, but his impulse was arrested by how drawn she seemed, how stretched out, bleached. She looked older. He hadn't noticed until then, as physically she had become invisible to him, sensitive only to her words. He put a hand feelingly on her shoulder. The look in her eyes shifted. Suddenly she was glaring at him. It was his fault.

'I have more work coming,' he said, 'Nathaniel Burt has promised another book or pamphlet, and there is a woman called Mary Cary I am talking to who has a long book.'

'Talking to her, are you?' she asked.

'Edna, she is a writer. A religious writer.'

'So you say. And here I am, wasting away, and you're with some whore, seeking your next wife.'

He wanted to tell her that she knew that this was unkind, but that would only have angered her. 'You're not going to die. I was only saying that I'm going to be earning enough to put good food on the table. I can stop speaking to her. There'll be other work.'

She coughed, and it racked her narrow-shouldered frame.

That night she coughed so much that it kept them both awake.

The following morning he is downstairs composing type when he hears a coughing fit, and it frightens him. He pictures her whole body convulsed by the expulsion of air, the trembling

166

of her hands, the pain expressed in her face, the utter lack of control. Then there is silence. He runs upstairs, and she is standing before the mirror, which is spattered in blood. The droplets form a scarlet rainbow arching over her reflection.

He buried her a week later, in St Botolph's churchyard. The physician said she would last longer than this, but she did not seem to want to last. Her family attended the funeral, and her mother told James that he had not cared for her daughter properly. She should not have lived to see her own daughter in her grave. The father led her away by the arm without looking at James. He drank too much that night, a Friday night, in a pit of grief, and the next day he was sick and full of misery and self-pity. But on Sunday he washed himself and went to church and prayed, then walked east, around the wall, past Cripplegate, the Lord Mayor's dog house in Moorfields, past Bethlem hospital and Artillery Yard, and thence into the woods beyond Spitalfields. As he walked a burden lifted from him. He didn't know if the fresh air or God was to be thanked, but he felt lighter and more content than he could have imagined possible. He walked home.

On Monday he scrubbed the floors and rearranged the furniture in the workshop and the bedroom. He looked in the mirror too. He didn't like what he saw. He had lost something he couldn't put a name to. This wasn't the person he wanted to be. He pulled a cloth from his pocket, and wiped the rainbow of blood, now brown, burnt umber. It didn't move, and he felt foolish. It had dried hard, stubbornly hard. He spat on the cloth, and wiped again and again. With effort it smeared, he spat again, and it dissolved, disappeared. Now it was a mirror again, telling untruths.

Her clothes were scattered around the bedroom, hung over furniture, some kept in the closet, some on a shelf in the larder. Everywhere, he hadn't noticed. There were more than he'd ever been aware of. He went from room to room, and folded them neatly. Some he recognised, some he didn't, and some even had memories that he traced back. Was it all bad? No. But was any of it true, was he in any real sense present through any of the good memories? Of this he wasn't certain. But he folded them neatly, respectfully, and all the while looked for sentiments he might have overlooked.

When he'd finished he wasn't sure what to do with the tidy piles of clothes. But on Tuesday he took them to Spitalfields. The mirror too, he laid upon the clothes, and transported with care.

He took the mirror back to the Frenchman, who remembered him.

'Your wife, she changed her mind?'

He prevaricated. Would he want the mirror, if he thought that it was fated? Then he resigned himself to being direct. 'She died.'

The Frenchman nodded. 'I'm sorry.'

'Do you still want it?' he asked.

'The mirror wasn't at fault.' The Frenchman nodded in assent.

'These dresses?' James asked, holding the folded clothes before him.

'Try Williams,' he suggested, pointing across the way. 'He's honest.'

Then he heard Edna's voice again, telling him to make sure he wasn't cheated. James thanked the Frenchman.

'I'm sorry about your wife,' he said as he left. James turned and nodded. He didn't know what to do or say, but he didn't want to seem heartless. He was glad he no longer had the mirror.

The clothes he sold to an English mercer a few doors down. He learned that there was a considerable market in used clothes. He knew that this was so for books, but he was a little surprised at first at what the clothes were worth, though after a little reflection it seemed obvious that fine, used clothes would be bought and used again.

He started the commission from Burt, as Cary had found another printer. He continued to hear her voice for some years, usually when he was uncertain whether he'd done something right. It never reassured him. It was distinctly her voice, and it sounded as though she was there, in his head, in a dialogue, and it would question him or challenge him, and he wouldn't know what to do now, and the more he deliberated the more it spoke. He wished it were a different voice.

From time to time he felt a pang of shame because he did not feel more grief. Though he wondered why he did not feel more of anything, why so much was blocked, stopped up, locked away, forgotten. He went digging for the grief, in conduits he'd covered over. And after a while he found it. There was something there, a grief, though it was grief for something else that died before she did. It took him a while to identify it with any confidence. It was sadness about the hopes he'd once held, hopes that had been long buried. He wondered if she had felt this too, regret for something that was possible, or should have been, or that she had once thought possible. But it wasn't enough to make him cry. There were no tears. For some years he examined himself, wondering why this was, asking if there was something missing inside him, something unloving and unkind, but after those few years he simply forgot her, and she was no more.

CHAPTER EIGHTEEN

He has seen enough of commerce, and he understands that he must visit another aspect of the city. St Paul's is now behind him, so he walks ahead, to St Andrew's Undershaft, then steering between St Katherine Cree and Duke's Place, which was once a priory and then a secular home for a knight, with a new church, St James, untainted by popery. And he feels the others near him that he doesn't see: St Gabriel Fenchurch and its church-yard, All Hallows Staining, St Katherine Coleman, St Helen's, and, beyond Aldgate, another St Botolph's, though not the one he attended in an earlier life. Everywhere God leaves his footprints; He has stepped all over James's body, again and again.

There are churches everywhere, at least one in every parish, each making a family of believers and a community of neigh-bours. The second commandment according to Mark's gospel reminds us to love our neighbours. Except neighbours fight, and parish priests disagree, and other churches spring up, sometimes in secret, and the old church oppresses them, and everywhere there is discontent and dissent and persecution. The churches form a web over the city, covering it and protecting it but perhaps also weighing down and afflicting it.

Take St Katherine Cree, which is called by other names too, including St Catherine Christ Church. Many names, but it is as old as anything. He feels this in the soil, that there was something here even before the Romans. It is a modest church from the outside, a small stone tower at one end with a bell at the top, and a short nave with no transept. The row of windows in the nave, viewed from the south, is very pretty, but also strange, because the tower is at the west end, and both the door and the windows face south, as though they don't really match. They were built at

171

different times, he guesses, and he feels this within him, the tower being a century earlier than the rest, and the rest squeezed into the space that was available.

Inside it is different. The coloured glass window is probably the most beautiful in London, a sun with a burst of rays, or a corn marigold with petals of blues, greens, oranges and reds, filling the most ornate and finely sculpted stone frame. The vaulted ceilings are high, the nave wide, the aisles narrow, with a bold row of columns. The ceiling bosses show the arms of the livery companies, representing the most prevailing merchants and craftsmen of the city. There is a good organ, and some fine musicians have played here. And Holbein the painter is buried here. Many of the arts meet here: the craft of the builders, the stonecutters and carpenters, the architect, the glassmakers, and then the organ-builder, the organ players, and at least one painter. And speakers too, because the late Lord Mayor, John Gayer, who held office during the civil wars, left in his will a fee to support a sermon to be preached once a year. This sermon is known as the Lion sermon, because Gayer wished to be remembered for his deliverance from the paws of a lion while travelling in Arabia. He was a merchant before he became a politician, but James is sceptical about this story of a lion, because the tale, as reported by Gayer, was too favourable to its teller, and besides, he doesn't see why God would have lifted a finger to save him. But there is a sermon, preached every October, and in it men, always men, reflect on the myriad of things that threaten their faith.

So even this one church has signs, marks, scars, of all the history of the city and the arts locked within its improbable exterior and in the lives of those who worship, speak, perform and make things there. It is a microcosm, just as London is a microcosm of the world, and just as he is the spirit of the city, containing all of it within him.

The bells strike as he passes. The church is so old now, so deep in the city's roots, that it is sinking into the ground. To arrive at the front door you have to descend seven steps. This is not because the earth is swallowing it, however, or because the foundations are weak. Rather the city is being built up around it, as Leadenhall and surrounding streets receive new pavements and so creep up. In a thousand years, if the earth survives so long, it might be entirely underground. A passer by would then look down upon the roof.

He is the city, and so every stone and brick matters to him, they concern him because they are part of his own fabric. But do they matter to God, who enjoined people to love their neighbours, and not war with them over which religion is the more true? And this is the saga of the churches that he inhales into his very pores now, St Katherine Cree, St Gabriel Fenchurch and beyond. The buildings come to seem more than the people who worship in them, as if devotion consisted in the stonework rather than the human heart.

And there, with the flames pouring upward from his skull, he feels for Ellie, reaches for her with his conscious mind, because he needs her with him now, needs her to see and feel this, to counsel him. More than anyone he knows she could winnow what was the church's and what was the believer's. He cannot find her, and his anxiety grows with this absence, but as he touches with his mind all the baptismal fonts in all the churches of the one hundred and thirty parishes, he remembers his baptism, then hers, and she is with him again, and he is back in the grounds of St Bartholomew the Less with Ellie and they are discussing Thomas Bishop, which reminds him of their first meeting, until everything flies away from him, like a series of candles. She has heard a man called Kiffin who, unlike Bishop, preaches against infant baptism. How can a Protestant, he asks, believe that a sacrament doesn't demand that the worshipper understands what the sacrament means and does? Without that understanding it's empty, a mockery. But more than that, what does it mean, as Paul tells us, to be washed in the blood of Christ when we are baptised?

He walks with her through the churchyard.

Today, as he walks between the churches, he knows that if they were to walk through the churchyard now he would be speaking with all the bodies layered up beneath them. Which in a sense he is, and he is among the dead, and perhaps that's why he can't find Ellie with his mind.

* * *

Ellie sits before the fire, a blanket wrapped around her. Setting the fire made her dizzy and she fell and struck her head, but she needed the direct heat of the flames. And perhaps the smoke would purify the air of the particles of plague. She sits there, her forehead bleeding, stroking Tobias who stands at her side. He is sleepy, because of the heat, but he stands and leans against her leg.

She is remembering the search for new preachers, the appetite for hearing new words, almost a haunting. A spirit chased her, the desire for the truth, and she was convinced that she didn't know it. The parish preachers would always tell her what to think, and her response was to walk from church to church. A neighbour, learning this, told her he disapproved, and she replied by asking if he thought his parish had a monopoly on the truth. When he had gone, and she looked at James, she laughed at her neighbour's look of surprise, and at her use of this word, monopoly. She had only learned it a few days earlier, reading it in a book, reading together with James. She had stored it up for future use, because a word like that is potent. It was in a book about an imaginary place where the rich were not able to buy up everything in the market and keep it all for their use. The book had made her laugh, despite the hard words.

She went from church to church, hearing two or three sermons in a week, and debating them in her head. But she also went to other places, the secret chapels and the private houses where worshippers would gather outside the embrace of the Church of England. She covered her head and looked at her feet when she went, but she would not give up seeking for the truth just because it was against the law. She was never caught, but sometimes she heard that a gathering she had attended two or three weeks earlier

174

had been broken up and the preacher arrested. She was lucky, or perhaps it was more than luck.

The dissenters' preaching had more life in it. There was less written down; they spoke more from the heart and mind. They were usually easier to follow. The path to Kiffin was through a man named Spilsbury, who she heard by accident, if it was accident, speaking in a house in Cripplegate, outside the wall, near the conduit. It was a private house, belonging to a baker, and Spilsbury had spoken about Paul's first epistle to the Thessalonians. Abstain from evil in all its appearances. Even when, he warned, the powers that be are evil. He made her think about her own doubts about preachers who didn't persuade her. But it was a passing remark about baptism that caught her attention. He said that just as the whole body needed grace, not just the flesh, or a particular organ, but the whole body, so to obtain grace the whole body must be immersed. If you wanted to know more, he added, there was no better place than the sermon to be heard next Thursday in the village of Stoke Newington.

A long way from here, she thought.

She found a ride on a cart, and Thursday found her in a big house in Stoke Newington listening to Kiffin. He speaks about a verse from Paul's epistle to the Romans, where the apostle says that 'we are buried with him by baptism into death: that like as Christ was raised up from the dead by the glory of the Father, even so we also should walk in newness of life.' And he is so fierce and confident in his opinions that at first she is repelled, but then she concedes that he has something. It is when he digresses in the middle that she is hooked. He tells her, and though she is in a crowded room she is sure he speaks directly to her, that hostile and ungodly men, the writers that are salaried by the state to suppress all who question, tell the gathered churches that they are Anabaptists. These writers, he says, do not listen to the doctrine, but only hear the challenge to the church as it established in England. And, he reminds them, each truth first emerged under the name heresy. All names are given by enemies. And that was true back in the days of Queen Elizabeth when they burned Anabaptists in the streets of London, and when the Anabaptists captured Munster in Germany a century and a half ago, in 1534. But, Kiffin says, we are not Anabaptists, whatever they say. And we do not bring anarchy, but only the truth, and it is the truth that will set us free.

The history hooks her, and she is susceptible to his message. He is saying more than that someone has to believe in order to be baptised, and that the sacrament is violated when given to a child; it is also debased when given to someone who is not saved. Christ's blood is what brings us grace, and we die with Him when we are washed, head to toe, in his blood. We are united with Him in His death. And this is only for the saved. Not for infants, who have not had a chance to examine themselves, and not for the unredeemed. Some are saved, and some are damned, though all are depraved.

Perhaps it is his voice too, which crosses the room without impediment, and bears the marks of a Welsh accent. She hears something before this present moment, before 1662, something from her childhood and before.

She thinks the same after the sermon, when she listens to him speaking to another of their congregation, where she learns that he is a successful merchant, a member of the Leatherseller's company. She learns that he has been imprisoned repeatedly, that the new government arrests him but then releases him after a short spell, almost as though they are trying to subdue him and make him fearful, without the public show of a court case. 'Abstain from evil in all its appearances,' he says. He quietly enjoys the persecution, she thinks, but he is right all the same. The power and the mystery didn't lie in Christ's sacrifice so much as the union we have with Christ in death and rebirth. And what he has said about being baptised into death and resurrected with Christ has affected her. She does not speak to him.

She walks the long miles south west from Stoke Newington to their printing shop in Farringdon Without the Wall, and all the while the scripture he has quoted and glossed and conferred resonates within her, and she sees that she is going somewhere with it.

When he passes through Aldgate he turns right onto Minories Street, and heads in the direction of the Cross by St Mary Graces. He passes the remains of another ruined Abbey, now almost invisible but for some of the walls that have been incorporated into other, less grand buildings, warehouses and houses of residence. He feels the ruins underneath him, and the residue of former plagues. Once at the cross he faces a small common, smaller every decade as the surrounding houses encroach upon it, driving out the possibility of any man or woman surviving by farming the common land. In recompense there are also Alms Houses built upon it, to provide for them in their poverty. On the far side of the common, surrounded by a moat, rises the most potent symbol of power in London, the Tower, though it's one he cares little for. It's a palace, an armoury, a mint, and a prison. He shrugs at it, and turns right, and walks towards the wall, the ditch, and Postern Gate.

He remembers that day that she came home from Stoke Newington, her boots all muddy, speaking at such speed and with such passion that he thought she might burst.

She takes the Bible from the shelf, and takes his arm.

'The printing can wait.' They leave John Smith to clean the press, and sit at the kitchen table. As soon as they were together she started to learn to read. When they remembered this, she thought it was his idea, and he thought it was hers. By now she is already competent, though slow, and she can write her name and numbers too. She finds Romans and they read it together, and she tells him what Kiffin said.

He looks at her face, at her wide and grave chestnut eyes, at the convex of her lips, at the pock marks from the smallpox she contracted when she was a child, and he feels how much he needs her, how incomplete he is without her, how he cannot understand what he did before he met her, and then he remembers that he has to concentrate on the doctrine of what she's saying and not his desire. She is explaining that God has prescribed very nicely the particular ways in which He must be worshipped, and that to swerve from them endangers all modes of worship. We must restore, as carefully we can, the institutions of the church as they were practised by primitive Christians, not by the inventions of later generations.

He follows what she says. 'But what about modern writers, don't they have anything to say about this? Should we reject them just because they're modern?'

She thinks for a moment. 'No. They're to be listened to as long as their reasoning is strong. Otherwise, no, their authority is of no consequence.'

Over the next few days they talk about this. John Smith is gloomily silent when the three of them work in the printing room, and Ellie and James discuss salvation and baptism. They attend together another sermon by Spilsbury, also in Cripplegate, and then two more sermons by Christopher Blackwood. Spilsbury preaches about predestination, and James is diffident. He is unpersuaded by the Calvinist tenets, cannot swallow the doctrine that Election is only for those whom God chooses, and that their own merits, the goodness of their life, isn't free. He thinks that their perseverance in goodness, their meekness in shouldering the burdens that this world puts on them, must count for something. And the notion that Christ's atonement was limited, that it was for the 'many' and not all, he finds hard to stomach. He and Ellie don't agree on this, but their disagreement is hard to put into words. Blackwood is impressive. He is an old man, but still ardent and defiant. He has lived in Ireland, was loyal to Cromwell, and his life was threatened when the king came back in 1660. He is a man who sticks to principles. This is also in evidence in his book, which someone in the gathering carries with him, a thick volume of commentary on the first ten chapters of Matthew's gospel. It's almost the length of a Bible.

The first time Blackwood preaches, James and Ellie agree that he is a shrewd expositor of scripture. They go to hear him on Water Lane, in a fine, tall house a few doors down from Baker's Hall. He speaks about the second chapter of the epistle to the

Colossians, where Paul tells the believers in Christ that they will be 'Buried with him in baptism, wherein also ye are risen with him through the faith of the operation of God, who hath raised him from the dead.' And for Ellie this fits so closely with what she has heard from Kiffin that she thinks she has been directed to this moment of illumination. She must die and be raised again, through total immersion in the blood of Christ. She speaks to Blackwood after, and they arrange for him to baptise her after the sermon the following week.

At the second sermon, there's a buzz in the room. The congregants expect the meeting to be broken up at any moment. They look for signs of government spies. James thinks: they're excited by this. They think the danger brings them closer to the truth. He doubts that this is correct. But he is admiring Blackwood's way of speaking, which for all of his professions that he will speak plainly and directly and without ornament is very clever, when he is ensnared. Blackwood is speaking of the third chapter of Matthew, and about Christ's baptism, an act which seems to James to make little sense. How could sinless Jesus wash his own sins away with his own blood? But, Blackwood says, Christ has taken on human sins, and so he offers himself to John the Baptist, and washes his own sins away in himself, and in doing this, he says, 'he did, as it were, bury the old Adam underwater in his burying, and, rising up from the water, he did as it were lift up the world of believers that were drowned.'

And this, James thinks, is true. And he is seized, and he is the new Adam, and he must be buried and rise. He feels to his side, finds her hand, and holds it tight. And so, when the sermon ends, he says, 'I see it. I must be baptised too.' And they speak to Blackwood. And then, together, the three of them walk down Water Lane, then down Watergate to the Custom House, and they are at the Thames. Blackwood says little, though he warns them that he is not permitted to baptise them according to the laws of the king and the Church of England and, though they have a higher law behind them, it would all the same be better not to be arrested. They walk along looking for a quiet place where they can get down to the water. They walk away from the Tower towards Billingsgate. Because the stretch of waterfront between Billingsgate and London Bridge is so populous, they have to find somewhere nearer than that. They settle on a spot between Andro Morris quay and Smart's quay, where merchant shops dock, and find some steps leading down to shingle and shells where they are not so likely to be observed.

Blackwood has brought gowns, and they change into them discreetly. He catechises them about their faith, then claims his commission from Christ. Then he takes Ellie's shoulders in his arms, walks into the Thames up to his waist, and pushes her under the water. He speaks a few words under his breath. She rises, coughing and shaking her head. The water smells. She stumbles back from the water, while he guides her. Blackwood does the same with James. He holds his breath. He thinks of the rats in the water, the filth, and it's hard to see this transformed into the redeeming blood of Christ. He can't hear Blackwood, only the beating of his own heart. When he thinks he can last no longer, Blackwood lifts him and he is resurrected. He and Ellie change back into their dry clothes. Blackwood is soaking from the waist down, but does not seem to mind. James sees the old man smile for the first time.

'Welcome,' he says.

Now James remembers all this as he passes through Postern Gate, walks along Tower Street, passes All Hallows Barking, and turns, once again, into Water Lane to follow it down to the river. On the banks of the Thames he smells it again, the sweet smell of rot, the promise of another life. He thinks that he might throw himself in, but then he remembers he is the city, and he cannot sink. Instead he must find Ellie and complete her salvation through his own sacrifice. Just as she led him to be baptised, guiding him through the right scriptural texts, patiently showing him the way to the quay, now it is his turn. It might have been twenty good years, or twelve, but it is to be six.

In a printing shop in Farringdon, just a little beyond the wall, Tobias watches Ellie sleep. She is cold, bitten raw with the bitter cold she feels inside, as he lies in front of the dwindling but still hot flames. She turns her head as she sleeps, moaning in a language he does not understand.

CHAPTER NINETEEN

So he walks home, past Smart's quay, Billingsgate, Somar's quay, Lion's quay, Botolph's wharf and Fish wharf until he arrives at the Bridge. It is populous again, when a year ago it had been deserted. Traffic and commerce flow into and around the shops. Drawbridge Tower catches the evening sun, and he squints at the spikes for signs of grisly remains. But that's not where they put them now, he recalls; instead, decapitated heads are displayed at Westminster and the Tower of London, where they draw sometimes fear and terror and sometimes only indifference from those who look up at them. Seeing that he is here, at the entrance to the sole bridge, he could walk to Southwark. But he has to return to Ellie. And the anxiety grows in him, because he cannot reach her with his mind, but he is torn between walking the history of the city that he embodies, and returning to his more human life. So instead he keeps to this side of the river and passes Fishmonger Hall, the Steelyard, the Vintry, where much of the wine brought to London is stored, Worcester Hall, which used to be the home of a great man but now houses the Hall of the company of Fruiterers and many smaller tenements, then Queenhithe, Broken Wharf and Chertsey House, and then he is at Paul's Wharfe, and he walks the familiar route home, past St Paul's and Christ Church and then through the small gate, turning right past the tree towards the printing shop, without retracing any of his steps.

A warm wind blows from the east. The nearer he is to her the more he detects her with his senses, as though the obstacle had been the distance he has walked, and the time he has travelled back into memories, and as both diminish so does her absence. He opens the heavy oak door and Tobias is already waiting for him, as though he felt him coming, with footsteps of stone juddering the floor, making the city shake. He falls to his knees and embraces the dog.

'Is she well?' he asks, though he knows the answer because he can feel, without looking, that she sits by the fire, and despite the heat and pain, she is asleep and restful. 'You looked after her? You stood guard?'

Tobias follows him to the kitchen, where he rewards him with another bone from the larder. The dog carries it through to the hearth in the printing room, and sits on Ellie's foot while he worries it. James contemplates her. She has a cut on her forehead, and has wiped the trickle of blood into a smear. She does not look comfortable, with one foot on the floor, the other tucked under her on the chair, her arms holding a blanket, head on one shoulder, but he assumes that she must be comfortable enough, as she is deep in sleep. He would find it uncomfortable. He pulls the other chair closer, and sits next to her. But he speaks to Tobias.

'I walked all around the city. I didn't see any dogs inside the walls, but plenty outside. And I saw the city dog house, where the Lord Mayor keeps his dogs. They're hunting dogs, like you, but also not like you. And I saw the plague pits, one expressly for dogs, outside the city, between Bishopsgate and Aldgate. It was enough. I've had enough of walking. The city is suffering too. It wants to sink into the earth, but it can't.' He strokes the dark streak along Tobias's spine. The dog moans low, then shakes his back. 'What did you see? Anything?'

He stokes the fire, and puts another log on. He's feverish, but he can sense Ellie's chill.

'Tobias, you will look after her when I'm gone?' The dog lies back in front of the fire as the flames increase, and he licks the marrow.

'Ellie, are you asleep?'

She doesn't respond.

'I was remembering about Jeremiah. I think you were too. I was remembering his birth. About how you breathed your way through the pain, and shut everything out until he appeared. And then you were so tired, but so happy. And I was remembering all

184

those restless nights with his colic. And how you blamed yourself, and sank into a void. There was no light anywhere for you. And I was thinking that, perhaps I should have …'

She moans and he stops. He wraps the blanket over her shoulder, from which it has fallen.

'Are you awake, Ellie?' Now he is in the room and touching her shoulder, but he is also the room, and he doesn't know which he is the most, if he is James White, printer and husband, or if he is the spirit of the fabric of the city and its guardian. He sees both, one with his body's eyes, and the other with the eyes of his mind. So when he speaks to her he does so as himself, but also sees himself speaking, as from a distance, and wonders what he will say next, and what he means. His bodily self speaks with an astonishingly narrow perspective on where he is, and from within a confined moment, whereas the other self sees many places at the same time, and sees time stretch forward and back.

'I should have grieved more openly, so you didn't feel the burden of doing it for the two of us, or think that you needed to conceal it. That was all part of blaming yourself.'

'Enough,' she says, 'not now.' She reaches her hand out from under the blanket and fumbles for him, The first thing she touches is the top of his head, and her hand reactively recoils. 'You're burning. Like a flame.' She gingerly returns her hand to his head. 'My hand will cool you.' But it doesn't. 'It is cold in here?' she asks.

'No, it's warm.'

'I remember now. I had a dream. We were sleeping, and when I woke up you were on fire. I tried to cover you to douse the flames. But the flames weren't hot, and I didn't put them out. Instead you sat in bed and talked to me about Jeremiah.'

'Did you eat?'

He brings her some bread and cheese. They sit and say nothing for a while. Then she breaks the silence.

'It made me think. Please don't be upset by my saying this. I wish we'd had another child.'

He sits with this for a while.

'I do too. I would have liked to leave someone for you to care for. And it would have been like leaving some of me with you. To be with you, every day.'

'I'm going to die, James.'

'You're not. You can't. You'll live. You've already survived longer than most do, and you're getting better. The buboes are hardening, and they're getting smaller and seeping. You're going to recover. I'm going to die instead of you.'

She shakes her head. 'I don't think so. I can feel death coming. I can feel a new life coming.'

He wants to say that he'd rather hold onto this life, at least for a while longer, but that he knows that he can't, and that is his covenant. And because he's received signs that his offer at St Paul's was accepted, he also suspects that her doctrine of predestination, the sticking point in their differences over baptism, is shown to be wrong. What we do in this life does affect God's judgement. Perseverance is rewarded, and election can be bargained for, atonement isn't only for a few. It is even for people like him, whose clumsy good efforts could be rewarded with her survival. He has bargained for her reprieve, and while he would like to live with her for another six or twelve years, it's enough that she will live.

'I need you to live, Ellie.'

'I'm sorry.' She finishes the cheese. 'Let's go to bed.'

He helps her upstairs, which, as they both have sores in their armpits, is painful and impractical. He is out of breath quickly, not even halfway up, and they stop. The room spins as he breathes. Everything is rebelling against him. He can support St Paul's, Christ Church, Guildhall and Bridewell prison, the Royal Exchange and Austin Friars, and yet he cannot help his wife to climb the stairs. Even his hands are weak. He wants to cry in frustration, but he will not let her see this. He holds it in, and breathes.

Tobias watches them go up.

'I should be carrying you!' she laughs. He takes a step, grips the rail with one hand, and with the free arm guides and supports her as she takes a step, and then they repeat with the other leg. Together, they make it into their bedroom. He holds her as she uses the chamber pot, and then they climb into bed, breathing heavily.

'Tomorrow we'll recover,' he says, though inwardly he qualifies this, '*You* will recover, and I will accept my bargain.'

'Yes, perhaps.'

It is dark already. They lie under the blanket holding hands, as their breathing eases. Each listens to the other breathe. And they fall asleep together.

★ ★ ★

He wakes, as he always has, for an hour parting the night. There has always been for him a sleep followed by a time of prayer and reflection in the dark followed by another, deeper sleep. In the waking hour, though he has no means of measuring the duration of that hour, he sometimes remembers his dreams, and he weighs and turns them over, and wonders at the jumble in his mind. In the morning he seldom remembers them, because he springs awake, contemplates Ellie and dwells in a moment of joy, kisses her, on the mouth or forehead or eyes, then rises and heads, cup in hand, for the front door. That is his ritual, and he rushes into it. But at night, ruminating on patches of dreams, he finds the things that bind him to life and make him settle with adversity. It is the time when prayers feel most earnest and direct. As a child he would get out of bed and kneel and speak them formally, muttering. These days prayer is a silent meditation, a contemplation not so much of God but of His works, the book of nature, the days here. Ellie does this with him, sometimes waking him, sometimes being woken, by movement in the bed, by a change in breathing. They don't speak but become aware that the other is awake. And they pray together, meditate and reflect together, then fall asleep in quick succession. Then at dawn he wakes. But since the plague she has stopped waking, and instead sleeps through, deliriously deep.

He wakes, as he always has, and tries to hold onto the dream that drifts swiftly into shadow. He is in a great church, it may be Paul's, with many colours of light falling through patterned glass onto the floor. He has that sensation in his heart and stomach again. He's waiting for something calamitous to happen, but he doesn't know why. He looks around for signs of it, but there's nothing. He's thinking that perhaps it won't happen, that he may be safe, provided the hour passes without event. That's all, that's when he woke, with the chance of disaster dwindling to nothing. His dreams have been full of fear and vigilance for months now, he's tired of them. He'd like some variety.

He prays, noiselessly thanking God for listening to him, for accepting his words and his offer, for the covenant he made at Paul's, and he reaffirms his submission, his devotion, his faith and his sacrifice. He enjoys praying in the utmost darkness. He likes the fact that everything is still and silent, except for Ellie's breathing, and there is no business going on in the world beyond sleep and prayer. He feels then that there's just the two of them and God, and that the rest of the world is excluded and kept at a safe distance. Nothing can intrude. They are a shrine to their intimacy.

He searches the city, feels it within and without him, and everyone is asleep apart from some of the bakers, the merchants, the lawyers and babies.

Something stirs, and he senses that Ellie is conscious. He touches her with his mind, with a tendril of flame, but keeps as still as he can. He feels her hand creep across the bed and take his, then interlace their fingers. For a second he thinks that she wishes to join hands in prayer, but then his mind leaps to their wedding, when she did just this as they stood before the minister, and the way this ordinary gesture had become transformed by their union into one flesh, under the watchful eyes of God, and there is something more carnal than prayer in his thoughts.

As so often their thoughts are mirrored, as she pulls his hand over and places it on her breast. This isn't what usually happens in the peaceful, watchful hour in the dark. But he senses what she wants, the need she feels, her anxious sense of privation and loneliness. She is finding it hard to move, so he touches her and kisses her, and for a while he thinks that will satisfy them both, but then she pulls him on top of her, and they make love, their faces almost touching but invisible in the complete darkness. They move together sightlessly in an abyss of knowing. The senses are unfathomable, perhaps because they are one flesh, undivided, unsevered. He doesn't know why, but the sensations are acute, amplified by the fire in her heart and his head. There is an exquisite oblivion when they hold onto each other afterwards.

She retreats into sleep, tightly bound. He thinks he will sleep too. But the fire won't leave him. It's a dry heat, as though he's run out of fluids to sweat. She's asleep, her mouth open. Unseen, though he knows the exact position of her limbs, where the curves lie, the elbows and knees, the precise arch in her spine and the twist in her neck, the acute angle of her feet, the lie of her hair over all her body. He doesn't need light to discern this.

Nor does he need light to know the contours of the city, or to comprehend the actions and lives occurring there, because he is the city, it is within and without him. And he knows that something is not right. Inside him is a new conflagration, and it is not only the resonance of their lovemaking, which devours him in an ache of simultaneous joy and lacking, a sense that it's wrong that she's actually a distinct being from him – it is more than that. He can't stop the calefaction, and he grows hotter inside. But still he doesn't sweat. Is this what death feels like, a burning that increases till he explodes or expires?

He knows that a year ago, when he and Ellie stayed in the city in the months of August and September when thousands were dying daily, that they weren't only risking death, but were rushing straight at the flashing hooves of the four horsemen of the apocalypse. Is the sensation he experiences now what they were defying? It feels like everything and nothing to him. It is a pain, and it is awful, but it is not overwhelming, because he is still himself, he is still able to contemplate death, and look the grey horses in the eyes. He will manage this, and will not cry out. After all, it is what he agreed to, what he asked for.

He coughs a little. He is too dry, he must douse the flames inside him. He disentangles himself from Ellie, now rapt in dreamlife, and drinks from the cup he left by the bed. He sits on the edge of their big bed, and drains it. He stops coughing, but he doesn't stop burning. It is a warm night with a warm easterly wind, and the night air doesn't cool him at all.

Something is nagging away at him, an idea or a voice. It's saying to him that there's more to this than a fever, that his fever is meaningful, a sign. Yes, he says, I know that, because I made a covenant with God, and this is a sign that the covenant was accepted, and that I'm fulfilling the terms of the agreement. But the voice says, yes, but it's more than that, the flames won't stop because the fever is in the city too, because you are the city. Well then, I must die all the sooner, he says to the voice within him, because there's no air here, just fire. His cup is empty.

He staggers to the stairs, and sees Tobias's eyes blink in the darkness. Without a candle he fumbles into the larder and fills his cup, leaving a finger over the edge so he knows when to stop the spigot. He is blind, but knows where everything is. He reaches out with his mind, and walks back to the print shop's door. He feels out into the city, back through the day's perambulations, and he is boiling inside, witnessing his blood turn to vapour, and he transposes back towards the river, vaulting over Paul's, and all is calm, and then east along the river, striding back and forth as he takes streets now closer to, now further from, the water, and he knows he is seeking something, because the city within him is leading him towards it, and as he approaches the bridge he is sure that he has understood it correctly, that his combustion is ruining the city too, and as soon as he traverses New Fish Street, which leads down to the bridge, he knows he has found it. He hears the sigh of wooden houses as they submit to the flames. He hears the cries and the panic in the streets. It is happening. He is destroying the city. This is his work.

He moves towards the front door, vigilant of the flames he brings within him, seeing and feeling in the dark, his human eyes worthless now. He steps out, Tobias at his heels. He stands where he always does, and sees the heat ripple from his body, disturbing the cooler air outside, shifting light and sound. He looks towards the city, east, beyond the bridge, and he doesn't need to see it but he does see it. Vertical reflections of flames grace the air, and the semi-illuminated smoke is enough to justify his apprehensions. He is on fire, the city is on fire. It is beautiful and it is terrible, it is wrath and mercy intertwined. He has ruined the city, and this is his sacrifice.

CHAPTER TWENTY

Growing up in Smithfield he witnessed a lot of killing. Throats slit, with that first violent effusion, a spurting arc of blood. The sound of blood splashing on stone, different from water, distinct from brick. Bleeding corpses hanging from J-shaped hooks. Flesh skinned, hanging in curls to the floor. The crack and crunch of bone, and the soft crackling of boneshards underfoot. The smell that sits halfway between savoury and rancid, the smell that never goes away. The texture of a carcass, that always gives to the touch, is never hard, but gives without acceptance, an inert lifelessness, organic but obsolete. You press, and you hope that it is not you. The colour of death, only briefly or rarely crimson, but more often brown, warm pale brown, with splotches of dark brown that harbour blue. The offcuts, clogging the gutters, conduits, sluices and drains. Rats and cats and dogs dragging them away, furtive and beaten. The pooling blood, staining the grass and stone. The smears on aprons, imperfectly scrubbed by hand, leaving layers of traces, palimpsests of butchery, unhurried accumulations of cut and hack wiped away. The smears on knives, frequently washed and sharpened because no one wants to use a blunt knife with its unclean cuts and unnecessary effort. The spray of droplets on whitewashed walls. The buckets of organs put aside for the poor: intestines, brains, eyeballs. The smell of organs, different, sweet and pungent. And so much more. He doesn't need to remember any of this, it's all too human for him now. Too corporeal. Mortality is omnipresent.

He thinks, as he wakes, of a pig hanging from a wall opposite him, the head down, as always, legs tied, struck with fear, and the butcher's knife approaching, its ribs writhing so you could feel the beating of its barely-larger-than-human heart, its eyes black, shining with death, and the first feeble cut, the sweep of blood, the smell, taste, sound of that, then the frantic and belated struggle against death, lashing against the forces of gravity and the irresistible expulsion of blood, and, here is the thing that he holds onto, the wild, fearful, terrified, entirely conscious and uncontrolled thrashing, fully aware and wholly distraught, with every sense and thought and complete understanding in its mind, and yet unable to feel anything but desperation and fear and the slither of perfect apprehension. That dying animal, that's who he is when he wakes.

He waits for all the fluids to drain from his carcass into the wide bed, and for his flesh to desiccate. It doesn't happen. All the terror and anxiety sit there and won't go away. His body won't fail him that easily. He would thrash and flail his limbs, but they are leaden and unresponsive. His thoughts batter against his mind instead. He's a slaughtered pig at that moment of extremity, and unable to leave that moment.

It takes some time to stumble through the disorderly recoll-ections of yesterday, to identify why he feels that way. Some of the day before returns, but none of it is entirely intact, and he can't recall the order in which things happened. He steps among the broken pieces, and after a while finds the night. Shards: a conversation about death, though he can't remember half of it, returning home from a long walk, speaking with Tobias, waking for prayer and making love, burning with a dry and searing heat, a covenant made and kept, and a razing of everything that stands. The vision of a city aflame.

He tries to shrug off the moment, because he knows it is the kind of madness that comes with waking from a bad dream. Delusions rush in during the night, and especially when night turns to day, when the wolf of a dream becomes the waking dog. He knows this, but he cannot shake the sense that he is hanging from his feet and the life is flooding out of him. The soul has been ripped out of the city, and he, the cocooned soul, is trans-forming from life to death, while the mortal form lies outside him, below him, immovable and unresponsive. The pig's consciousness drains into the atmosphere. He is empty and still the vision remains.

Ellie is there, the susurration of her breath reassuring him. She is dreaming of faraway hills, he knows this, almost as though he can see into her. Her skin glistens with perspiration, like the dew on the hills. He risks kissing her on an overheated cheek, and she doesn't murmur or stir, before he stumbles downstairs.

Tobias stands waiting at the foot of the stairs, bone in his mouth, tail wagging. You'd never know, thinks James. He reaches to stroke him, but when he stands upright again he has to find the wall and lean against it. He is dizzy, the room spins, and he cannot find enough air. Once steadied he breathes, breathes deeply into his stomach, seeking that steadiness that stills the world and grounds him. But this fails immediately. He breathes in smoke, the smoke that blows down his streets. He chokes and coughs, falls to his knees. It is some time before his lungs are clear again, and his breathing anything more than a shallow and painful gasping for air. Now he worries that he has disturbed Ellie. He looks at Tobias, but the dog isn't troubled by any noise upstairs, just his master on the flagstones. He rises, breathes more tentatively. If he focuses on breathing in the right air he can avoid the smoke, but this shallows his breaths, making them slide through narrow streets and casements, and he can't get enough air. Why can't I breathe? he silently asks himself, What is it about this disease that deprives me of air? What lesson am I meant to learn from this?

He fills his cup, closes the spigot firmly, heads towards the front door, wonders if he turned off the spigot, goes back to the larder, stares at it, watches it not drip, returns to the printing room and the front door. His legs are heavy already, as though the day has been too much. He cannot imagine standing at a press today. Something is weighing on him, something in addition, a burden across his shoulders. He feels around his thoughts and sentiments, and decides that it must be something from yesterday. Something he cannot remember or hasn't fully understood. Waking or dream, from the day or the hour in the night, something that happened or something that did not happen, a presence or an absence? Something known or unknown? Nothing good, he knows that.

Tobias reminds him of where he is, and he opens the door and steps out, and there it is. His vision is real. Either he has brought the world of sleep and fantasy into his own world, as though by a magic bridge, or the terror had been real all along, and he had mistaken the horror he recalled as too improbable to be real. It is substantial, a matter of truth. He can see the smoke rising from the city to the east, a little south of east, being blown westward by the wind. It rises high above the walls, broiling grey and black, scattering particles of destruction, so that the city's history is no longer buried under the accreting matter of new years, but is instead dispersed upward and into the wind.

He and the city are burning up, are hanging from their feet, and the blood and life are flowing from them, drained as their flesh grows more tender, more seasoned for consumption, ready for the butcher's knife. This, he tells himself, is a propitiatory sacrifice. They are a burnt offering. The city will be razed, buried under ash, and will rise again, a new life made possible only by death. He will die, as the city burns without he will burn within, and this will be a purging fire. Not the kind of purgation that his mother spoke of with such relish, not the cleansing by suffering of a soul in purgatory. He will burn and purify Ellie's meagre sins, his own more considerable ingratitude, his slighting of the blessings he has been given, and, by bringing this destruction upon the city, he will purge it of its infinite sins, of pride, greed, concupiscence, anger and violence, the endless appetite for food and drink and anything in limited supply, the desire for anything that belongs to someone else, simply because it is another's, or is needed by another, and the extraordinary laziness that governs the motions even of the active and devout. Without these sins the city barely lives: there is no church, no trade, no politics, no war. He thinks that while both died one of the thieves was saved, the other damned, the wheel of fortune ever turning, and he knows that he will not see paradise, and that he is not that fortunate thief. The city will rise again, and he will not. This is a purging fire, and it is his fault, and he has brought it upon the city, and it is what he asked for, though perhaps not exactly, and he and the city will be destroyed in order to save what is worth saving.

★ ★ ★

The dilemma comes upon him as he ascends the stairs. He wonders whether he will ever descend them. The buboes are large, still swelling, sensitive to touch. His shirt is stuck to his armpits, where the pus has leaked and encrusted it. The skin around the buboes is inflamed and cracked. He stops and looks down into the room, at his press. He can't remember for how long it's been idle, but does know that he needs to set and print the fourth forme. Then he realises how he must descend the stairs again, how he must spend at least another two days printing, because he has to finish Eagle's book.

He does feel indebted to Eagle, and obliged to complete the work he promised to finish by tomorrow. It is a matter of pride in his labour, in the skill, and in the honesty with which he under-takes his trade. Because he has said that he will, and taken the money for the job, he feels bound to complete it. For all he knows, Eagle lies dead of the plague somewhere, or imprisoned for preaching illegally in a private house. That doesn't matter: he must finish the work, as much as he must do it well. But there's another reason he has to do this, and it's because he's dying and Ellie is living, and she will need the money. When he dies she will have very little to live upon. She must have something to see her through the next few weeks, so she can begin to establish herself as a printer's widow, and a printer in her own right. The other printers, and especially the widows, will help her in this, he knows that. And she will succeed, she will, he also knows that, because she is clever and resourceful, and because she will have to. Just a few pounds will afford some time to find commissions for new works to print. And she may need some time for grief too. So he must finish Eagle's little book, to help see her through, and heaven knows it will be little enough.

Did I finish printing the third forme, even? he asks himself, halfway up the stairs. He peers at the press below him, squinting. The plague has affected his eyes and he can't see as well as he used to, so he can't determine whether or not bound and framed pages of type sit on the bed of the press. So he may need to do more than a couple of days' work before the commission is finished. He can't remember. And it's too far to go back down and look for printed sheets and check the press. He can't see a pile of half-printed sheets in the room, nor can he remember whether he printed a full ream or just a handful. He despairs: he wants to be angry with himself, with his own failing faculties, but he doesn't have the will or the resolution for fury. He's too feverish and too tired and too devoid of hope. And then he remembers John Smith and curses him, because his fleeing was so unnecessary, and Smith could and should have remembered his obligation and helped him print this book, and he should have been there to help Ellie take over sole responsibility for their printing house, the White printers. And Smith was shaken and fled when he should not have, and may now have ruined his chances to become a printer and complete his apprenticeship. And he taught Smith well and they treated him kindly, and he has now made things more difficult, for no good reason.

And then he remembers: they have the plague, and if Smith had stayed he would probably have it too. Smith was wrong to flee, but the choice was, as fortune would have it, the right one. It may have saved his life.

He looks at the stairs. He must try to continue up them. He cannot work today. Perhaps he will improve enough by tomorrow to complete Eagle's book, recover if only temporarily, if he even survives until tomorrow. His body aches; he walked too much yesterday. He ascends a couple more steps, pauses. Breathes, tentatively. Tobias watches him from below.

'Damned plague,' he says.

Stopping once more, he reaches the bedroom. Ellie is muttering in her sleep. He can't make out the words. He reaches into her thoughts and they are green. He breathes, and climbs into bed beside her, the big, hot bed, and his limbs are released. He lies on his back – though this used to be uncomfortable, it's now the only way the swellings don't trouble him – and he breathes through dry and cracked lips.

It is Sunday, and he has not been to church. He cannot remember when he last went to church, nor when was the last Sunday he did not. He senses death rushing upon him, feels the ground trembling, hears the hooves.

Soon his mind begins to leave his body and he blows into familiar streets, walking or floating through them with his eyes close to the pavement, as though he is a dog. He walks through the city, seeing but unseen, and observes the panic in the eyes and faces of its citizens. They are thinking of themselves and their belongings, of which goods they would most want to save, for sentiment or monetary value. They perform shrewd calculations by size and weight. And now he runs like the fastest dog chasing a hare through open fields, and he is swift enough to escape smoke and flames. He is a spirit, a thought, a fancy, released from all corporeality and its burdens.

★ ★ ★

A hoarse voice calling his name wakes him.

'White!'

He contemplates this for a while. Why would a man address a running dog or hare? Could he hope to stop it through language? Must people always fear the things that move unencumbered?

He wakes a little more, and recognises the nasal voice, in spite of its newly-hoarse tone and the effort of calling through closed shutters.

Then the thought that someone, perhaps an observant neighbour, has seen a sign that he and Ellie have the plague, and that they are to be shut up in the house, brings fear upon him, and he is suddenly fully aware. He stands and walks to the window, then realises that he must disguise his condition, so he puts on his jacket before throwing open the shutters. Down in the street stands Eagle. It is just as well that James is not printing, for Eagle would object to this on a Sunday. The tall, uniformly grey man looks up at James in the window, and frowns.

'Abed?'

James shakes his head. 'Praying,' he says, mistrusting his own voice not to crack or break.

'Not at church?'

'Already been. The sermon wasn't good.'

Eagle nods. 'Bramhall,' he says, as if that explains everything. 'You prefer the darkness for prayers?'

James shrugs. 'The times are dark.'

'You've heard the news?'

'I've seen the signs.'

'It's prodigious, a terrible wonder.' Eagle's voice is excited with terror and satisfaction. 'You've not been to see?'

Eagle explains: he approached the city early this morning to preach one of four sermons, and he saw it long before reaching Aldgate. Smoke blew along Fenchurch Street like a pack of wolves, or sheep fleeing wolves. Pudding Lane was destroyed, and St Magnus church with it, and St Margaret's almost down. Churches gone, levelled with the angry finger of God. A lesson unheard. And now Fish Street was ablaze, and it would go the same way. The talk everywhere was of pulling down houses to stop the flames; on every corner where fleeing people collided, that's what they spoke of. Destruction to prevent more destruction. But the city authorities had done nothing, nor the mayor, and the Duke of York had done nothing, and the king was said to be frozen with trembling at the meaning of this judgement. And after Fish Street, then St Michael, and where next? The bridge itself? St Paul's? All of London?

'God forbid,' mutters James, after half an hour of this.

'But He doesn't,' exults Eagle. 'It's His will, His message, His judgement. The plague was only the beginning of this, and, as I've testified, more was to come.'

'And what are people doing?'

'Some are doing nothing. They stand their ground, thinking

that the Lord will save them if He doesn't want them to die. They tempt providence, like Turks or Ranters. They don't understand.' James shakes his head. Eagle continues: 'Others are fleeing the city to save themselves. Like last year. Running has become a habit. I stood on the corner of Fenchurch and Gracechurch and saw carts loaded with cases and furniture slip over cobbles. The things they couldn't leave behind. Children trailing. Mothers walking to make room for chests. The poor emptying from their tenements and carrying what they could in their arms, or wrapped in sheets over their shoulders. And it's only the start.'

Eagle says that he stopped to give an extempore sermon, without premeditation, on the wages of sin, outside St Edmund on Lombard Street. The minister there had not appeared. Perhaps he was saving his silver and gold. So instead he preached himself, and told the crowd that a new life was coming. They listened, they were all ears as the smell of smoke reminded them of their predicament.

And afterwards, everywhere was the noise and obstruction of carts, and a shortage of horses, and on the river, boats heading both east and west with more goods spilling into the water, and other boats with spectators, come as though to watch a play, approaching as close as they could to the flames, and backing away again when the heat and ashes were too great. He pitied the watermen rowing them.

'Now everyone will say it's a judgement. And they will say that they knew all along. And perhaps one day they will learn. Perhaps one day they will see the signs, or listen to those who read the signs. But not today,' says Eagle. 'I must go back,' he adds.

'Be safe.' Eagle has turned his back and is already walking away when James remembers. 'Your pamphlet. Did you come to ask about it?'

'I forgot. I remember you said that it would not be tomorrow, but Tuesday. I thought I would come by to ask about progress, and to tell you the news.' Yes, thinks James, you were excited.

'I wouldn't print on a Sunday, of course. I think it will be done by Wednesday. I will let you know when it's close to ready.'

Eagle nods solemnly. 'This is not a time for distributing books in London. But as soon as the fire is extinguished, then people will want to read "The judgement and warning of the Lord against the people of England". They will be ready and ripe to read it. I was right, again.'

He turns and walks away. I concealed it, thinks James. Eagle didn't suspect. How did he not see the marks of the plague upon me? He only sees what he expects or wants to see. Doesn't ask questions.

He has been gripping the casement in order to steady himself. With Eagle safely out of sight he closes the shutters again and climbs back into bed. His body rebels. It hurts and aches, it oozes, it smells and burns.

No longer the incorporeal dog tearing through the burning streets, once again he is the corpse hanging from a meat-hook, as the blood drains from him, splashes irresolutely, and runs in narrow rivulets between Smithfield flagstones and cobbles. He is surrounded by the groans of the dying, the grinding of bone and scrape of skin, the cracking of boneshards, the slow howl of terminal breaths, the hacking of a cleaver, the sawing of a blunt knife. Rats scurrying, sniffing the air. He smells the fetid, rotten discards, offal, the uncleaned bones, the sweet and stale butchers' blocks, the rancid drains, the lifelessness of draining blood before it acquires its bitter honeyed devastation.

The light forms warm stripes across the dark of his eyeballs, red smears on black. Unexpected sparks threatening to disturb the balance of things.

Flesh is soft and vulnerable, taking impressions of the harder steel of the world, sometimes resisting, sometimes break-ing. A yielding smear on brittle bone. It is red and brown, cochineal and cursed.

He is a dying animal, hanging from a hook, as he falls into sleep.

CHAPTER TWENTY-ONE

Death feels like a baker's oven. Yesterday, or was it the day before, his skull had been opened to the heavens, and flames coursed in and out. Today, his every pore is open. He wishes his body would melt, but instead it remains firm, a porous hunk of pumice, the heat rushing through. The pain is not confined to any one part, but absorbs him entire. His thoughts are a cocoon within the fervid broil.

Dreams are never free from the lived stuff of life, but now his life isn't entirely distinct from dreaming. He is thinking of Jeremiah, and he is dreaming of him. When people speak of dreams they mean things that are not real, that are insubstantial, or things that are erroneous or misleading, and things that are imagined or fabricated. These dreams are none of those things, though. They are material and real and more truthful than the world he has lived in for the past year or more.

He is in a field, north of Finsbury, sitting in the passing shadow of a windmill. Each time the blade turns he sits in light, then out of it. He has plucked a handful of hollowed-out corn from the edge of the field, unharvested last autumn. He has wetted it with water from his flask. He is conscious that he must get back to the shop, back home soon, but there is something he wants to make in a little window of escape, running from near Moorgate to Farringdon Without, though he knows that this is not on any direct route. He is a touch delirious from sleep-deprived nights. But this is about surprising Ellie and Jeremiah. He is also rewriting the history of corn dollies, so they will now have a completely new meaning for him. His childhood efforts, only a mile or so from here, will disappear. A corn dolly will mean a smiling baby, and Ellie laughing at his childlike pleasure.

Jeremiah does smile at the doll, and his eyes sparkle. He holds it in the air.

'Is it too sharp? Will he scratch his face?' she asks.

He shakes his head. But he hadn't thought of that, so he checks. He runs his hands over the stems, their cut ends, the wheat ends. He finds nothing too sharp. Harder than the baby's skin though, which he touches. Ellie holds him from behind. He makes the dolly dance on the bed, where Jeremiah lies. He sings:

> 'To market, to market
> To buy a plum bun,
> Home again, home again,
> Market is done.'

He sings this when Jeremiah cries, and it silences him, temporarily.

He gives the dolly back to the baby and lies down on the bed holding him up above him. He makes a swooshing noise as he first holds the baby high, then brings him down so he is closer to his own nose, then lifts him high again. Jeremiah dribbles on his face, rapt. He shakes the dolly, then drops it so it falls on James's face.

He lowers the baby so he can reach the dolly. His arms thrash at first, and he touches the dolly without clasping it, but then he stretches for it more deliberately, and his fingers close around its arm. He lifts the dolly triumphantly, as James lifts him.

Jeremiah and the corn dolly are impervious to the fire, to the flames that pour from him, lighting the big bed, the room.

Around the bed and the room people flee the city. They look anxiously down their street to see if the fire is approaching. They walk to the end of their street, then along another, until they can see the flames, and they gauge whether the wind will blow the fire towards them, and how long it might take before their own house or tenement and their possessions are jeopardised. They begin to think about what they will take with them when the moment comes. Those who have cellars place their valuables there. Others run around the streets looking for a horse they can borrow or hire. Some run to Hackney looking for horses, and hire them at raised prices from doubtful owners. Many carry their possessions to neighbours who live further away from the wards of Billingsgate and Bridge Within. They don't know how long this will last, how far it will spread, whether they will have to go further afield. Some load handcarts in the street, to find themselves stuck as others block the way. A shower of sparks blows unexpectedly into faces when the wind changes. The fire makes its own weather. Its force lifts a great column of smoke high into the air, as tall as the Colossus at Rhodes or the Tower of Babel, and then more air is sucked in, hot and dry and full of sparks and ash. Onlookers fear stumbling into the inferno with the hot wind behind them. They are fascinated too, shuffling towards the flames, choking on the smoke, lumbering back when the heat is excessive. But what scorches changes over time, and they lose a sense of danger until hot ash wakes them.

He sees them flinch and lurch away from him. He is deep in the inferno. The pus that seeps from his buboes evaporates as soon as it touches the air. He prowls around the buildings of the city, looks inside them, scales their walls, opens their shutters. He is a question that cannot be answered. There is no answer, only longing.

He is at the wedding, on St David's Day. He is watching himself as he stands before the altar with Ellie. He looks happy. This might be a dream, but he has been seeing himself, if not from outside, at least from slightly to one side, ever since Thursday night. His body is not his own, not entirely, and he is aware of so many things outside his body. She wears pale brown, whiter than tan, with cream and gold. He now sees, as he did not that day, the cream ribbons tying her shoes. His jacket is newly tailored, the seams crisp and flat. It is made of a fine brown wool, and it is still his best. His white shirt collar stands above it. He cannot see it from where he stands, but he remembers too that he wore a posy, pinned to his new jacket, of dusky purple Lenten roses, also called hellebore. He learned the name from a book, where he read that hellebore eased fevers. Nothing like this he learned from his family or from Smithfield meat merchants. It was country magic, but the kind that found its way into books.

Around the church are more hellebores, in purple and white, and daffodils, snowdrops, crocuses, jasmine and primroses. They sit throughout the church in pots loaned by neighbours. Ellie has gathered blue flowers from the meadows too, lungwort and violets, and things she calls wildflowers. These sit underneath the windows. The church is a profusion of colours, colours inexpressible; there is nothing restrained about it today. Thomas Bishop makes no objection to his church being decorated, a mosaic of speckled brilliance.

Ellie holds a posy. She already has a ring on her finger, which he presented to her on the last day of the previous year. She asked him what it meant, and he told her. The ringed hand holds the posy, and he sees the glint of silver beneath the white, yellow and gold flowers; the other hand holds his. Every word he said was true, except that they would not live for ever.

He stands next to his sister Jane, in the fourth pew. The pews in front of them, though mostly empty, belong to the better families of the parish. He inclines his head to whisper to her.

'Thank you for coming.'

'Don't be silly. I'm so sad Mary isn't here.'

'Me too. She would have liked Ellie.'

'Yes,' she laughs a little. 'She had her own ideas.'

He touches her arm.

'I mean what I'm saying up there, I will be loving and faithful to her, I will be her comfort. Richer and poorer won't matter at all. She doesn't need to obey me either. I told her before asking her that I would love her for ever, and I will.'

'I know you mean it, James.' She laughs again. 'Margaret might object to poorer.'

'I don't like this prayer book,' he says. 'We should be allowed to say what we mean.'

She nods silently, not because she disapproves of the prayer book and the Anglican marriage that returned with the king, but because her attention is now fixed on James and Ellie before the altar, as he puts upon her hand another ring. She has to move the posy to her right hand before he can do this. The flowers catch the light of the stained glass.

'You won't remarry?' he asks. She shakes her head.

'Not again, not unless I have to. I hope to get by.'

'Perhaps I will be able to help.'

'I wouldn't ask that.'

'I know you wouldn't want to. But if it comes to it, and you need it. I want you to promise that you'll ask.'

She nods.

As he lies burning, hot blood and pus and fumes seeping from his body, he realises that it is a year since he heard from her. He doesn't know if she is alive. The town of Reading, where she lived, is far away, more so when plague has shut down the city and all of its hopefulness. He should have written to her. He should have made enquiries. She might have died of the plague for all he knows, might have encountered exactly the same fate that now greets him. He wouldn't know.

He turns to ask her, but she is gone, St Bartholomew the Less is gone. Ellie is there, though, and he reaches out to her hand. She stirs, takes his hand and squeezes it. She is awake, and perhaps also dreaming at the same time. They always echo each other, he thinks, as though a pair of mirrors faced each other, with their reflections repeating into a contracting infinity.

Except now, he thinks, they are opposites. He is dying, and she is recovering. As if to confirm this, she stirs and speaks.

'Were you dreaming?'

'Of Jeremiah and of our wedding.'

'I thought so,' she says, without further explanation.

'You're feeling better?'

'A little. My head is a little clearer.'

'That's good. Eagle came by. Do you remember that?'

'I don't,' she says. 'I don't think I was awake.'

'I spoke to him through the window. He didn't notice there was anything wrong.'

'What day is it? What time?'

'Sunday. The middle of the afternoon, I think.'

'I've been asleep for how long?'

He tries to remember when she was last awake. He cannot. 'I don't know. Perhaps you were awake earlier.'

'What did Eagle want?'

'To tell me about a fire. There's a fire in London. Destroying parts of the city. He thinks he predicted it. All part of his prophecy.'

'How bad is it?'

'I don't know.' He doesn't want to alarm her. 'They will pull down buildings to stop the spread. People always panic.'

'I hope no one dies.'

'And he wanted to check on the progress of his book. Which I can't finish for a few days. I don't think I can. I will try. You will need the money.'

'I feel less feverish.'

He is suddenly full of hope and energy. He rises, goes down the stairs and heats a pan of water. He thinks: is this what dying feels like? A sudden burst of life, a few final, thrashing gestures, then into the shadows? He brings two cloths with him as he carries the water up the stairs. Then he washes Ellie's sores with hot water, cleaning the pus, softening the hardened crusts and easing the stiffness of the joints.

'That feels good,' she says. She takes a cloth from him and, sitting up, washes his armpits. Then she suddenly tires. He finishes cleaning himself, though he cannot reach his own armpits. He concurs, it does ease the pain. And he is tired too, so he leaves the pan and the cloths on the floor and falls back down on the bed.

She takes his hand.

She is dreaming again, a dream of things that happened outside this room, as they occurred but with brighter colours. It was a Monday, the last day of the year. Winter honeysuckle bloomed on Fish Street, yellow and white brightening the grey of the none-too-recently whitewashed walls of the houses leading down to the bridge. Sarah Cooper had released her for the day, and he had promised himself he would work late to make up for the lost time. They'd met at St Bartholomew the Less on Sunday, and he'd asked her to walk with him the next day. They had an afternoon to themselves, the thirty-first of December in the year 1660. The dream is concrete in detail, vivid and vibrant.

They walk, hand in hand, towards the bridge. She thinks he seems a little distant today, as if he has something on his mind. She hopes that he isn't having second thoughts. The air is mild, but the high winds make it cold, and they are wrapped in wool coats and scarves. Their exposed hands keep each other warm. When they arrive at the Thames they see that the water is high, and the gusts whiten its crests. They walk onto the bridge, and feel momentarily exposed to the wind, until they are in the shelter of the many tall houses that line the bridge. Except for the gaps where the buildings stop, and where they look out onto the river on both sides, along the Thames towards the Isle of Dogs or towards Whitehall, the houses form a continuous street, and you can forget that you are on a bridge.

The ground floor of each house is a shop, and there are haberdashers, pinmakers, metalworkers, grocers and others. It is sometimes a busy street, if not the most fashionable to shop in, though not on a windy December's day. They look into each shop in turn. It's interesting to see how people make things, what skills a pinmaker and needlemaker have in common with a type founder. Haberdashers use different stitches from bookbinders. A clothmaker is weaving wool into a marvellous pattern of squares and circles. It might be magic for all that she understands how the weaving works.

They walk as far the drawbridge, which is down. There they stand, their feet on the eastern edge of the bridge, their toes almost above the water, and face the direction of the Tower, St Katherine's, Greenwich, and beyond that, places which she has never seen and of which she has little idea, Gravesend, Tilbury, the Medway. They lean out to see some of the nineteen arches, and the starlings around the piers on which each arch stands, but the jutting houses conceal most of these. It's as though the bridge is a floating city, she thinks, defying the water, defying the ordinary weight of things. James holds her shoulders as she leans. It's frightening, as she fears that she'll lean too far and be swallowed by the bleak grey turbulence of sea and air.

They walk on, as far as Bridge Gate, and the entrance to Southwark, and there they turn around and walk back. The light is fading, and they have no time to adventure in Southwark.

The old chapel, now a house, is covered with ivy, which turned red months ago and is now frozen into position as a backdrop for more winter honeysuckle. Imagine living there, she thinks, in such a grand house, on the bridge, floating in the air, with the wind screeching over the roof at night. And the people passing by, always passing. She stops and leans against the wall. He wraps around her as best he can, within the confines of a heavy woollen coat.

'Ellie,' he says, and her name seems strange in his mouth, as though it makes him more remote. He should have a more direct way of speaking to her. Then it turns around, 'I love you.'

This is not a phrase she has heard uttered before, not in this way, not as directed to her or to anyone else. He has a biblical seriousness about him when he says it. She thinks about what it might mean. She knows that the Bible is all about love, but that is the love of God, or the love of His laws, or desire for worldly things, which is bad but also goes under the same name of love, but here, standing on a windy bridge, between a man and a woman, what exactly does it mean?

She squeezes his hand.

She thinks of Proverbs, when a nameless woman dressed like a harlot, who is loud and stubborn, approaches a young man who isn't subtle enough for her, and proposes that they take their fill of love until the morning, that they take solace in love, and he accepts, and that is the way to hell and to death. Not that love. Love in sermons, when it is not the love of God, is usually destruction. Otherwise it is an empty sound. There is the Song of Solomon, though. Perhaps James has been reading that. By night on my bed, I sought him whom my soul loveth … she knows that a clergyman will tell her that the song refers to seeking the Son of God, but when she has woken in the night and longed for someone to embrace her, for the past month it has not been the Son. She thinks of his arms, his mouth, his teeth like sheep on a hill, of searching for him in the city, of the fig tree and tender vines, of the dove's eyes within his locks. That's what he means. Or perhaps he has been reading old poems, sung hundreds of years ago in France and Italy, songs of love for a pure mistress who will never yield. He has told her about those, and read her one from a book, and she wondered at the time whether it was his way of saying the same words to her, about her lips and eyes and pale skin, but then she put the thought away and listened to the sound of the words, and the sound of his voice. Poetry reminds her of legends sung on the hills of home, on the edges of the Black Mountains, and those are full of love too, and it seldom ends happily.

He's still speaking, he hasn't finished.

'I think we're good together, and good for each other. We fit together very well. We don't agree on everything, but we always find a way of talking about it. and we know how to talk. I've never talked like this before. Time passes differently, time's changed, like you've always been here. And because you are here, there's an empty space in the house, in the printing shop. I've not noticed that space before. I already know that I want to spend the rest of my life with you. I was wondering if you felt the same way.'

She thinks she knows what he means. She had been entirely happy working for the Coopers, and counted herself fortunate. She deserved and could expect no more. Her position was stable and secure. She was comfortable, or had been. And then she had heard that voice in the churchyard, asking her ironically if the preacher should speak more of the sins of this world, and things had gone slightly askew. The thing she couldn't account for, over the three, almost four months they had known each other, was that he seemed to speak directly to her. Not over her shoulder, or in some other direction, but to her in person, to her whole person. The remark in the churchyard seemed like yesterday, but it also seemed half a lifetime ago, and she couldn't make the two feelings meet.

He is looking at her, expectantly. Is he asking her a question? Was that a question? She is not in a place to think about or answer any questions. And no one asks about her feelings. She is lost there, seeing things in the spaces between the words.

'What do you mean?' she asks.

'By what, which bit?'

'By love. What do you mean by it?'

He is entirely still for a moment, body, hands and face. She waits, time gone awry.

'I mean that I will always care for you and treat you well,' he says. 'I'll look after you and protect you. I will always be honest and faithful. All of that. I would lay down my life for you. I will show it in the things I do, not just the things I say. But also, I mean that we're entangled. In a way I can't put into words. You're already living in here,' and he touches his chest, through the heavy coat. 'Everything was fine before, but now it's different, as if I've been made more perfect by you being here. There's no falsehood.'

'That,' she says. 'That's what you mean.' Then she remembers he was asking her something. 'What was your question?'

'I was asking if you felt the same way. If you felt your life would be better if we spent it together.'

'Then yes,' she says. 'And I love you too.'

He lets go of her hand, and she panics for a moment, because she thinks she has said something wrong, and the cold wind touches her palm. But he is fumbling in his pocket, and he pulls something out, a small drawstring bag made of leather. She is puzzled, because now she wants more words, and he takes something from the bag and shows it to her. It shines, it is a ring, made of silver, polished. And she understands: it is for her.

'Oh,' she says, in surprise, and takes it from him. There is writing inside. She is learning to read, and she tries to make it out, but she cannot discern the letters now, standing on the bridge, while he looks at her and all these feelings rush through. 'What does it say?' she asks.

'Love is as strong as death,' he says. 'Will you wear it?'

Time is broken, slowed to a standstill.

She offers him her left hand, and he tries to put it on her fourth finger. It is too small, and sticks at the knuckle. He is suddenly deflated, and she feels a rush of sadness for him. But she remembers. 'We passed a silversmith's.'

'We did.' They walk to it, handed, and he asks the silversmith to make the ring a fraction wider. And within a few minutes it is done, and the man is polishing the ring up, and James slides it on her finger as they stand there in the heat of the shop, protected from the winds that whip along the Thames and howl over the roofs and under the nineteen arches.

She looks at her hand with the ring on. Her hands look different. She will need to get used to this being her hand. She will need to get used to the idea of having a ring there. She touches it, rubs it, to tell herself that it's real, to remind her that she's there, in this moment. It is the most valuable thing she has ever owned. It doesn't bind her to him, she understands then, because she was already bound.

She thinks through everything he's said. That it's true, what he says. And she's listened and said yes, but no more. Did she even say yes, or consent silently? She's left him to say everything, though it's not that she doesn't feel things. But the words, they feel wrong, compromised, blemished. They won't do to name hallowed things. She wants to give him something, some words to express everything that's too much to say. 'I love you,' she whispers in his ear, there in the silversmith's shop, flushed and embarrassed because it sounds like something profane. The words are hers, and she means them, but they're also not hers. They're not his words either, they're the words of the prophets of the Old and New Testaments. They've been spoken, she imagines, by other lovers too, over and over again for hundreds of years, each one of these lovers meaning them, she hopes, but also meaning something different by them, something known only to them, quoting and misquoting into eternity.

She is holding his hand now, lying there, and he is burning as she is burning. The big bed she has made her home, and which she had hoped to lie in forever, is a furnace hotter than a silversmith's. She doesn't know if this is real, if her senses are overwhelmed, or if she was dreaming or remembering the coolness of the bridge on the eve of the new year, though she feels the ring on her finger, now one of two, and it is speaking to her, and it tells her something she knows from the Bible, and which all of the old poets knew, that love is as strong as death.

CHAPTER TWENTY-TWO

He can see that it is morning from the light that edges around the shutters. Orange September light. He considers what day it is. What happened yesterday? Fire, inside and out. How much was dreaming? It will never be clear. He smells smoke. I set fire to the city, he thinks. That wasn't a dream, because Solomon Eagle came by to confirm it, though Eagle did not know who was responsible. He reported a fire in the east, around Fish Street. That was yesterday. And the fire began in the night, in the early hours, when they were awake and not praying but making love. And he was too exhausted and inflamed to move. And before that was the walk, the walk around the city, full of memories.

It is Monday, he thinks. The original deadline for the book. That was why Eagle came yesterday. Unless he has slept for a whole day, or two. Then it could be any day. Does it matter? He is sliding down, into the flames. But Ellie, she matters. He reaches for her hand, she responds, squeezes his. He can hear her breathing, which tells him that she is sleeping, dreaming. Her hand feels a little cooler and she is resting, which he takes for a good sign. She will live.

The city will not. He is not today as sensitive to the destruction, or to the news that passes through the streets. The opening in his skull has closed a little, the flow of information is thinner. This he takes for a good sign, that she will live while he will not. But though he knows less, he can still feel the devastation. No traffic enters the city, because the outward flow of citizens is so great. It began again as soon as the sun rose. The wind still blows, the fire still spreads, the fear extends, more people understand that they should flee. Still they carry their belongings, as many as they can, and people with gardens bury valuables there. Threadneedle Street is on fire, he can see that clearly in his mind's eye. There is a great conflagration of letters flying into the air unread, secrets forever lost. Words between companies, friends, letters of news, of love, all turning to ash. He sees the wax drip from them as they unfold and lift. The Post Office is gone.

Sparks and ash soar into the air and swirl. The wind deposits them on distant roofs, some tiled, some straw, on window ledges and shutters and gutters made of wood. Thus the fire leaps unexpectedly, unpredictably. Now fast, now slow, now here, now there; people flee unnecessarily or spend too long watching its progress, fascinated by its blind power. Sometimes its magnificence traps them, steals their reason. Splendour masks ruin.

Yes, the city is doomed, even if its denizens aren't. And it is his fault, because he is the city and he made a pact to sacrifice himself for Ellie, and so in sacrificing himself he also sacrifices the city, which burns just as he burns. He hopes not too many will die on his account.

Another thing weighs on him, though he can't see what it is yet. Has he had a troublesome dream? Another almost-empty building with many rooms, with strange light and stranger echoes? He feels around, but if it's there then it's not disturbing as others have been. Something urgent then. Of course: the book. He must finish Eagle's book. Not for Eagle, but for Ellie. He must put something aside for her, and he must live long enough to complete it. So he has to rise and work. Yesterday's inactivity, his sickness, he will forgive himself, but today he must work, even if it makes the plague worse and shortens his life. Has he failed to work for two days or three?

He releases her hand, moves on his back to the edge of the bed, and slides his legs over. He stands, pushing his torso off the bed. He is stiff, but is surprised that there's not more pain. His arms move. This is good, he thinks, my resolution hides the pain, and this means that I will get through today. He touches the bubo under his right armpit, and finds not only that it's hardened and reduced in size, but that his left arm moves freely. He's pleased. This is a brief respite.

After using the chamber pot he descends the stairs, and fills his cup with small beer. Tobias trails.

'I forgot to feed you, sorry.' There's a little meat left over. He hopes it's not rancid. He sniffs it, but can only smell smoke. There's some dry bread too, which he breaks up. 'I should take better care of you.'

Then they go to the front door. He will pretend this is an ordinary day, will clutch the few tokens of normality, will make a show of it, with the hope of deceiving the world and himself. They stand outside and look over the city. It's later than he thought: the sun is already up. The light enters his skin, and a warm wind touches his lips. He breathes. There's a twisting knife. But also a spark. He's hungry. He'd like to buy some food. But he'll make do with stale bread and cheese. There may be some old ham too.

Under the sun there is smoke, writhing, pulled away from the rooftops by the wind. It entrances him for a few moments. Why is there no noise? In the buildings from which the smoke ascends the noise must be fierce, deafening. The crack of beams, the collapse of roofs and the smashing of tiles, the din of flames biting, chewing, gnawing, swallowing, consuming every little chattel that has been left. Fire eats almost everything. Not gold, which will withstand the heat, but those with gold will have transported it from the flames in good time. Books not so much, and he thinks of all the editions that will vanish, abandoned in favour of lighter, more valuable possessions. Might a work disappear entirely because all copies of it are burned, as happened in the Library at Alexandria? If a book were to be printed this week, then the whole run of copies might be sitting in a warehouse near the bridge right now, anticipating the flames that would erase it from history. And it might be a great book too. Fire is no critic.

But as he studies the horizon, the devouring flames make no sounds audible from here. He has to rush into the streets for that, feel the surging panic, sense the heat on his skin, singeing the hair on his arms, be stirred by the cries, and there they are, the sounds, harsh and brittle, a quiet yet deafening roar followed by a frightening silence. The flames' intensity scars ascending images on the backs of eyeballs. It is all there, far away, removed from him, but it can be returned to when he walks into the flames.

'Can you hear it, Tobias? It's hard for me.'

Tobias watches the horizon too.

James dives into the thoughts of the thousands of people who surround the conflagration, despite the warnings that they should stay away and not clog the streets for the fleeing citizens. As he rides the wave of these thoughts he crashes into so many things, fear and apprehension, sadness and dejection, all of which he expects, but he also collides with and trips over unexpected minutiae, little thoughts about broken pots, lost blankets, a passing smile on the street, the mewing of a cat, a scratch on the back of a hand, the shape of a cloud, the tilt of a hinge, the scrape of a door, a cracked button in a stitched buttonhole, and worries about little things, a word a friend didn't say, a silent child, a bad cough and a rash, a house unlocked, an unclean table, a book misplaced, a disorderly desk, a missed appointment, an excess of work without time to do it, a bridge burned a decade or more ago, a road not taken, a question unanswered. All of these, and more weighty things too: hunger, disease, a blow to the face, a forced kiss, a grief too consuming to bear; all of these thoughts lie in the minds of those who look at the flames, as if the flames aren't so much an immediate threat as an occasion to stop and consider all of the other dangers and regrets, and all of the things seen that morning that have lodged in the memory, however trivial.

For some time, as he drinks his small beer, he is lost in the inconsequential. Then he steps out of these thoughts, disowns them, and wonders why inconsequential things preoccupy those who look directly upon destruction. Is this what death feels like?

He hears a faint rumbling. He looks along the street. A cart approaches, pulled by a single horse. The metal rims of the wheels clatter on stone, slip on cobbles; weight murmurs. The horse struggles with the burden that's piled high on the cart. A weary figure holds the reins and walks alongside, pulling the horse, not wanting to add to the load, or, more likely, having calculated that he can save more of his worldly goods by walking. He wears two coats, but it is dejection and not these that makes him stoop.

'Good morning,' he says, and stops.

'Good morning,' James replies, and wonders when he last heard his own voice aloud.

'The price of carts,' the man says, without gloss. He is perhaps forty years old, sweating because of his exertions and the excess of clothing. Perhaps he is glad of an opportunity to pause.

'Where is it now?' James asks, though he thinks he already knows.

'Almost at the Exchange. It may be there by now. It moves west with the wind. The east end of Cheapside. Lombard Street. Cordwainer Street. Bread Street. You know them?'

'I do. The goldsmiths' shops then?'

'They've fled, those with any sense. They know they will be plundered if they leave it to the last minute, when their shops catch fire.'

'And the merchants?'

'Some of them too. And the bankers. Those with plenty of money in hand left first. That's why it costs so much to hire a cart and horse. Ten or a hundred times the usual price.' James looks to the load on the cart. Furniture of fine wood, several small casks, a bundle of silks; a silver candlestick protrudes from under a protective tarpaulin that conceals the more valuable debris of a life.

'You are a mercer,' he guesses.

'You're right,' the man replies, surprised.

'You've come through Aldersgate. Why this way?'

'I have a brother near Smithfield. The fire won't reach there.'

He wonders who the brother might be. This man is a little younger than him, but they might have met before, years ago in the market. But at this time it doesn't matter, as personal connections and memories have no purchase, and nothing is at stake. He reckons the traveller wishes to avoid being seen as he brings the cream of his wealth, and so has chosen this lesser path. He thinks the mercer travels to Clerkenwell, and that he names Smithfield as a petty evasion. It doesn't matter.

'You're frightened.' He doesn't know why he says it. It falls from his mouth, conversationally, as a matter of fact. He doesn't regulate his passions or even rule his own speech.

The mercer is startled, says nothing, and pulls his horse's reins. It takes a straining moment for the horse to get the cart moving again. Their eyes are cast down.

He smells the smoke on them, witness to how close they were to the flames. Then he breathes, and breathes, and though there is smoke there is also air.

★ ★ ★

He re-enters the house and prepares some food for himself and for Ellie. There is a little ham, heavily salted, and some cheese and dry biscuits, a good store of apples. He takes it to her, and helps her to eat.

At first she says nothing, but after a long drink she wakes enough to say, 'Thank you.'

'How are you feeling?'

'A little better, I think.'

That's enough for him. He knows what it means.

'I'm going to print today.'

'Shouldn't you rest?'

'We need the money.' Though he thinks that it's she and not he who needs it.

'As long as you're well enough.' She squeezes his thigh.

'You rest,' he says, and goes back downstairs to the printing room.

He discovers that he has printed only a handful of copies of the third forme, and that the ream of blank sheets is almost untouched. He searches the room for a while, to ensure that he has not missed any. Then, his mind unexpectedly clear, he pegs one of the sheets to a board and begins to proofread. He looks through pages nine, twelve, thirteen and sixteen. Most proof errors are of a limited number of kinds: where a wrong letter has been accidentally picked up, usually from a compartment next to the intended letter in the tray of type; or where the compositor's hand went to the right box, but a letter had been accidentally misplaced in there; where the manuscript has been misread, commonly a punctuation mark; and where a piece of type is upside down because the hand didn't notice the groove was on the wrong side. This means that when he proofreads he doesn't have to think about the meaning of the words, though he has to attend a little, just in case he accidentally skipped a whole line. He has no inclination to concentrate on Eagle's argument or his rhetoric. But it seeps in nonetheless.

We are drowsy. In all of us there is a child who, without understanding the consequences, thirsts for everything that we know to be wrong. We have to listen to the light within, the true guiding light, not once but for all time. When we bring the darkness upon us, it won't be with our whole mind. A passion will topple us, cloud the inner light just a little, obscuring the clear illumination of right and wrong, and we will want to sin just a little. A part of our mind will lead even the righteous the wrong way, not the whole mind. We are not clocks, we are not animals. The mind is divided. That's what he reads, that's the sense he makes of Eagle's writing, while trying not to interpret it.

The mind, he thinks, is a thing made of impressions and of memory. It is a place of thinking and choosing. All of its actions are reactions, based on recollections. It is a storehouse and today, he thinks, his storehouse has been pillaged, and all of its wares lie in great disorder, pulled from the shelves by hasty thieves who don't understand the value of the things within it.

Why does the Lord work hope? Eagle asks.

None of this matters, he thinks. The darkness has come and gone, and now we are pursued by a burning light. Eagle's prophecies were right. No one needs to read this. It is a thing already done. Eagle also says that a darkness will follow the burning light. This could be the night, or the smoke that will settle over the remains of the city once it's razed, or it could be the darkness of the heart when there's nothing left, and most of the people of London have few possessions left and no home to keep them in. But there will be a darkness, for certain, and by the time anyone reads Eagle's book then the darkness will already be upon them.

He marks seven corrections in the four pages. He takes the sheet to the press. There's the bed of type, which he forgot to clean when he stopped printing two or three days ago. He brushes and wipes the dry ink off now, loosens the type in the frame, and replaces seven pieces. He tightens the frame, retying the string and tapping the quoins with a small hammer. He scrapes and cleans the ink tray and removes the caked ink from the inking pads. So much of this delicate art involves scraping, scrubbing, cleaning. Then he pours fresh ink into the tray. He rubs a little oil into the press.

He breathes for a while. Then he applies the ink to the type, secures a piece of paper in the frame, pulls the lever, and presses a sheet. He releases it, hangs it to dry, and returns to the far side of the press to ink once again. And again, and again. The day ekes away. He is lost in a fog within his own mind and body. He can scarcely see where he is going. But he keeps on moving, step by step. Confusion and pain seep into each other, and he ignores them, trusting his body to keep doing what it knows how to do. At one point he stops to take Ellie more food and drink, and eats a little more himself. Then he continues as though he doesn't know how to stop, as though he really is a clock. A clock unwinds until the spring is fully released. Then it is dead until someone comes to wind it again.

The ream of paper diminishes and diminishes. He lights two tallow candles, one either side of the press, and continues. Monday, he thinks it is Monday, is almost over. In truth now he feels very little of anything, confusion, pain, tiredness. Little except an out-of-focus grief. Is this what death feels like?

CHAPTER TWENTY-THREE

Is this what love feels like? He has reached out for her hand, felt her tactile response, breathes again.

'How do you feel?'

'A little better.'

'Better than yesterday?'

'Yes, I think so.'

She coughs. He imagines the droplets in the air, cutting through the rays of light, making rainbows.

'Is it Tuesday?' she asks.

'Yes, I think so.' He tells her that the night before he completed printing the third forme. Today he will set the type for the fourth and final one. His arms ache. He's glad he can sit to the compose the type, though he usually stands to do it.

She coughs again. He feels her forehead. It's cooler than his.

'Would you bring me a drink?' She seldom asks him to do anything. He fetches her one and it eases her coughing. He warms some water and washes her skin, cleaning her buboes.

'That feels better,' she says. He looks at her nakedness, her long limbs, her round hips and breasts, her stomach, the matted hair falling on her shoulders. He feels love, and it's an awareness that she is a missing part of him, and the other way around too, that peace of a kind unknown elsewhere comes to them both when they're together, and when he's inside her, and so this love involves physical desire as well as spiritual. She is perfect, he thinks. But she's too unwell, and he pushes away temptation, just as she pulls up the bedcover. 'It's cold.'

'I'll bring you something to eat.'

But when he comes back upstairs she is asleep, murmuring, turning, restless, distant.

★ ★ ★

Standing outside the front door he reaches into the city. He can still do this, though this morning he senses that he is less the city and more himself. He seems more grounded. The sun has risen, again, he is later than customary. The smoke this morning is greater still, darker and wider. A wind still blows from the east. In the city he finds that people are fleeing, approaching every gate except Bridge Gate, which is now blocked because the bridge has burned, though not all of it, on account of the wide gaps between some of the houses. People also flee by water, descending the narrow steps and loading their goods and themselves and their families into whatever half-seaworthy vessels they can find.

He wishes that someone would pass along the street so he could ask them for news. But the street is empty. He has to rely on his senses, trust that what he finds inside himself is reliable.

The wind expands the fire more westward than eastward. Nonetheless it is approaching the Tower. He feels the panic there. They fear for the Tower because of what it symbolises, what it means, the same reason he dislikes it. The power of the state, the power of life over death cannot be allowed to burn. And the armoury there is at risk, full of guns and powder. And another symbol, the Royal Exchange, what of this? He probes. It is gone. The centre of trade, the meeting point of merchants from around the world, the storehouse of the city's present and future wealth, is ruined. He can see, even with his bodily eye, where its carcass stands, under swirling grey-black wreaths.

He breathes. The Tower, the Exchange. Cheapside is burning, with its shops and craftsmen. What next? The churches, he imagines. St Margaret, St Andrew Hubbard, St George, St Antholin, St Mary Le Bow, the churches of Billingsgate Ward, of Bridge Within Ward, of Langbourne Ward, St Martin Vintry and all the churches of Vintry Ward, the churches of Cordwainer Street Ward, Bread Street Ward, Queenhithe Ward, so many churches. What else? The hospitals, poorhouses, prisons. Flames approach the governors and the governed, merchants, consumers, craftsmen, criminals and victims, worshippers and preachers. It's all of London life, he thinks, but not thoughts or passions, not love or death, except it's all imbued with love and death, which are everywhere.

St Paul's stands in the path of the conflagration, and the little world of the booksellers around it. What will be left of London if these are burned down? What is London in its essence?

He searches around again, listening to the emotions expressed in the voices that resonate in these buildings. The clearest is fear, but many others resonate: anger, bitterness, confusion, denial of what's happening, resentment at God and poor city-planning, recriminations too, sadness, dejection, resignation. These are the new cries of London, its chorus, moans, groans, the ceaseless brawl. These are what the citizens vent, all of which he anticipates, but there are other things there too, less expected. There is loneliness, regret and guilt. He has to listen harder to comprehend these. Loneliness. When the plague struck in May the year before, even before the City authorities began to reduce the contact between people and stop traffic into and out of the city, before the rich fled, as soon as the Bills of Mortality began to record the deaths and attribute them to plague, people began to shun their neighbours. They feared the contagion, and soon they feared people altogether. Conversations, touching, company, all seem threatening. They tell themselves that it's not rational, and that they must continue to speak with neighbours and friends. But they still sit behind a veil of anxiety, and so they keep their distance even when they speak, and they keep their thoughts and feelings private. They are suspicious, doubtful. And so they grow lonely, trapped inside their tenements or houses with their families, trapped inside themselves. They are lonely, more than they know or understand. When they speak now, even though they have agreed that the plague is gone from the city, they speak suspiciously, and they find it hard to say what they think.

Regret is worse, as it conjures up before their eyes the things that they do not have, that they might have had, the things they have left behind. Here the past is a cage. When the plague came, they say, their lives turned. Things did not happen or could not happen, and so much life was lost, and so much of them was lost when they were shut down and went into hiding. And the friends and neighbours whom they neglected, their closeness was lost too. So much time lost, and so much wreckage. And, more strangely to him, he hears voice after voice that regrets wasting time with the people about whom they cared less than those whom they forgot, people whose only effort was to keep in touch. Time spent unwisely. Plans that were delayed and then abandoned. People who died and who would not be seen again, family members gone, and all their secrets with them, faces rendered faint in memory. Friendships abruptly aborted. Intentions thwarted, opportunities crushed. Love unspoken or ungiven. Skin untouched. The plague stole so much, long before the consuming fire. All of this is regretted, as the flames rush on.

Guilt is worst of all. Guilt absorbs the regret, and transforms it, like pitch defiling everything it touches. The voices he hears say that it was their fault, that they should not have spoken to this grocer or that farmer, and that by doing so they brought in the danger of plague that killed their son. It was their fault, because they took a risk and spread the disease. They feel guilt because they should have made that journey to see their father, or because they should have spoken more kindly when they did. They feel guilt that they were too lazy or too tired to chase after such a person when they left and walked away, in order to tell them what they really felt, and now that person will never know. They feel guilt at not doing something when the opportunity was there, and now all opportunities have passed. They feel guilt at what they said, and what they did not say, and now they have made their own life, and the lives of others, worse for it. They feel guilt because the disease has suddenly shone a bright light on all their failings. They feel guilt because they have colluded with the plague, and it exposed them for who they really are.

It hurts to have the top of your skull opened, so you can feel the connection with heaven, and examine the thoughts of your fellow citizens, to have hearing this acute. Feelingness can be a curse, he thinks. No wonder the angels weep as they look down on us.

A warm wind blows along the street, from east to west. It brings the taste and smell of smoke, and fragments of ash, like dry black rain. If only it would rain. But it will not, he can see that. Autumn rains will come too late. He goes inside, Tobias at his side.

He will print while the city burns. He forgets so much though. Where is he in the book? The shop is full of sheets hung to dry. These are the front of the second sheet, so he must set the back, the fourth and final forme. He collects them, five hundred and sixteen copies, unless he spoiled one or two. Four of them will be slightly different, different in seven characters, he thinks, it's strange the details that you remember and those that you forget. He doesn't know which are the different ones, and it doesn't matter. They're good enough to use. Eagle won't notice them. They stand by the press for use later, or tomorrow. He's feeling hot again, breathing the smoke.

The type is still on the press. He must break up the forme, and put each piece of type back in the right compartment in the right case, lower-case, capital, lower-case italic and capital italic. He rubs the type down to clean it, which he also forgot in the haze of last night. He can't remember much of last night, as he was so tired. And distracted too, now that he considers it. The fire sits there inside him, he carries it in his mind and in his body. He can feel it approaching.

He takes the frame of type to the composing table where his four cases stand, unties the string, removes the quoins, and puts each piece of type in its correct place. There are thousands of them, he doesn't know how many thousand. Each space is a piece too, and, except for the largest, they are thrown higgledy-piggledy into a single compartment. Punctuation marks have their own place too. Spaces and points and pauses are as important as letters; the typeset page has no particular respect for words, let alone meaning. Words are only letters, and letters are only ink marks, and ink marks are only the contrast between black and white space.

This runs through his mind over and over as he breaks up the forme and redistributes the type. He takes apart Eagle's arguments, and turns meaning into ordered lead pieces that simply press black into white. He does this for hours without really noticing time passing, aware only of the shrinking pages. Eagle's outpourings dwindle into a few lines, then nothing. Noise into silence, disorder into order.

When he is done he goes to the kitchen, takes Ellie something to eat. He thinks it may be time for her to eat again, but he's lost his intuitive apprehension of time passing. She is asleep. And she is hot, he senses this as soon as he enters their room. She is burning, while he cools. Something clouds his mind, like the smoke that forms a canopy over the burning buildings. He cannot look the shadow in the eye, but he knows he must. So he breathes, feels the flames rushing towards him, towards them, and looks straight at it. What if he is wrong? What if she isn't getting better? What if it's he who is recovering? She lies in bed, burning, asleep, while he's downstairs working in the shop. He'd thought that the pact he'd offered to God had been heard and accepted. Had he just convinced himself of this? He tries to remember why he had thought this covenant was being honoured. Yes, that's it: he has the plague. That was the bargain. That was the sign that the bargain was made. But what if he'd simply caught the plague by virtue of lying with Ellie? What if it was the property of the disease and not providence?

He lies down next to her. Her skin is soft, smooth, tender, newly washed. But it is hot to the touch. The flames now approaching are obstructed, so he cannot see or feel them, by a wave of fear, a towering, crashing wave of desperation and panic. He runs his hands over her and whispers in her ear, 'Ellie, my love.' He feels her elbows, the hair behind her ears, the back of her knees, the parts he seldom touches. 'Ellie, you have to get better.'

She moans and turns to him. 'I will,' she says, 'I will. As soon as this headache goes I'll come down and work with you.' Her voice is tremulous, high.

'You will?' He clutches at her words, imagines that they might be true.

'All this death,' she says, 'I won't be part of it. I won't be part of his empire. I'm stronger.'

He wraps his arms around her, holds her, knowing he can't and won't let go. She begins to snore, gently, breathlessly. She turns and twists, as though his arms impede her sleep, and he releases her. She needs rest. He pulls down the bedcover a little, kisses her forehead, and rolls over on his back.

★ ★ ★

He drifts into sleep. Despite the anxiety, which he feels in every part of his body, and overruling the sound and feel of the onrushing flames, he succumbs to the tiredness.

After all the cleaning, the repeated scrubbing, the tidying of the house and shop, the retidying, the incessant working. After all of the silence, all of the turning inwards. After the shock, the refusal to believe that he was dead. After the crying, the rage, the burying herself in shadow, not coming out, not wanting to come out. After sitting at the bottom of a well, in the darkness, for so long that the brickwork in the well became visible. After the first few stumbling words, in a tongue that no longer felt comfortable. After lifting her eyes and looking directly at him for the first time in so long that she was surprised at what he looked like. After thinking, he's handsome, I forgot him. After trying to work again, scrubbing the floors, whitewashing the walls, polishing the furniture, and discovering that it no longer worked, that the memory was still there, still present in her mind, intently observing her. After learning that she could live with it, if barely. After accepting that she could be present, some of the time, speak, some of the time, listen, some of the time, feel, some of the time, touch, some of the time, hold, some of the time.

After all this, some of which he observed and understood, and much of which he did not, and guessed or heard her try falteringly to explain, she appeared again, and he sees her, and he sees that she sees him. They are standing on opposite sides of the press. John Smith is in the city, on an errand to borrow a tray of Hebrew type, which James refuses to buy and uses only reluctantly and in small quantities because he cannot read the characters and is prone to introduce errors. He catches her looking directly at him.

'Is the ink running out?' he asks.

'No it's not that.'

He stares for a moment, puzzled.

'Do you want to carry on working?'

'No,' she says. 'I'd like to go out.'

He hasn't heard this for a long time, not since before.

'You mean for a walk?'

'Yes, exactly that.'

He is apprehensive, and has to push back the rush of happiness in case it's a will-of-the-wisp.

They put on coats and scarves. A fire blazes in the shop, as it's cold outside and has been for weeks. Christmas has come and gone, ignored. A new year beckons, uninviting and unwelcome. They step outside and the cold strikes them without remorse or remission. It bites and stings. At least the wind that's rattled the door and fretted the roof tiles has died. They have to steady themselves against the shock, which takes away their lungs, pinions them, and brace themselves before they start to walk.

She leads him, through Aldersgate and down the graceful strait of St Martin's Lane, past St Michael Le Querne, so all the while they can see ahead of them St Paul's, towering ever higher, a north star for the walking Londoner. The moment she sees St Paul's, something stirs in her and she takes his hand, fumblingly, as though she's forgotten how they do it, how their arms latch. Now he can detect how she's feeling by the way she squeezes his hand. A little pressure here as they turn onto Old Change, because she remembers something, how they walked here one day, before she was pregnant, in the spring. She tilts her wrist as they turn onto Knightrider Street, a little more bustle here, and pass St Nicholas Cole Abbey, before finally heading down Old Fish

Street Hill, from which they see what he knows to be her destination: the river.

They walk east along the river, traversing the wharves where they can, keeping as close to the water as possible. The water is quiet and still, without traffic, without even the watermen ferrying passengers from bank to bank. The Thames has frozen, its surface a crazed and hazy mirror, reflecting clouds and heavens in a pale shadow. As they cross the Vintry and approach the bridge they see something new. People are walking on the water. Children run and glide over it, on their feet and knees. One man pulls a small sled by a rope, while a woman and a child sit on it, huddled for warmth. There, a sight he thought he'd never see, a man leads a horse across the frozen Thames, an apprehensive horse that balks at the notion of walking over slippery, shiny water, and dislikes the feel of ice under its hooves, while its elongated shadow ripples over surface, stretched to a giant's proportions.

'Let's go,' she says excitedly, and she pulls him into a run until they find steps that will take them to the ice. These they descend gingerly, holding onto the sides, until they stand on the first step that rises above the ice. She's laughing, he's caught it too, while still worried that her laughter will turn to tears. They pause and look at each other, momentarily apprehensive about committing themselves to the wonder of ice of unknown thickness. Then, together, they step out. He almost slips, letting go of her hand, then recovers. Hand in hand they walk out and east, towards the shadow of the bridge's arches. She's laughing at others who find unsure footing in trying to cross the river, at the sheer miraculousness of such a frozen expanse, the unfamiliar made so alien. Then she falls and her eyes are wide with surprise. She pushes him and he falls, he gets up and they try to run, hectic, slipping and skating, until they are between the piers supporting a middle arch. Here they are alone, unseen, and something he doesn't know about or understand causes her to cling to him and bury her head in his shoulder. He thinks she's sobbing, but he lifts her head, and, though her eyes are red, she's not, at least she doesn't seem to be. She kisses him then, and they kiss like they haven't for a long time, he can't remember how long. Lips sting in the cold, and they keep on kissing.

On the ice memories return, unfrozen after too long, and these memories are almost perfect, but disconnected from the time they happened. Little structures are preserved in place, while the greater ones are lost in the flow of meltwater.

They walk back, until they no longer trust the ice and take to the stairs. Their hands, her left, his right, are frozen now. It's too cold out here, and they're tired and content but also a little sad. He doesn't know why he feels this, perhaps it's for the time they've lost, perhaps because he has had an insight into her sadness. He feels cracks running through his chest. He wonders, for a moment, if it's not only Ellie who has been closed off from the world. Have his own tears been stopped, frozen in place and time until it seems possible to thaw? This passing thought opens up a new window into Ellie's suffering, into her privation and desolation, and this pierces deep, and so as soon as he thinks it he is again focussed on her, how close she was to breaking, how much he needs her, and how he must keep her together in order to save himself.

And she is now back with him, and he is happy. He must hold this a little longer, and not breathe too heavily, never trust in providence, and never take anything for granted. They walk home, find the fire still burning, and the printing room embraces them. Its warmth is a promise of thawing. The skin of their hands and faces stings as the numbness dissipates. After taking off their coats they hold each other a while. He thinks, but does not say: after weeks and months of grief, the skin's grown hard and calloused, but we peel off our skin and are more than naked.

★ ★ ★

He wakes, though he thinks this dream is no more or less than a memory of what happened, and he doubts whether he was just now asleep. He washes Ellie's sleeping face with a damp cloth, and listens to her moan. Then he goes downstairs to set type. He doesn't know the time. His head spins, his insides churn with uncertainty and distress, he grieves that he is not in more pain because the suffering would give him greater certainty, or at least cloud out his fears.

Finding Eagle's manuscript, he sits on a stool at the composing table and locates the places he needs, which will make pages eleven, ten, fifteen and fourteen, all on the final forme. He starts with eleven, starting to fill a rule with pieces of type. For all he tries to block out the meaning of Eagle's words, to turn them into black shapes seeping across a white page, it sits there, impressing itself upon him. The light that burns brightly cannot be excluded, not even by the tightest shutters, or the hardest heart. The truth will remain the truth even when trampled on; in fact, like thyme, it will grow back more flourishingly. The prophet cannot be silenced, for even his silence speaks. Judgement cannot be averted, because everything ultimately serves it. Eagle's words beat into him, through the aching in his head, lead letters hammering into tin.

He works, and can feel the flames approaching, destruction blowing west across the city, heading his way.

CHAPTER TWENTY-FOUR

S ome hours later the noise of the flames inside his head is too much. He has composed the type for two pages, and is some way down the third. It is mechanical work, and his internal mechanisms are disordered, so he knows that there may be many errors in what he has done. He has tried to let the work shut out the sound of the city burning, but it will no longer do this.

He reaches out with his mind, but something blocks him, impedes his connection, his union with the city. Have his fears for Ellie broken something? Then he wonders if it's the city that's broken, if all of this obliteration has taken it away from him, or if the human suffering and distress, the cauterised sensations, the rack, the grief and loss, all centred in so small a place, have stopped all meaningful communication. As though the city's confusion mirrors his own disorder. And he considers all of these possibilities together and he is even more confounded.

I have to go out, he says to himself. Then he says it aloud, to Tobias, 'I have to go out. I have to go and see it for myself.'

But first he must check on Ellie. She's asleep but restless, turning, moaning. He doesn't want to wake her, though he would like to tell her that he is going out, that Tobias will be watching over her. But she is resting, he tells himself. He kisses her forehead and it burns his lips. He pulls down the covers a little, but she pulls them up and mutters something he can't understand. He says nothing. What more can he say to her? So much left unsaid, but there aren't words for those things, and he's struggling to find words anyway these days, words choke in him, or the wrong words come out, words that sound like the right ones but mean something completely different. She knows it anyway, he thinks, she knows it all. This was how they fell in love, they felt the same things, so he knew how she felt and she knew how he felt, and so there was trust and understanding. He would like to say something but all the words he can find are crushed under the weight of what he can't put into words.

He leaves her, puts on his coat, and walks towards the small gate through the ditch and wall, on to the gravel path.

★ ★ ★

Her body is a cauldron from which her consciousness barely emerges. When they escape, her thoughts have only a passing purchase on the world, they are mayflies in the breeze with transparent wings. They are day lilies, budding, blooming and falling in a single movement. She tries to hold them together in a garland but the petals droop and wither in her hands. Then they plunge with the mayflies and disappear into the agony that is almost all that's left of her.

She remembers walking on the ice in wonder, thinking that this must be how angels fly, as though the air on which they glide is solid. The ice transforms her body, making it as light as air so she can walk across the water. The miraculous transvection, conveying her from the bank to the middle of the bridge, is also how she imagines flying because it changes the light. Light strikes her from all around, and it is airier, shining through her. The only thing holding her to the ground is James, and he is corporeal, and she loves him for it.

She remembers when English became a foreign tongue again, walking back along the same path she'd walked for years, reversing the doubtful progress. The fortifications of Welsh surrounding her, the consonants too hard for the English. There she could shelter and hide when the wrong questions were asked. Her grief was protected by her tongue, and this same shield defended her from her own grief. People never understood when to stop, except when they stopped coming and stopped caring. And at some point the English came back and dominated her again.

And the printing. Days and years of printing, but especially in the latter days, and not only because she'd grown better at it, but also because the work had brought new meanings with it. She was making things. Things that would last. The paper, soft and strong to touch, would last years, decades. It might even outlive her if someone looked after it. Caring for it was simple: do nothing and it would survive. As long as it wasn't too wet or too hot. The books could sit on shelves, neglected, and live. Best untouched. She had learned how to make something, unfamiliar words in writing she'd recently learned to read, sealed in ink on paper and bound, something that would last.

And she remembers the cleaning. Sweeping, scrubbing, scouring, polishing. Chasing after every trace of dust and dirt. Because when she saw the dirt around her it crept inside her and contaminated everything. She felt defiled. Whatever had taken him from her, she knew, might lie out here, in some infection in the air or walls or floor. In some almost invisible putrefaction. And if it did, then it was her fault. And this was her penance, to clean, to scour and scrub, too late. If she could rid the house and all it contained of any trace of uncleanness, then she would be purified inside. And then, and only then, perhaps it would all stop.

She crushed his hand, she remembers that, when they lowered the coffin. As if that would transfer some of her pain, or make her wake from a terrible dream. The coffin was tiny, weighed nothing. Gelert and the corn dolly keep him company. He throws on some soil, she does too. The prayers are jumbled. She remembers desolation, masking the fear and grief that lie behind. Not saying goodbye, not having been there, the doubt over whether he called out for her, the terror of her not responding, the loneliest last moments, all in her mind, which can only conjure these moments, because in truth she knows nothing, only the outcome, this narrow coffin under a layer of dirt. She rubs her palm with her nail until it's chafed, which helps a little. It blocks out the parade of mourners, all seeking to comfort, none able to say a single thing that consoled her. Their pity is full of her terror, perhaps theirs too. There is a dry-stone wall between them. She crushed his hand, but it wasn't really his, he isn't really there. Something is broken.

He was standing in the doorway, a silhouette, a little breathless. She was in the printing room, by the hearth, rocking Jeremiah, who was asleep. She needed the fire, not just because it was cold but because there had been rainstorms, and everything seemed damp, especially her bones. She'd been colder since he was born. She was tired of the kitchen, so she sat in the printing room instead. The book beside her rested untouched. As her eyes adapted to the light of the open doorway she saw that he was holding something. He sauntered to where she sat, and from his manner she could see that he was proud. 'This is for you, Jeremiah,' he said, holding up a pale human figure a little smaller than his hand. He was smiling, and it was a different kind of smile, as if father had been added to husband. She felt tears. She asked what it was, and he told her it was a corn dolly. She knew them from before, but they were different on the Black Mountains. This one had plaited hair and a skirt. She tried to look more closely, as he held it above Jeremiah's cot. He made a little noise, as if the dolly was shuffling through the grass and singing. The incipient tears disappeared, and it made her laugh to see the child in him. And the strangest thing happened. The baby smiled, as if he understood the game. A tiny baby smiling at his father. He reached for the dolly, and she thought, he's too young to do that, he's just a tiny baby. So tiny. The big, sparkling eyes are unseeing. 'Is it too sharp? Will he scratch his face?' she asked. Then she felt guilty, because she saw that he hesitated. He nodded, but she knew he hadn't thought of the risk. She didn't want to sound like his mother. She wishes that she'd explained, about legs scratched from running through uncut cornfields in Crickhowell, and her mother cleaning the blood from them, and telling her that she should be more careful, but she didn't say anything, and she watched him check the dolly for points and sharp edges. She wants to say that she's sorry.

Her dream carries her to Aunt Rosie, who had moved to Llangattock to marry a shepherd. Rosie taught her to knit, when she visited her sister, Ellie's mother. Ellie's mother could knit too, but Aunt Rosie was a more patient tutor. They said she had been wooed by a poet from Llangattock, but had chosen an illiterate shepherd instead, though one who, like the poet, lived across the bridge. Ellie sat with her woven knitting basket, a bag of needles, a fat ball of wool that she'd carded and spun herself. Ellie squeezed it, and couldn't believe how soft it had become since leaving the sheep's back. Rosie taught her how to add loops to the needle, to make row after row, to close the stitches. She made a doll under her aunt's eye. A ribbon made the neck, a button in the middle of the chest dressed it. And then she knitted other more ambitious things. Decades later she finds herself uncovering this latent knowledge, remembering how Rosie had helped her knit a dog, like the sheepdog on the flagstones. Rosie had been so clever; she can't recall what happened to her, though in her dream she thinks she died. Now, with him across her belly, she knits a second dog, and she wants to call it Rosie, but she remembers the legend of the dog Gelert, who protects a child from a wolf. Rosie will live in the making of the toy, though not in the name. It's a sad story, though, because prince Llewelyn sees only the blood and that his son is missing, so he kills Gelert before finding that the dog has saved the child and killed the wolf. The blood is the wolf's. In her dream she stands there, wishing she could tell Llewelyn, and every other person, to search the room before blaming the dog. When she finished the dog, though, she felt proud, and sees Rosie telling her that she's a clever girl, and a spark from the fire flies over the hill and through time.

Next, and before that, there's the birth. On her knees, with her bottom in the air, trying to hold the pain back with the fragile defence of a breath. She doesn't remember where James was, perhaps in the doorway after Mistress Grey had tried to shoo him out. Grey wiped her with a warm cloth, and said something indistinct. 'Say that again,' and Grey repeated herself, but she still couldn't understand. Then the pain surges over the breath, flattening it. She feels like she's going to tear. And then Grey was shouting at her to push, and it hurt too much, she thought she'd be submerged under it all, the pain and noise and the fear, but then there was a moment of relief, just a fraction, and it gave her some hope. And much of this is forgotten and it won't even come back in her dreams, but then there's a time when she's lying in bed, and Jeremiah, wrapped in a blanket, is at her breast. She is wiping the baby's head with a warm damp cloth, washing the mucus from the matted black hair. James lies beside her, holding her, trying to find his way back in. The pain still pulsed on, though, refusing to let her go. When it did, there was still the emptiness, the ghost of something hardly there, and she felt that she preferred it when there was a little pain. When he was fixed on her breast the sense of lack disappeared, but her love was so fierce and all-consuming that she worried they weren't connected all the time.

She thinks of herself as a fruit, because he joked that she was like an apple, flushed and round, but she holds her belly, feels the heat and the subtle, stirring movements, and it's as though no one else is there.

She was under water only a few seconds, she thinks, not long enough to die and be reborn. She dreams that she swam away, along the Thames, to Gravesend, and saw the community of the dead living there, living after their own manner, in a solemn procession of days. They wear rags, and communicate by movement rather than words, though their faces are all bone and they have no eyes. There are babies among them. They sit in rooms under the shadow of the riverbank and dine together on passing fish.

Then her dreams take her to the preachers who brought her to the dipping. They take her to her appetite for preachers, and it was an appetite, and the more she heard the more she understood that there was more to hear, so that feeding made her hungry. There had been so little of this in Brecknock, with so few visitors. In her dream she can walk to hear whatever she wants, she only has to hear the rumour of a good speaker and she's there. She moves by magic. Each one gives her a piece of wood. She collects them all in a bag, and when the last word has been spoken, and she returns home with a full bag, she sits there with the pieces. By the time the sun is rising she has solved the puzzle by putting the pieces of wood together. They form a chair, which she assembles, knocking the dowels into holes. She sits on the chair and looks back over the day, and she wonders: why did I hear no women speak?

And the only woman to speak in the dream of her wedding is her. She says her vow. In the dream the vow she speaks is her own, not the one prescribed by the church, but one that says what she feels, makes promises that are deep and rich, words of endearment and commitment that reverberate along the rivers and over the hills, all the way home. The audience isn't sitting in the pews, but hears long before and long after.

The ring newly placed upon her finger after these words takes her back to the first ring, the one that tells her that love is as strong as death, though as her life ebbs away this is a hard fact to hold onto. Sometimes she wishes she'd just said yes right away, but then she remembers that all the questions she asked were the right ones and they set her on a path that led to times that had some sadness but were much richer with things that were real, not imagined or dreamed, things that made her apprehend the world around her and love it dearly, even if they were also insubstantial. And in her dream she asks herself, but is it true, isn't it even stronger?

And she looks at the first ring and reads the poesy, and it says that love is stronger than death. She knows this because he's taught her the letters and how to join them. They sit at the kitchen table in the old house, which she never really liked, and she spells them out with a hornbook. He keeps on having to tell her that the letters make the sounds, but often the sounds they make change, so there's no sense in the whole. She breathes and reads nursery rhymes that sound all wrong. He did this before asking her to marry him, as though he always knew. She wonders if she knew as early.

It's Sarah Cooper who appears next. Well-meaning and usually kind, if always a little interested in herself. She leads her to a crossroads west of the city and points to the road she must follow. Sarah hugs her and gives her a penny when she sets off. She heads west, on the road home, as she has to see home one last time before this is all done. And as she walks the skies turn grey-blue and the fields even greener.

By the side of the road there are places she thinks she recognises, houses where she might have been, but she doesn't need to visit them again, nor speak to anyone in them.

And then she's back in Crickhowell, and it seems like such a short walk, and it was never so easy to climb the mountain. Her legs are light, but it's when she sees the front door of her house that the weight comes, and it's in her chest rather than her legs. She walks through, and there's her father, and they say goodbye, and he heads out into the fields, where he has to cut back the hedges, and she goes upstairs to say goodbye to her mother, who's lying there, dead, with the baby in her arms. She walks over and licks the smear of blood from her mother's breast. She wants her mother pristine, but if she's honest with herself she misses the breast where her brother sucks. She loves William, and won't begrudge him the nipple, but sometimes she feels sorry for herself, and then a little guilty for feeling sorry for herself. She climbs into bed with her dead mother and her brother, and closes her eyes.

When something stirs she opens them, and her mother has wrapped her arms around her. The smile is pure April generosity, and for a moment she remembers a shut-off part of her life. A liquorice part, warm and protected, with the two of them, pregnant with hope, buried in warmth. But it doesn't last long, because her mother looks over and the baby is dead. She freezes, and is lost to Ellie.

She runs to get away from this. She runs over the mountains. Through hay and grass, with or without cuts on her shins and ankles. She loves running because it is freedom, it defies the landscape and tames it, and because she knows how to do it, knows where to place her feet, when to lean into the stride, when to raise her arms. She doesn't know how she knows, but she knows that she can outrun not only Iolo Morgan but any child near her age, because her feet defy the weight of the earth, just as angels do, just as the skater confounds water.

And in her dream she runs over every hill and mountain of the Beacons, and they're all hers, and perhaps there is some truth in the story that her family are descended from a Welsh prince. Here her shins are never bloodied, she glides, she flies with impunity. Her body is back where it was when she was older, old even, it's hers.

There is a bird sitting on a tree behind a dry-stone wall, *cornicyll*, lapwing in English, she thinks, her adult brain interprets, though she's unsure. It whistles from its throat, two rising calls and an intricate trill. She doesn't move, because she wants it to carry on singing. She will try to imitate it later. It flaps its wings, then stays. She drops to the grass. She lies splayed out, holding the earth, and it's hers, and she is hers. This is the place she was looking for, this and the wide bed. The two goodbyes fold into one, and he's there, in everything. And she thinks yes, this is who I was, yes.

CHAPTER TWENTY-FIVE

James is standing at Paul's cross and it unfolds before his eyes. The warm wind blows in from the east, bringing the flames before it. It's evening; his hunger and the descent of the sun tells him this, because all other measures have been dislodged.

He sees Miller and approaches him.

'Christ's blood. Christ's blood. Christ's blood,' the bookseller effuses.

'Do you think it's going to happen?'

They watch sparks cross the air high above the wide empty square that surrounds Paul's. Miller nods grimly.

'I can't imagine it. Now I have to. I stored my books there, to keep them safe.'

'What?' James asks incredulously.

'A lot of us did. In the crypt. The fire can't reach them there, we thought. It's so far away, and there's a break between all the buildings. And the crypt should be deep enough. But now I wonder. It's like the fire's moving with a sense of purpose.'

'All of your stock?'

'Most of it, yes. The rest waits for the fire there,' and he nods towards Ave Maria Lane. James sighs.

'When will this end?'

There's no reply, but he is suddenly distracted when across the piazza he spies Eagle, running with a pile of papers to the west doors. That's it: he doesn't see him again, but his mind piles up with questions.

'Do you think St Paul's will burn?' Miller asks.

He looks inside himself and considers, and then he realises he knows. He is the city, and the city is him, and Paul's will burn. He will burn, because once you've measured the merchants and the lawyers and the politicians, then St Paul's still towers above them all, and it is his heart and mind. He will destroy the city, and unwillingly ruin the livelihood of Miller and others, and then the city will rise again, slowly. Perhaps no one will know that it was his fault.

He wonders: I'll die with the city, but how? Will it be the plague or the fire? I can't rush into the flames, because that would be self-murder. It will be the plague. It has to be the plague. His brain is wide open again, and he feels the destruction east and south, and he begins to burn inside, and he thinks about the pact he made in this very building, and he feels a comfort and he knows that Paul's will burn.

He forgets Miller and walks towards the cathedral. There should be some goodbyes here. He wants to go inside, but when he tries to enter a beadle stops him, blunt and wordless. But this is mine, he wants to say, this is me. He knows it would not be understood. And the beadle has real fear in his eyes, so he doesn't want to speak with him. The creaking and the crackles rise.

He doesn't have to look, he can feel the fire devour his body, that it's passing along Watling Street and has crossed Old Change, and the backs of the buildings there are on fire. He feels it rolling over him, and the air is now like a night sky full of stars, but the stars are burning cinders and ash, drifting through the space between the buildings, now brighter, now darker, rich with uncertainty and peril.

He walks around Paul's. The repairs have crept for years, with scant and only occasional progress. The scaffolding forms a squat carapace. It holds the crumbling building together, keeps the walls and what's left of the tower in place. So it contains, supports, and provides access to the upper levels, all at the same time. He could climb it if he wanted, perhaps up to the roof, and see the city from there. It looks flimsy, he thinks, wood supporting stone. How can that make sense? As though a vine could support a tree. Resting his hand on the scaffold he feels the woodworm inside, thriving after a dry, warm summer. The wood vibrates with their slow devouring, as though they're singing, their tune in a different time from human music. How could anyone think that anything will last forever?

The upper parts of the scaffolding are on fire. He feels it before he sees it, registers it in his hand and in his senses. Flames split the sky, high above his head. Then flames curl up from the arched windows in the tower, licking the stone. The fire begins in the middle, spreads towards both east and west ends. He watches it from below, a firmament of flame. Then a board falls from up high, and crashes into the cobbles near him, sending charcoal and cinders everywhere. He runs to the far side of the square and watches. The flames rip across the scaffolding, roaring like an injured, incensed animal. The heat ruins his vision, and he doesn't know if he's watching with his eyes or his mind. The flames move like a salamander, crawling purposefully, licking, sometimes flickering, sometimes holding steady, but always encroaching. At first he thinks the building will resist, that the scaffolding will burn and fall away and the stone remain. But then he sees that the fire is within too, and that the whole frame is in jeopardy, is being consumed by the salamander.

Something crashes near him, grazing his shoulder. It's a flaming beam from the building behind him. He's hot, but he's so used to being too hot that he's hardly noticed that he's almost surrounded by the fire. He spins and doesn't know which way to flee.

He runs to the west end, towards Stationers' Hall, to the Atrium before St Paul's, and to the tree that stands there, where he takes shelter. The heat is less intense here, but the hot ash still showers down on the gathering crowd. He sees other booksellers he knows, standing rapt before the spectacle of woe and destruction. They lose sight of the danger they're in, because devastation, force and violence are spellbinding.

With a thunderous crack, the scaffolding on the south side of Paul's collapses, sending a flurry of embers against the fronts of the row of facing buildings, the east end of which is now already ablaze. They rebound in a wave that sprawls upward, swirls, and disperses into the air before spiralling down again.

Some land in his tree. He smells the charring. The air is congealed with smoke, he can't breathe, he coughs. He doesn't want to leave though, he needs to witness this. This is a kind of testimony. Paul's will fall, and then London will have fallen, and then it will all be over, and he will have witnessed it.

But now the tree's on fire, and he has to retreat from the heat and flames, back towards Ave Maria Lane. The booksellers do the same, withdraw towards their homes, where they feel safe, though all know that their homes aren't safe. This is the reckoning. They debased their art, he thinks, they made printing merely mechanical, they made pamphlets and abandoned poetry. Now all the pamphlets will burn.

So it is at the top of Ludgate Hill that he stands, at the intersection with Ave Maria Lane, directly facing the doors of Paul's, with the perfect view of the church as the salamander crawls over its walls and roof and turns it all to the element of fire. At one point the beast raises its head and looks him in the eye. He returns the gaze. I know you, the salamander's eyes say. And then it turns back to its prey and continues to devour it.

He thinks of himself and Ellie, of what it means to love, to be in love, and lose yourself in the thoughts and feelings of another, to burn inside rather than let them go, to sacrifice your life because it seems the better course. Fire is stronger than the most ancient, most ambitious tower. He touches his ring to remind himself that she is there and he is here.

He watches the lead of the roof liquify, trickle down the walls in molten globs, and drop to the floor. Glass explodes and shards plummet, but the noise is drowned out by the crackling jaws. Pictures of apostles and of saints flash into a thousand coloured fragments. The beast shifts and the remaining planks of scaffolding tumble. The tower crumbles and charred lumps crash into the upright structure. The frame holds, but the scorched walls decay and totter, leaving only a skeleton with an agonised rictus. Now he cannot distinguish between the fire and the building, between the skeleton and the salamander.

St Paul's is gone. London's haughtiest, most imperious,

most heavenly work has transmuted into a single flame, in which he can catch only glimpses of wall, buttress, shattered bone. At last it's his turn. His mind boiling, he can go home and die of the plague.

He hasn't reckoned how fierce the flames were, even at a distance. The trance partially broken, he steps back and realises that his skin is burning, his body parched from exposure to the heat. His head spins and there isn't enough air. He coughs as he retreats up Ave Maria Lane and Warwick Lane, past Christ Church and Hospital to the gravel path and the small gate in the wall. The streets are littered with ash, the sky dark with smoke. He coughs, then breathes, then coughs, alternating unstoppably, passing through the gate, over the ditch and into Farringdon Without the Wall. There the air is a little clearer, and he bends double, hands on knees, trying to catch his breath. The space around him is closing in, his eyes fading. Not here. He wants to die in his own bed. He manages to regain his feet and stands upright as the dry air swirls around him, confounding his balance. He finds the shop, stopping only once more to lean against a tree, and at last enters his home. Tobias is sleeping at the foot of the stairs.

'What's wrong, Tobias?'

The dog raises his head listlessly, looks at him, then curls up again.

He stumbles to the kitchen and drinks three cups of small beer. He retches, coughs up some thick, black phlegm into the sink. He washes his face with cold water. Its bite restores him a little, his vision opens up, his mind settles, cools, focusses on what's next: his death. He will at last let the plague rip through his body. Eagle's pamphlet will go unfinished. Perhaps Ellie will be able finish it, in a rush of grief, as happened before. But watching Paul's burn has told him that his days are over, that he's as a man already dead. He must resign himself to it. Paul's was all that was left of his heart, his spirit, his resilience.

He goes upstairs, carrying a tallow candle, already the shell of a human. Tobias stirs a little. Does he know what's happening?

The bedroom is dark, and he brings the odour of smoke with him. He throws his outer clothes onto the landing outside, because of the acrid smell. It will be bad enough with just the air creeping around the windows. Ellie does not stir. He will lie beside her and give in. Perhaps that will help revive her: as one falls the other rises. He hopes she does not mind that he chooses to die here, in their wide bed, that the shock when she wakes will not be too great. After all, she must know, must comprehend what is happening. Perhaps he should have told her about the covenant, though on the whole he is glad that he did not, because he would rather that she blamed God than blamed him.

The candle scatters only a sparse light. He places it on the little table on his side. Her illuminated face is still, like marble, rare, like her thoughts, immaculate. He pulls back the bed covers, blows out the candle, and climbs in beside her, wrapping his arm around her chest to pull her to him, wanting to whisper in her ear, whether she hears him or not, how sorry he is to leave her, how she was the only thing that mattered to him, how she had made the world make sense, made it new and old. But as he wraps his arm around her chest he feels that she is cold, lifeless and cold.

CHAPTER TWENTY-SIX

There is a night of grief and terror. He holds her body and lies awake, remembering. He tries to recall each and all the days in order as they passed. The first time he saw her in the churchyard. The second time, when they went for a walk on a Sunday. The third, and fourth times. He tries to arrange every day in succession. The early ones he can locate; the most recent ones too. Some days are easier to remember than others, some easier to place in time. Many are missing, he can tell, lost in the years. Six good years, not enough. Two thousand days, and he can't even remember all of them. He is frightened that he will forget more of them, that the memories will slip and he won't be able to bring them back. Like dreams in the morning.

She is dead, and he's realised that he's not going to die, not yet, that the plague has abated and he'll recover.

Around the time of the first birdsong, more subdued this morning as most birds have fled the fire, he falls asleep. He wakes and she is still dead. He drifts away again. He tries to find her in his dreams, but she's not there. The streets are empty, most of the buildings razed, ruined. Some are shells, their insides ripped through, others are piles of smouldering timber and the detritus of lives that could not be carried away. He looks through the streets, but can't find her. He wakes and she is still dead. It is light outside, the shutters tell him. He is dried up inside, parched, desiccated.

He has to pass water, so he gets out of bed and uses the chamber pot. He looks at her. She seems at peace, lying on her back, tranquil, an untroubled expression on her face. No creases of concern. He wonders whether she was asleep when she died. What was she dreaming?

251

He's uncertain, and he stares at her for a while, then decides that it will do no harm if he goes downstairs. Tobias, lying at the foot of the stairs, looks up with weary eyes. He understands. The dog follows him to the kitchen, and he gives him another bone before pouring himself a small beer. They stand together in the street in front of the shop. He has recovered from the plague. The buboes are now hard, lumpy scars, but no more.

The fire has spread further than he imagined. How long was he in bed? It's travelled far west of the wall, over the River Fleet. Judging by where he sees the smoke, he thinks it's marched along Fleet Street, perhaps over Shoe Lane. The Bishop of Salisbury's residence, an ample court along the river, may have been overrun. While he lay with Ellie, awake and dreaming, the fire moved relentlessly. And still it moves, and it is approaching him, steadily encroaching on that part of the city wall that is only a few minutes' walk from where he stands. The smoke rises over the wall, curls, licks the air, drops.

He drinks. 'It's coming for us, Tobias.' The dog has carried the bone with him, deposited it on the floor, and now gnaws it. 'What shall we do? What shall we do about Ellie?'

He is not yet ready to part with her.

He tries to breathe, but it's still hard because of the smoke. He goes back inside, Tobias following. He sees on the table the pages of type he has been composing, and sits in front of them. He remembers. He was working on the fourth forme before he went out to investigate the progress of the fire. That was yesterday, but it seems like a lifetime ago.

Something is wrong. He knows this. He is empty, broken, but the grief is stuck there in his head, making him dizzy, as though there's no air. Immobile, charred. There is no present, only a sideways glance at the past. He breathes and it does no good. He grabs a handful of type and turns the pieces around in his fist, feeling the weight of the lead. It doesn't help. He puts them back in the composing tray. He looks at the typeset page he was work-ing on, the third of the four in the forme. Eagle's manuscript is there in front of him. He looks at the first word of the next line and, without really thinking, adds the letters to the slide. When the slide is full and the line done, he transfers it onto the bed and fits it tightly underneath the previous line. He builds the rest of the page, character by character. There's no mind involved. His thoughts spool out silently, without touching the world.

But words leap out at him, goading him, like demons' spikes in hell. Raised, forgiveness, fire and brimstone, whipped, putrefaction, deprived, whipped. Eagle's vocabulary is choice, and it stings. The dark iniquity of solitude.

Until she comes.

He hears her voice in his head, as clear as if it really is her voice, and she is full of hope and grief and remorse, and she is saying that he's alive, full of life, she says this from the grave, or from the underworld, she says that even when things are awful he keeps on going, keeps holding things together, she praises him, because he always does that, always bears adversity, offers forgiveness, and because when Jeremiah ripped him apart he just bore it and worried about her instead, while she lay there, lifeless, unable to move, as if it wasn't his grief, his loss, too.

The voice is so real he is confounded. She's alive, he thinks, and he runs upstairs. She's there, frozen in the moment of her death. Her face is perfect, but immobile. She's not speaking. The voice is in his head, and still he hears it there, and it's saying, you held all those things together while you were broken, and instead you worried about me. And he hears himself saying back, you know it's not true, I was just doing what I had to, you were the one who bore all the grief and all the mourning. All I had to do was stand upright. And he hears her say, but you didn't get to grieve and mourn, and it wasn't right, you just made it easier for me, and now you're stuck. And he says, you're right, I am, I am stuck.

He kneels by the big bed, beside her, takes her hand and rests his forehead on her face, and it doesn't feel right because she's cold, and he can tell that she's not really there, but this is the closest he can have to a connection with her, so he lies there and waits for the grief to come. It doesn't. There must be a path he can take, there must be a way to say goodbye and feel the separation and the end of things and keep on living. But he can't see it now. There are no tears.

If he goes back downstairs he can carry on as though she's still here, sleeping, recovering from the plague. He'll sit with Tobias. So he goes downstairs again. Why does he no longer feel ill? Where is the fever, the aching, the pain in his armpits? There's only the dizziness now, an overwhelming brainsick confusion of understanding and sight. He sits back at the table. Her voice is still there in his head, a soft low voice with hard consonants, but sing-song. She says, it tore you apart and you're stuck. And now this, he says.

Without really thinking, he finishes the third page of the forme, and now on the bed of type there is a space to fill, the final quarter, before the forme is finished and ready for printing. So he turns in Eagle's manuscript to the final page he has to compose, which is page fourteen, the antepenultimate page of the pamphlet. Quickly he completes the first line, and slides it into place. Characters drive out words and voices. But then he begins to notice Eagle's words again. Combustion, depressed, inspired by voices, repentance, instruction, enlightened, dipping, darkness, consumed, prostration, cinders. Eagle chooses provoking words, they jostle and thrust. Cinders, fire and brimstone, loss, privation.

Tobias sits at his feet. As hard as he tries, he cannot imagine that she is alive again. She sits somewhere between life and death, in a netherworld from which he can't bring her back. A shade, a spectral presence, an absence from this world and from his body. He thinks of her face, made thinner, lighter, drawn, by the loss of her soul. As if she breathed her soul out, and the body became less material by it. He wonders if she drifted peacefully into death, or if she cried out in pain, while he was away from her, watching Paul's burn. And then he sees it: that's when she died. He thought it was he who died with Paul's, but in fact it was her. That was the loss and omission, that was his misdeed, his distance, his faithlessness.

He composes line after line, caught between Eagle's

provoking words and the voices in his head. He thinks that some-times he inadvertently puts those voices, rather than Eagle's writing, into the letters on his slide. He composes quickly, line after line, and soon the final line is ready. He pushes it into place. Then he inserts, below the final line of text, the page number and the catchword, which indicates what the first word of the next page will be. The catchword on this page is 'unravel'. He fills the empty space, inserts the quoins and wedges, and ties the whole tight. The composing is done, only the presswork remains. He carries the set forme to the press and positions it squarely, careful not to disturb it. He checks it is tight one more time.

He doesn't know if it is early, or the middle or the end of the day. Time has disappeared into the gulf between the world and his thoughts. He won't contemplate doing the printing now; he must stop for a while. He can't eat, but fetches a cup of small beer. Each step he takes, he's aware of her lying upstairs, there but not present.

'Bring your bone, Tobias.'

He opens the door, and it's there, immediately, the fire. Right in front of him, just over the wall. They stand in the street, in their usual spot, but now the sky, the horizon, the presence of the city is unimportant. Now there is only the fire. It is coming for him, and quickly. Flames rise from rooftops, shaking build-ings to the ground, visible over the top of the high city wall. Above them great swirls of eddying smoke, peppered with black fragments of ash and red-hot sparks, track the movements of the air. The warm wind blows towards him. He hears it devouring, the sharp crack of bones, the grinding of the walls and doors and floors, the slow chewing of the broken, falling matter. It eats the streets noisily, and the creature is approaching. It towers above him, and brings death.

He will die with her after all.

And then it unwinds before him, he sees it: a life imperfectly lived. They walk on ice, and he sees another world underneath them, their own world inverted. They walk, glide, fall, and it makes them laugh, for the first time in months. They kiss between the arches. He is almost present. He wants her to stay like this, and worries that she might retreat again, disappear back to wherever she's been.

He remembers her slipping away from the present, the people around her, even from words, becoming once again uncomfortable in English. As though she was retreating, like Eurydice, into another world, not able to communicate with or reach her friends and neighbours. Neither understood the other, but it wasn't just because of language. He stood there, like Orpheus on the banks of the Styx, in the doorway, unable to bring her back, helpless.

And the compulsive ardour for work, for printing, even when his limbs ached. He remembers that time. They did some good work. Her reading was fluent, she helped him with the proofs. She laughed at the theology. He liked to study her as she inked the type, her hips especially. Sometimes he would watch her and be reminded of their lovemaking the night before, and he would involuntarily close his eyes and inhale sharply, dislodged from the moment and place he occupied, transported to somewhere in-between. She worked furiously, perfectly attentive to detail, and was closed to him, except sometimes when they woke at night.

And before that she cleaned. He would come in from his morning salutation to the dawn, and she would be on her hands and knees, scrubbing. The floor was clean before she started. Then she would continue with the kitchen. She would barely acknowledge him, not till they ate, when she would lift her eyes and say something about the food, or the work he was doing. They'd already stopped saying prayers aloud by then, preferring unspoken, informal prayers, direct from the heart. There was no dust, everything was in order. But there was nothing between them, just a fallen-down bridge.

He can barely see, ahead of him, the flames hurtling towards the wall and his printing shop, high and merciless and contemptuous of all obstruction. They don't concern him now.

It unwinds further, to the graveyard at St Bartholomew the

Less. He sees his hands, the dirt on them. He has just thrown a handful of soil on the coffin. Now he can feel it, loamy but pungent like vinegar, clinging to his fingers. She's there, but also not there, turned in. But he's turned in too, perhaps, sealed up with the coffin. He sees the body in there, Jeremiah's tiny body, swaddled with the corn dolly and the dog she knitted. She throws October flowers into the grave, orange buds wrapped in pink petals, spindle fruits he thinks. It's a shock when more dark soil lands on the bright colours. He fumbles around for her hand, and misses.

And then more passes before his eyes, a procession of days and pictures, and he sees mourners, Ellie in bed, and himself by Jeremiah's cot, sobbing. He is a man enclosed in a transparent carapace.

And then there's more light. It cracks through broken cloud and he's more frightened of this than of the gloom. The cracks are made by the reappearance, in his memories, as he unravels backwards, of Jeremiah. Being with Jeremiah makes him learn everything anew. He hears his voice differently. He learns to play. He remembers how to make a corn dolly, and the very idea of a corn dolly is reborn. He lies on the floor, holding the baby in the air above him, and moves him up and down, bringing their faces together then apart, and a line of saliva dribbles from the corner of Jeremiah's mouth onto his nose. He laughs, and it's a different kind of laugh. He hears himself laugh for the first time. And Ellie, he sees her hold him, and he lies next to them in the big bed, and there's something that wasn't there before, she's become a bigger person, incorporated more multitudes within her, so they're more than the three of them, and the light that breaks through the shutters reveals the sheer multiplicity and the magnitude of their togetherness.

Tobias barks. He looks down; Tobias looks up. The flames are coming. He feels the wind on his face. He stands firm. There's no need to change anything; he and Ellie are bound in this conclusion, and if Tobias wants to run then he should. But he looks at the approaching flames, and he stays because even though he knows that his God forbids it, he wants the fire to consume them.

And then there is the cleaning of the baby, the bathing, the feeding. The fear that comes from uncertainty, because they don't know what to do and they have to rely on the advice of others, especially Mistress Grey, but still they worry that what they do isn't right. And you'd think a baby would be simple, because so many generations have cared for babies, from their parents through their grandparents and their great-grandparents all the way back to Noah and Adam and Eve, it should be second nature, and something you just know, but it's not, and it's full of terror and apprehension with all of the beauty.

And then he arrives, as all his memories unravel, at that moment when he first lies beside her and Jeremiah. And it's at that point that the threads are loosened, all tension is gone, and the unspooling ends and the pressure releases. There he is, looking down at Jeremiah lying on her breast, sucking as she wipes the crown of his head. Her other nipple is the same, familiar, fat and proud, not yet transformed. Mistress Grey stands there, at the window, then turns her back, in tacit acceptance that this is their moment. He is the most perfect, most beautiful thing he's ever seen, except for his mother, but they make each other more beautiful, and in a way they're the same thing, a two made of one, or a three made of two, or a one made of three, a miracle of numbers. He is dumbfounded by what he's feeling, because there is a beauty in this moment that he cannot accommodate, and at the same time the moment contains the purest loss. He sees a scene that he knows is common, a family and childbirth, because people must reproduce and this is how it happens, but at the time it astonishes him to think that this moment was once his, that he was there, and that his heart was so full of love and splendour that he can't, and never could, put into words. He sees himself there, without the armour of his carapace, surprised and overtaken by happiness.

That's when he breaks. The tears come, and he doesn't recognise what they are. Whatever happened days ago, years ago, was only the mildest foreshadowing of this. The dam cracks. His eyes are wet, tears run down his face, leaving streaks in the grey deposits of smoke. His hands are shaking, he sees them and his whole body trembles with the quaking of unaccepted grief. All that's been accumulating is released, and the store is mountainous. He sees the flames coming towards the printing shop and he knows that there won't be time for all the tears he's hoarded to flow. He's howling too, in a voice he hardly recognises. No one will hear him over the crackle of flames. He puts his hands over his eyes to stop the tears, but the pressure's too great and they burst through anyway, prying between his fingers and running down his arms. He thinks they should evaporate in the heat, but instead they soak him, his skin, his shirt. He cries and it is a great roar of desolation.

There's scarcely space for a thought, but as he sees the advance of the flames, he finds just one to console himself with. At least the period of mourning will be brief. Soon he, Ellie, the printing shop and all their memories, will be eradicated. The flames will rush over them. All this love and grief will be reduced to ashes, and to three rings, together with an iron press, lying in the embers of a razed shop.

'Run, Tobias, run,' he says. Tobias disobeys, and lies down, disconsolately watching the fire.

He would say a prayer, but none comes. This is the risk of not praying with the formulae of set prayers. He wishes his prayerlessness concerned him more, but he is absorbed by the prospect of his imminent death, and the great store of grief, the grief of this world and this life, that it will carry away from him. He lies there with Ellie and Jeremiah in their big bed and knows the beauty, joy and loss, his final thought.

The ordinary workings of time abandon what happens next. He feels it in the tears that still run down his face. The wind changes, the warm wind that had been blowing from the east. It drops, stops. And the obedient flames follow. The conflagration that had been approaching, that was about to sweep over the city wall and consume him, instead hits the wall and dies. It rolls back, discouraged. The beast's roar is subdued. The inferno will progress no further. It will not pass Aldersgate, won't squeeze through wall and ditch. A boundary the length of four or five men from where he stands will be its terminus. Though not yet fully extinguished, it's defeated, attenuated. Like the plague, its threat has weakened, for those it's not already destroyed.

He watches it dampened and dispirited, and another thought creeps upon him, casting a new shadow upon the memory that he is holding onto, though by no means stopping the universal lament and the flow of his tears, and at first he doesn't have a name for that shadow, but then he looks within himself and he can see what it is, he knows that it is fear, a nauseating, over-whelming fear, and the fear that racks him, that shakes the tears onto the cobbles below, is the fear that he will, after all, live.

ACKNOWLEDGMENTS

ACKNOWLEDGEMENTS

While we endured the dense fog of long Covid, Georgina told me to embrace the moment and to take the time to write, and without her *All the Colours* would not exist. George Capel was full of kind praise and ensured it would be published. Thanks to Daniel Defoe, William Harrison Ainsworth and Ralph Agas, whose map of London, originally drawn in 1561, was invaluable when I followed James through the streets. There is a brilliant online edition of Agas' map < mapoflondon.uvic.ca /agas.htm >. Now go, little book, find a new life.

THE AUTHOR

Joad R. Wren is a Welsh writer based in London and Folkestone. In a previous life he was a professor of renaissance studies and wrote and edited numerous books on the literary and political culture of early modern Britain and Europe. These days he divides his time between writing novels and non-fiction and making music.